C000174261

David Shepherd
Lancaster, in 194
School in Derb
Durham. He ha
"Yugoslav-Bulgarian Diplomatic Relations, 1918-1941"
(M.A. 1968) and "The Royal Dictatorship in Yugoslavia,
1929-1934" (M.Litt. 1976). After University, he was a
probation officer in Linlithgow, West Lothian, and a
student at the Episcopal Theological College in
Edinburgh. From 1968-1979, he was Chaplain of
St Paul's Cathedral, Dundee, and Anglican Chaplain in
the University of Dundee from 1973-1979. Since 1979,
he has been Rector of St Mary Magdalene's Church,
Dundee. He has served on many boards and committees
of the Scottish Episcopal Church, most notably as
Convener of St Serf's Home, 1976-1992 and as
Convener of the Diocese of Brechin Administration
Board since 1984. In 1985, he opened the Meadowside
Bookshop which has now sold over 100,000 books.

To celebrate his 50th Birthday, he published his first
novel: "Who killed Sophie Jack?" In view of the great
enthusiasm with which that book was received, he feels
compelled to offer his readers a second helping of
MEADOWSIDE CRIME.

MEADOWSIDE PUBLICATIONS

MURDER WITHIN TENT

DAVID SHEPHERD

MURDER WITHIN TENT

A DETECTIVE NOVEL

BY

DAVID SHEPHERD

MEADOWSIDE PUBLICATIONS

DUNDEE
1994

Meadowside Publications
75 Meadowside, Dundee

© *Meadowside Publications, 1994*

Printed by
Burns & Harris (Print) Ltd.
Dundee, Scotland

ISBN 0 9520632 1 2

Meadowside Crime
is a © imprint of
Meadowside Publications,
Dundee.

CONTENTS

*The story is set in a small
university town in England
in August 1988.*

1 *The Night Visitor*

Colin Fisher awoke with a start.

Who was it making that strange snorting noise in the middle of the night? Heavy breathing was not unknown in Scout circles, but it seemed a bit unsociable – not to say downright inconsiderate – to be disturbing the other campers in the middle of the night!

What time was it?

He reached for his watch.

Five past eight.

Surely that could not be right?

He turned the watch the other way up.

2.35 am.

The noises continued.

Colin tried to imagine what was going on. He had a fairly vivid imagination for a boy of his age and he painted quite a colourful picture in his mind's eye. But then there was a slight sighing sound – followed by silence.

He cocked his ears to catch any whisper that might be exchanged. Even a vague mutter would be sufficient for an intelligent guess. But not a word was spoken.

There was a total silence for about five minutes. Then there was a slight rustling sound as if someone was crawling over a sleeping bag, the flutter of canvas in the breeze and the brush of feet against the grass. Someone had been into the leader's tent.

He could not explain it then – or later – but he felt a certain anxiety about what the night visitor had been doing. Perhaps he and Graeme were having it off? But Graeme wasn't like that! Graeme was as straight as they came. No one had ever made any such suggestions about Graeme. So what was happening? Perhaps because his bedtime reading had been one of Agatha Christie's novels, Colin was more than usually ready to suspect something sinister and unpleasant.

He waited several minutes and then said: "Graeme!"

There was no reply.

"Graeme!" he said more loudly.

But there was still no reply.

He shook his tent-mate, Ian Mackay.

"Wake up!" he said.

"What is it?" Ian growled.

"Someone's been into Graeme's tent and attacked him."

"Don't be stupid!" said Ian Mackay, who abhorred dramatics – especially in the middle of the night.

"I've tried calling him but he doesn't reply!"

"He's probably ignoring you. Trying to get some sleep like everybody else."

"Shut up, you two!"

The voice came from the next tent.

Johnny Cotton. A most unsympathetic character.

"What should we do?" Colin asked Ian.

"Shut up!" said Johnny Cotton again.

Colin felt a bit squashed. After all, he was one of the youngest members of the Troop; it was perhaps not for him to embarrass one of the leaders. If Graeme was saying nothing, then perhaps it would be better to shut up – as Johnny had said. But it was annoying – especially when you could not deny the evidence of your senses – what you had seen and heard. But, of course, being the middle of the night, he hadn't seen anything! Tomorrow, in broad daylight, he would soon see if anything had happened. One look at Graeme's face would be enough.

Colin snuggled deeper into his sleeping bag and thought about the holiday so far. They were all members of the 14th Grasshallows Troop, most of them pupils at Henslea, and they were ten days into their annual Scout camp, half a mile up the road from Picton Dale.

They were not far from home – only about six or seven miles out of the city – but for some it had seemed too far. There were twenty-four boys in his Troop; eighteen had said they would go on the annual camp; but only twelve had turned up. Garry Hogg and his brother, Stephen; Johnny Cotton and Mark Todd; Simon Wallace and Geoff Stewart;

Tony Mason and Harry Robb; the Armstrong twins – Pat and Doug. And himself and Ian. Was that twelve? Yes, it was. He counted them like sheep leaping over fences.

Their leaders had been a bit disappointed about the response. They had even thought about cancelling the camp, but they had eventually decided that if twelve of the boys were enthusiastic and had paid up, the show should go on. In fact, to their surprise, it had gone better than usual. There had been fewer fights, less quarrels, more willingness to do the dirty jobs and more general good behaviour than they had seen for many years. Graeme, Allan and Neil were feeling quite pleased – and a good report was in the making.

There had been plenty of food. A farmer had given them a couple of rabbits – skinning them had been horrible but the stew had been delicious. Harry Robb had smuggled in a few bottles of beer and Allan had cast a blind eye over their junketing. The weather had been remarkably good and only two people had fallen into the river – one had been pushed!

They had done orienteering, map-work and astronomy. They had gone on a nature trail, done some riding, been canoeing. Colin had made his first vertical ascent up an eighteen foot sheer rock face higher up the Dale and he was rather proud of his achievement. Simon Wallace had got stuck half way up. He had panicked and cried! Yes, he had cried. Colin was much more grown-up and mature for his age! Along with some of the older scouts, he had visited a rather bored and naughty woman on a nearby caravan site who had taught him more about anatomy than he had ever learnt in Henslea school. He was grateful for the experience but hoped he had not caught anything. Ian Mackay had said he'd been stupid – but Ian was slow. Like a tortoise, life tended to pass him by.

Finally, of course, there had been all those jolly scout songs sung round the camp-fire of a night, watching the wood burn and having cocoa and baked potatoes before they hit the hay. Colin reckoned that whoever wrote 'I'm riding along on the crest of a wave' should get a medal … or at least a five-star proficiency badge. It was a song that he really enjoyed singing … not that he had much of a voice!

11

Slowly, Colin travelled back to sleep and the camp was peaceful once more. Six dark green tents each holding two scouts and the old brown army tent holding four were arranged in a straight line facing the river. Two of the leaders shared one tent. Graeme slept on his own.

The dew fell, the sun rose, the dawn chorus opened up in full force over Picton Dale and by 7.30 am, the first brave scouts were crawling out of their sleeping bags and going for a swim. Two others emerged and set about making breakfast, measuring out porridge into a large pan and getting the fire going so that everyone could start the day with a large mug of hot, sweet tea. It was the usual lazy, hazy start to another splendid summer's day. No one hurried. No one spoke too loudly. People washed and dressed in a leisurely fashion. Gradually, everyone gathered around the camp-fire waiting for the large brown kettle to boil.

Neil and Graeme had been for a swim and came back pink and dripping. Colin was one of the last to come to life. Ian had had to kick him to get any response.

Colin was pleased to see Graeme looking as large as life – pulling on his green shirt and brushing his hair. He realized that his nocturnal fears had been completely unfounded. Ian had been right to tell him to go back to sleep. He must remember not to stay up at night reading lurid stories.

He looked at Graeme's tent. It was about six feet away from his own. The flaps were still tied. Someone was having a late lie. Colin looked around the assembled company to see who was missing. It was Allan Foster. But what was Allan doing in Graeme's tent? And why was he still sleeping? Allan was normally one of the early risers – always doing twenty press-ups before breakfast. But today, he was still asleep.

Ten minutes later, Graeme went into his tent to wake Allan up; but Allan had been dead for almost six hours.

2 *The Sandman cometh*

Raynes was still reading his morning paper over a leisurely breakfast at *The Green Man* when a message arrived from police headquarters. The manager, who took the call, bustled through to the dining-room where Raynes was considering the value of his shares in ICI. Should he buy more – or should he sell?

"It's a Detective-Inspector Carlisle on the phone. He says it's urgent."

Raynes raised his eyebrows at his colleague's sudden promotion, and ambled out to reception to take the call.

"Raynes here," he said.

"It's your lucky morning! There's been a suspicious death out at Picton Dale. A scout was found dead in his tent about an hour ago. I'm sending a car round to the hotel for you."

Raynes thanked him for his call and decided to hang on to his shares. It was obviously going to be a busy week.

The Inspector had been working in Grasshallows for about a month but had still not found himself a home. For the past fortnight, he had been terribly busy sorting out a very complicated murder and then writing up all his reports. Once that excitement was over, he had begun to look seriously at a number of properties. He had put in two bids but had been gazumped. So he was still enjoying the facilities of Grasshallows' best hotel where he was now treated with the utmost deference and respect. Raynes was too much of a cynic to let all the flattery go to his head but he reflected that, in his experience, success always bred success and he hoped that in this new case, he would not lose his momentum.

Scouts? What did he know about scouts?

* * *

The brand-new police Granada rolled up to the steps of *The Green Man*. The driver leapt out to open the door and Raynes joined Carlisle in the back seat.

"I'm not quite sure of the details," said Carlisle, "but it appears to be one of the scout-leaders who has died – not one of the boys. He's about twenty or so. Works as a desk clerk in a travel agency in Grasshallows."

"I thought you once said that murders never happened in this part of the woods?"

"They didn't. You must be attracting them!"

Grasshallows had the reputation of being a quiet, sleepy University town where nothing ever happened. There were occasional punch-ups between the students after a party, some drunkenness at weekends, the odd theft and assault – even a little cattle-rustling on dark nights – but the insurance companies rated Grasshallows low on the scale of criminal activity and the police had a correspondingly quiet life.

The car sped northwards out of the city.

"What did the chap die of?" asked Raynes.

"Asphyxiation, I believe."

Raynes was surprised.

"Someone put a pillow over his face?"

"I'm not sure, but I think they said he was choked to death."

"How very unpleasant!"

They reached the campsite at about 10.15 am. The camp was situated about half a mile north of Picton Dale, up a side road, over a little hump-backed bridge, through a gate and one hundred yards further up the riverbank. It was a good site. At that point, the river broadened out and formed several pools. The seven tents were set out in a row about twenty feet back from the river bank with six or seven feet of space between each tent. Beyond the tents were a couple of trees and a long undulating meadow used mostly for cows and sheep.

Much of the activity seemed to be centred around the third tent from the left. Two policemen were standing guard nearby and the police doctor and photographer were talking outside.

The scouts themselves were sitting in two dejected groups – one round the embers of the camp-fire, the others beside the river. No one was saying much. Each boy was trying to come to terms with the tragedy. Now and again, a few words of comfort were exchanged – even the odd smile – but mostly, people stared aimlessly at the ground or looked over towards the police as if hoping that by some miracle, Allan might be revived.

Raynes stomped over to the tent.

"Time?" he asked.

"10.19," said the photographer.

"The time of death?" said Raynes.

(My God! These people were thick).

"Oh? Between two and three o'clock this morning."

"Thank you. And the cause of death?"

"Sand."

"Sand?"

"Someone poured a couple of pounds of sand down his throat. He just choked to death."

"Good heavens!" said Raynes.

Carlisle too was very surprised.

"Where did they get the sand from?"

"From the riverbed, I should think." The police doctor looked around him. "It's a pretty coarse sort of sand. Not the sort you'd get on a beach or on a building site. I should think someone just dredged it up, dried it and then shoved it down his throat."

"What a horrible way to die!" said Carlisle.

"Quite quick really!" said the doctor. "Just blocked his windpipe and within a minute or so, it was all over."

Raynes went into the tent to look at the body.

It already had a grey, waxy appearance. The eyes were still staring resolutely upwards but the mouth was wide open and, looking into his mouth, Raynes could see that his gullet was packed with sand.

The body was still firmly encased in its sleeping bag. The bag was zipped fully up to the neck. Raynes pulled down the zip. The young man was wearing a pair of blue shorts and his hands and arms lay loosely across his abdomen. Beside the body, there was a torch, a book, a watch, a pair of binoculars, a map, a pair of stout brown walking shoes, a pair of dirty white gym shoes, a heap of clothes and a brown rucksack with the rest of his clothes and equipment.

Raynes sat on his heels, taking in every detail. The position of the book, the watch … everything registered in his mind. He came out of the tent and walked round it to see if any of the tent pegs had been moved or the guy ropes adjusted. He looked at the simple canvas ties which held the flaps open or shut.

"Fingerprints?"

"They're on the way."

Raynes looked back inside the tent where Carlisle was making his own inspection.

"Was the zip up or down on his sleeping bag?"

"Just as you see it – up. We had to run it down to take the photographs, but we put it all back for you – just as it was."

"No sign of a fight? No blood or skin tissues under his nails?

"None. I don't think he had time to get his arms out."

"And how do you think the sand was administered?"

"A bottle or tube of some sort, I should think. There's a small quantity of sand on the right hand side of the ground-sheet. Not much. Just a trickle. It was very neatly done. Neatly, quickly and quietly. He wouldn't have made much of a noise; not with that lot pouring down his throat!"

"No one heard anything?"

"I haven't asked them yet. I was waiting for you. The beat men have had a chat with the lads but I don't think they've taken any statements."

Raynes looked across at the scouts.

"What a lousy end to their holiday!"

"If one of them did it …?"

"We shall soon find out." Raynes looked back towards the gate. "Are we having an Incident Room?"

"I believe it's on its way."

"Good! I don't fancy conducting my enquiries in the middle of a field!"

Carlisle crawled out of the tent.

"What a horrible way to die!" he said again.

Raynes was irritated.

"For God's sake, don't keep saying: 'What a horrible way to die!' We're not here to appreciate the murderer's art. We're here to catch him – and as quickly as possible. You round up the scout-leaders and I'll see them one at a time in my car."

He turned to the beat man.

"Do you know the local farmer?"

"Yes. Bert Sheldon. Went to school with him."

16

"Well, take the rest of the lads down to the farm and see if he can do something to keep them occupied till I arrive. Weeding his garden … feeding the hens … anything. None of them is to go back to Grasshallows till I say. No phone calls to be made. Especially not to the Press! Is that understood? All their equipment remains here. Their tents stay just as they are. Get them to empty their pockets in front of you – one by one. And then march them off down the road as quick as you can. If you have any trouble, belt 'em!"

3 Our Chief Scout

Raynes watched the boys being rounded up by the policeman. They seemed very subdued and sheep-like. They would cause no problem. He looked at the two leaders whom Carlisle was bringing over the field to his car. They were both in their early twenties, he guessed; one with freckles and auburn hair, pale blue eyes and a receding chin – the other had a smooth, creamy complexion with glossy black hair.

Carlisle introduced them.

The one with auburn hair was Neil Gray. He was a schoolmaster at Henslea. He was in charge of the camp. His deputy, Allan Foster, was the victim. Graeme Wilson, the smooth man, was his Number Three.

Raynes suggested that Graeme might like to sit on the riverbank near the bridge where he could see him. He invited Neil to join him in the back seat of the police Granada. Detective-Constable Carlisle sat in the front seat, opened up his notepad, turned to a clean page and took out his pencil.

Raynes started in an affable way.

"Well, Neil," he said, "this is a very sad business."

Neil agreed that it was utterly tragic. In fact, he felt completely dazed and bewildered. He couldn't believe that such a thing could ever happen at camp. Injuries and accidents he was prepared for. But not murder. How, he wondered, was he going to explain all this to the parents – and, in particular, to Allan's mother? His pale blue eyes broke into tears. He sobbed uncontrollably. Raynes waited patiently. "How many scouts were there altogether at camp?"

"Fifteen. Three leaders and a dozen lads." He sniffed. "Have you got a handkerchief?"

Carlisle passed over a packet of tissues.

"And what are their names?"

"Pat and Doug Armstrong – they're twins. Johnny Cotton, Colin Fisher, Stephen and Garry Hogg – they're brothers. Tony Mason, Harry Robb, Geoff Stewart, Simon Wallace and Mark Todd …"

"That's eleven!"

"I've missed one. Did I mention Ian Mackay?"

Carlisle looked at his notes. "No."

"Well, that's the other one."

"And all these lads are pupils at your school?"

"Most of them. One or two have just left."

"And you are a teacher there?"

"I teach Maths."

"How long have you been a scout-leader?"

"Ten years."

"You must be older than you look?"

"I'm thirty-one."

"Not married?"

"Yes. I've got a wife and a small boy and girl. Five and three."

"Is your wife quite happy about you being a scout-leader?"

"Yes. She used to be in the Guides. That's how we met."

"And how many boys do you have in your Troop?"

"Twenty-four, when they're all there. Eighteen of them said they wanted to go to camp but in the event, only twelve paid up. We did think twice about going, but we didn't want to disappoint the young ones. It was their first camp. I wish to God we'd never come …"

He started crying again.

Raynes waited till the storm had passed.

"Who was sleeping in which tent?" he asked.

It seemed better to concentrate on facts.

Neil looked out through the windscreen at the desolate scene.

"Johnny Cotton and Mark Todd were in the tent on the extreme left. Then there was Colin Fisher and Ian Mackay … Colin's the youngest …" He paused. "No, he isn't. He was here last year. The twins are the youngest. They were in the big tent with Tony and Harry …"

"That's the big brown one next to the river?"

"Yes. It's an old Army tent. Army surplus. Pat and Doug were in there. That's where we keep all the kitchen things. Allan and I were in Number Six; Garry and Stephen were in Number Five; Simon and Geoff were in Number Four; and Graeme was in Number Three."

Raynes looked confused.

"I'm sorry. I thought Allan was in Number Three?"

"He was last night. He wanted to stay up late to read some book. Graeme and I were both pretty knackered so they did a switch. Allan took Graeme's tent and Graeme came in with me …"

"So most of the stuff in Tent Number Three belongs to Graeme?"

"Yes."

Except the book …, thought Raynes.

"And whose sleeping bag was he in?"

"I'm not sure. It must have been Graeme's."

"A dark green quilted one with a single zip on the right-hand side?"

"That's Graeme's."

So Allan was murdered in Graeme's tent and Graeme's sleeping bag. That was the one night they had done a switch – and that was the night he had been murdered. It looked as if the murderer had been waiting for just such an opportunity to get him alone.

Raynes paused to absorb the information he had received so far. He continued:

"Did Allan have any enemies? Was there any aggro? Had Allan been too hard on any of the boys? Had he disciplined any of them too roughly?"

Neil shook his head.

If anything, Allan had been too kind, too indulgent. One of the lads had smuggled in a few bottles of beer but Allan had cast a Nelsonian eye over the misdemeanour. Neil had only found out about it when he'd seen one of the empty bottles lying in the waste bag.

"What kind of bottles were they?"

"Newcastle Brown! Quite the wrong thing to give to boys of that age! Two of them had diarrhoea … the others must have had iron constitutions … but it was a stupid thing to do. I told Allan what I thought!"

Raynes paused before asking his next question.

"Was Allan a homosexual?"

"I don't think so."

"That book he was reading," said Raynes, "I wouldn't have said it was Baden-Powell's ideal bedtime reading?"

Neil looked blank.

"It was called 'Camp Tales'. But it wasn't exactly the sort of thing that should be read around the camp-fire!"

"Oh, that? I saw Graeme reading it. He reads a lot of rubbish. He must have passed it on to Allan." Neil shook his head. "I must be a bit naive … I didn't realize what it was about … But I don't think he was a homosexual. I'm sure he wasn't. He never showed any sign of it."

Raynes turned to less controversial matters.

"Allan worked for a travel agency, I believe?"

"Yes. He was a trainee manager …"

"With whom?"

"Star Travel. It's the one on the corner in the High Street."

"And how long had he been working there?"

"About three years. He started as a desk clerk but they decided he had management potential so they put him on this training course."

"Was he doing well on it?"

"Oh, very well. Allan was a frightfully keen person. Anything he took up, he did it to the limit. That's what made him such a good leader. He was enthusiastic about things. He got people going. Made them give of their best. He was a bit of a fitness freak. He used to pride himself on running about five miles each day – and, before breakfast, he'd be busy doing his press-ups. He'd even get people to join him. That's the sort of person he was ..."

The use of the past tense touched off a tender nerve and Neil's eyes began to water again.

Raynes ploughed on.

"Who discovered his body?"

"Graeme did. He thought there must be something wrong. Allan was normally up long before breakfast. But there was no sign of him ... Graeme suggested throwing in a pan full of water, but I told him not to be stupid. Graeme's a bit immature at times ... So he just poked his head through the flaps – and then he called me over ..."

"What time would that have been?"

"About 8.00 am I should think."

"And what did you do then?"

"I sent Graeme off to Mr Sheldon's to phone the police. They were here by a quarter to nine."

"How did Graeme react to his death? After all, it was his tent."

"He looked a bit shaky to start with, but once he had something to do, he bucked up. Graeme's good in a crisis."

"Do the boys like him?"

"They seem to. But I think they liked Allan more ..."

"So it's unlikely that any of them would have murdered their favourite scout-leader?"

"Oh, very unlikely. They were absolutely shattered. They were all in tears. The twins were in a dreadful state. But they live next door to Allan. They've known him since they were toddlers. And Colin ... Allan was helping him get his mountaineering badge ... Colin just couldn't take it ..."

"Did any of the boys go into the tent?"

Neil looked very upset and his chin trembled.

"You know what boys are, Inspector. I tried to keep them out – but they all wanted to have a look. I tried to reason with them – but the moment I turned my back, they were all in having a look ..."

"So our fingerprints team will be completely useless?"

"I'm very sorry, Inspector. I was completely unprepared ... I didn't think ..."

"So they all know what happened? They all know how Allan died?"

"I'm afraid so."

Raynes silently cursed the entire Scout movement.

"How do you think anyone could pour half a pound of sand down the throat of such a healthy, active scout without him noticing and fighting back?"

Neil looked miserable.

"I just don't know. I suppose – in the middle of the night – you just don't expect such a thing to happen. It's like a nightmare. Before you know where you are, someone forces a bottle or bag of the stuff into your mouth. If you're fully zipped up in one of those sleeping bags, it'd be difficult to get your arms out in a hurry. They go right up to your neck. I reckon it'd take you at least fifteen seconds even if you were awake and in broad daylight. But Allan was asleep. It was pitch black. And it was Graeme's sleeping bag he was using ..."

Raynes nodded.

"... You've got to breathe; but if you can't breathe, you've had it. I imagine Allan did struggle but by the time he got loose, he would be choc-a-bloc full. And with all that sand pouring into him, he'd hardly be able to shout or scream."

Raynes thought Neil had put it rather well.

"What kind of bottle d'you think the murderer used?" Raynes asked. "Newcastle Brown, perhaps?"

"I hope not!"

"Well, it must have been in some sort of container ... if it had a neck to it, it had to be tough enough to stop Allan biting through it. Glass is pretty strong! Plastic would have been no use. A beer bottle or one of those returnable bottles of fizz. Have there been any of those around the camp?"

"Several crates of them. When we go off for the day, each boy takes a bottle in his knapsack and we go down to the village shop in Picton Dale for refills."

"So there's no problem about the means?"

"None at all."

"But you didn't see anyone filling a bottle with sand?"

"No …"

"You don't sound very sure?"

"Well, I saw Johnny Cotton and Mark Todd playing round with bottles near the river the other night – just before tea. They were trying to make them shoot the rapids. I was frightened they would break the bottles and we'd have people getting their feet cut. I made them put them back in the crates immediately … We had a scout cut his foot that way last year. He lost a lot of blood. We had to get him into hospital for stitches. He had quite a gash …"

Raynes nodded his head.

"So you have to keep a fairly close eye on them all the time?"

"You've got to."

"But at night?"

"Well, you hope they're so worn out, they'll sleep like tops. I must say this year's lot have been splendid. We've had a really great time. The lads have been co-operative. They've been no trouble at all. There was just one fight – and one person pushed into the river. Apart from that, they've been very well-behaved."

"So no one heard anything?"

"Well, one of them said he did."

Raynes raised his eyebrows.

"Why didn't you tell me that before?"

"You never asked. And anyway, I don't know that it helps much. Colin Fisher said that he heard sounds coming from Graeme's tent. He woke up his tent-mate, Ian Mackay. He also woke up Johnny Cotton who told him to shut up and go back to sleep."

"But what did he hear?"

"He said he heard grunting and groaning, rustling and finally footsteps running over the grass." Neil looked apologetically at Raynes. "Actually, he said he thought Graeme was having it off with one of the lads. That's what it sounded like, he said. But how he should know … I don't know! But he's got a very vivid imagination has Colin. I think you should take his story with a pinch of salt …"

"At this stage," said Raynes, "every detail is important. I don't suppose you happen to know what time young Colin heard these sounds?"

"He said it was shortly after 2.30 am."

Raynes nodded.

That at least seemed right.

"Is Graeme a homosexual?" asked Raynes. "I'm sorry to ask you all these questions, but I must know the truth."

"Graeme? Good heavens, no! Quite the other way! He's got an eye for the girls. And not only for the girls – some of the older women fancy him too. I believe there's a woman on the caravan site he's been seeing. Mutton dressed as lamb – but Graeme doesn't seem to mind. He seems to think that with his good looks, he's God's gift to women!"

Raynes was listening to Neil most carefully.

"You don't seem to like Graeme all that much?"

"Well, he's a bit brash, a bit vulgar. He likes everyone to think he's a real Romeo. Some of his dirty jokes are a bit sick. He always seems to think women are objects to be used – rather than treated as real people. Being a married man myself, I find his attitude pretty revolting. I've had to pull him up many a time, because I'm frightened he may end up indoctrinating the lads with his views. But he knows I disapprove. In fact, of late, I think he's been cleaning up his act."

"Did you appoint him as one of your deputies?"

"Well, I held up his appointment as long as possible, but the Area Commissioner twisted my arm. Grasshallows is a bit thin on the ground as far as leaders go, and with Graeme in his twenties, the Organization needs all the talent it can get. I didn't really want Graeme but, as I say, I think he's improving. He's a good man in a crisis but he does like his little bit of glory."

Raynes looked beyond Neil to the lonely figure pacing the riverbank and casting stones at some unseen target.

A show-off, he thought to himself. Someone who likes to impress. A man of the world who fancies himself. Who enjoys being a hero to the younger boys. Not at all like Neil who was an idealist – or Allan, who was a fitness freak. Graeme was a self-made man who worshipped his creator. Raynes could begin to see the picture fitting together.

He heard Neil speaking:

"Of course, he doesn't get much help from his father but you probably know that."

Raynes shook his head.

"I'm new round here."

"Well, perhaps I shouldn't say this, but his father's been up for assault once or twice – and he's been in jail for fraud. In fact, I think he's still in jail at this moment."

Raynes looked at Carlisle.

"Ron Wilson?" said Carlisle. "Yes, that fits. Up for reset. Thought I knew his face. He's a bit of a lad is Ron. Good-natured but as bent as a six-sided 50 pence piece!"

Raynes returned to Neil Gray.

"And what does Graeme do for a living?"

"He's a gardener. A landscape gardener. He works with his dad."

The pieces of the jigsaw clicked together very quickly. Almost too quickly? Raynes could see that beneath this peaceful camping scene, there were strong currents of crime and passion, envy and resentment. But who hated whom enough to commit murder? What had Allan done to cross his assailant? That was the question he had to answer. As he had told Carlisle again and again, the key to solving a murder was *motive*. Once you had identified the motive, you had the murderer. It was an article of faith which had stood him in good stead for many a year.

Raynes decided that he had heard enough from this earnest young man with the weak chin and the ever-watering blue eyes. He took a deep breath.

"Well, Mr Gray, I must thank you for all you have told me. There may be more that you ought to have said. If there is, do not hestitate to phone me or Detective-Constable Carlisle at any time of the day or night. Some small fact may be the key we are all looking for …"

Neil looked thankful to think that his interview was now nearly over.

25

"... I think it would be a good idea if you could go down to Bert Sheldon's farm and look after the boys. I shall interview young Romeo – and then I shall come down to the farm and have a word with the boys themselves. I should be very glad if you could say nothing – absolutely nothing – to anyone about this conversation. Is that understood?

"Perfectly."

Raynes looked him over. Grasshallows was certainly poor in leadership material if they had to appoint people like Neil Gray as scout-leaders. His knees were shaking and he looked vaguely sick. For all his leadership talents, Raynes decided that he was lacking in moral fibre. Decidedly lacking in moral fibre.

Carlisle drew a neat line under his notes, turned to a clean page and looked forward to a more entertaining performance from Graeme Wilson who – even if he had no morals – was at least blessed with guts.

Raynes waved him over.

4 *In Pastures green*

Graeme Wilson settled comfortably into the back seat of the police Granada and crossed his legs. He looked at Raynes with a slightly superior smile as if he was used to dealing with the forces of law and order. But although his eyes and lips showed him to be calm and self-confident, he tended to fidget with his fingers – something that Raynes noticed right away.

"What do you do for a living?" he asked.

"I'm a landscape gardener."

"That means that you are used to handling soil – and sand?"

Graeme rapidly uncrossed his legs.

"Are you implying that I murdered Allan?"

"Not at all. I merely asked you a straightforward question. Are you or are you not used to handling soil – and sand?"

Graeme seemed very guarded.

"Yes."

"So you would know what kind of sand it was that had been poured down Allan's throat?"

"I didn't look down his throat."

"But no doubt some was spilt on your sleeping bag?"

"I didn't see any."

"You were the first one to see the dead body?"

"Yes. I suppose so."

"Was there anything in your tent that was different to usual?"

Graeme looked thoughtful.

Raynes said: "I know about the book."

Graeme laughed: "Oh? The book?"

"The book was an addition to the scene … Was there anything else in the tent that wasn't there the night before?"

"I don't think so." Graeme looked serious. "I wasn't really looking at my things. I was just looking at Allan's face. I knew something had happened. I could see the brown stuff in his mouth. I thought he must have choked on his own vomit. It was his eyes – staring. I got out of the tent as quickly as possible and told Neil. He went in and had a longer look. He told me that his mouth was filled with sand and that he was dead. I felt sick – quite sick."

"What did you do then?"

"I don't remember. I think I tried to make a joke of it to the boys. Told them Allan had gone to join the heavenly gang show – and that, now he was there, he'd be as happy as a sandboy! I'm sorry, it was a bit sick, but I always think it pays to make a joke out of a tragedy. Helps you to cope …"

"Neil said you were very good in a crisis. You were a person who kept your nerve."

"Did he?" Graeme brightened at this unexpected compliment and crossed his legs again. Raynes noted the return of confidence.

"Did you like Allan?" he asked.

Graeme pouted with his splendid lips.

"Well, he was a bit of a prat! All those exercises! All that running! You don't have to do all that to be fit. He was a bit of a fanatic. Carried things to extremes. He was a good bloke. Ambitious. Good at his job. And the lads liked him. He was easy, you know. Sympathetic. Of course, he used to suck up to Neil and the District Commissioner." Graeme smiled. "But he was all right!"

Raynes noted that he had not answered his question.

"So why do you think he was killed?"

Graeme shook his head.

"Beats me."

"Had he any enemies?"

"Don't think so."

"Had there been any rows in the camp? Any fights? I hear that there was at least one fight."

"Oh, that was nothing to do with Allan. That was Harry Robb and Garry having a go at each other. Harry's very short-tempered and he lashed out at Garry. It was nothing important."

"Do you think Allan was a homosexual?"

"No. Why should you ask that?"

"Because one of the scouts said he heard grunts and groans coming from Allan's tent just before he died."

"Oh, that's Colin for you! Got to be in on the big act! He wants to be a detective when he grows up! Does nothing but read Sherlock Holmes and Agatha Christie. It's a wonder he hasn't come up with the murderer right away! I wouldn't believe anything Colin says ..."

"Why not?"

"Because he's a stupid little prat! Always nosing in on things that don't concern him." He looked at Raynes. "He'll probably make a superb detective!"

Raynes ignored the insult.

"Of course," he said, "it might not have been a boy in the tent with Allan. It could have been a woman ..."

"It could have been," Graeme sneered.

"I believe," said Raynes, "that there is some charming female on a nearby caravan site who is only too willing to share her favours with even the most foul-mouthed prat?"

Graeme looked thoughtfully at Raynes.

How much had Neil told him?

"You are referring of course to 'Grace the Lace'?"

"If that is her name?"

"That's what people call her. She's a bit of a nympho. Lives in a caravan just up the river."

"Would Allan have known her?"

Graeme hesitated a moment before replying.

"I should think so. Quite a few of the lads used to call on her. She had quite a queue some afternoons!"

Raynes raised his eyebrows.

"Did Neil know about this?"

"Probably. But he didn't do anything about it. Too spineless, if you ask me. Frightened of having to lay down the law. Or having to report it to the Commissioner. Might have blotted his copybook."

"I see … You don't like Neil."

"Not really. You see, he's blocked my promotion two or three times. He doesn't like me. I know that. But I try to get on with him."

"I think he recognizes your virtues but deplores your vices."

"Probably."

Raynes paused – wondering whether he should keep strictly to the murder inquiry or pursue the tempting prospect of finding out more about the Circe of the Caravan site. He succumbed to temptation – as Carlisle guessed he would.

"D'you think this lady – Grace the Lace – would have visited Allan in the middle of the night?"

"Shouldn't think so. She wouldn't have known what tent he was in."

"Quite so. You switched tents at the last minute. Allan borrowed your tent so that he could read your book?"

Graeme nodded.

"Could it be that Grace the Lace came to see you but then discovered it was Allan?"

"I don't think she'd worry who it was. So long as it's male, she never says 'No'."

"You paint a pretty appalling picture of this lady!"

"She's a cow!"

"Don't you think that perhaps she might have some grudge against you – or Allan – or the rest of the scouts for anything you've done to her – individually or collectively?"

Carlisle smiled to himself. Raynes had a superb way of framing the all-embracing question.

Graeme looked man-of-the-worldish.

"She'd probably be grateful for the experience."

"So you don't think she would have visited the camp-site at 2.30 in the morning? And you don't think she'd have murdered Allan?"

"No."

That's the end of Grace, thought Carlisle.

But he was wrong.

"You were talking about sand?" said Graeme.

Raynes nodded.

"Well, there's a whole heap of sand beside Grace's caravan. I think the farmer was planning to put down some paving stones. The slabs are there and quite a lot of sand. There could be a connection?"

Raynes nodded encouragingly.

He remembered quite clearly the police doctor telling him less than an hour ago that the sand down Allan's throat was coarse and rough, probably dredged up from the river bed. What interested him was why Graeme was introducing this red herring. Did he know where the sand came from – but was trying to mislead the police? Was he trying to involve Grace in the murder in order to deflect attention from himself? Or was he just trying to be helpful? Raynes was inclined to think that Graeme was like his father – too clever by half.

Raynes decided to puncture the balloon.

"Have you ever considered," he said slowly, "that you were perhaps the intended victim? That had you not changed tents at the last minute, it might have been you lying there and Allan talking to me in this car?"

Graeme looked completely unmoved.

"I can't see why anyone would want to murder me. I've no enemies that I know of. The boys seem to like me. I'm on good terms with all my girlfriends – and all my ex-es. Neil is always trying to bring me down a peg or two, but he wouldn't stoop to murder ..."

"... even if you were having an affair with his wife?"

Graeme went very red.

"What did he say to you?"

30

"Come, come!" said Raynes. "I'm hardly likely to repeat other people's evidence! And certainly not to you! When did it begin?"

"Well, it never really got started. We were all at a party last December – just before Christmas. Neil was on the bar, serving up the drinks. Home-made beer ... that was what he was serving. You have to pour it carefully or you get all the sediment into your glass ..."

He looked at Raynes nervously, realizing that the Inspector had already noticed the connection: sediment = sand.

"Go on," said Raynes.

"Well, his wife was at a bit of a loose end. She was hanging around, talking to people. She doesn't have much of a life – what with Neil and the two kids. So I thought I'd chat her up. And she seemed quite willing to be chatted up. That was unusual because, in the old days, she used to avoid me like the plague!" He grinned. "So I got her a glass of something strong – I think she'd probably had a couple already – and we found a quiet corner where we could have a word or two. Well, it just went on from there. We moved to the bathroom where we could have a bit of privacy. She got carried away – and I didn't stop. She was quite good. But Allan saw us coming out of the bathroom together and he told Neil. He and Jenny had a terrible row later that night. I've seen her a couple of times since then, but Neil doesn't know that."

Graeme shrugged his shoulders. "That's all there was to it. Nothing much to write home about. I can't imagine Neil wanting to murder me for having it off with his wife. He didn't even have the guts to hit me. All he said was that if I ever laid hands on her again, he'd have me thrown out of the Scouts for good!" Graeme laughed. "I said: 'Big deal!'"

Raynes said: "I can see why people hate you!"

"They don't really. They're just jealous."

"It's a small step from hatred and jealousy to murder. I think you ought to give me a list of all your 'conquests' just in case any of them decided to get their revenge."

Graeme smiled. "It'll be quite a long list!"

"I don't doubt it," said Raynes. "But we cannot rule out the possibility that Allan was killed by mistake. It was the one and only night you switched tents and that was the night the murderer struck …"

"Perhaps he'd been waiting to get Allan on his own?"

"But you've already said that he didn't have any enemies?"

"Not round here, he didn't. But it strikes me that there might be one or two people who would have been glad to see him out of the way. It's only hearsay but I think he was upset by one or two things at work. And I believe his stepmother might have been glad to see the back of him. He had a suspicious mind, did Allan. He liked to get to the bottom of things. Things that didn't concern him. And he talked! Boy! Did he talk! It wouldn't surprise me if someone had decided to silence him once and for all."

Raynes looked at Carlisle who had turned back his notes and was comparing what Graeme had just said with what he had said at the beginning of the interview.

"Detective-Constable Carlisle seems to think you've changed your tune. One minute you're saying that Allan didn't have an enemy in the world. Now you're producing them one after the other like a conjuror drawing rabbits out of a hat. Which story am I supposed to believe?"

Graeme looked hurt. "I'm sorry, Inspector. I was just trying to be helpful. I'm feeling very confused about all that's happened. Very upset. I don't think I'm thinking very straight. If you ask me – straight off – did Allan have any enemies, I'd say 'No'. Anybody would say 'No', because you don't expect people to come out all the way to Picton Dale in the middle of the night and bump someone off. But when you start to think about it, there are perhaps one or two people who might have had it in for him. People whom he might have been about to grass on … What better place to do him in … and put the blame on the 14th Grasshallows? It seems logical to me."

Raynes looked at Graeme long and hard. In fact, he seemed to look through him. Raynes had that remarkable ability to detect when people were telling him lies. He had listened very carefully to everything Graeme had said. He could not be one hundred per cent sure, but he felt that the young man had not told him any lies – but he had certainly laid a very neat string of red herrings across his path. Wicked stepmothers, corrupt travel agents, jealous husbands – and Grace the Lace! Graeme had definitely widened the scope of the investigation but he had failed to say exactly what he felt about Allan.

Raynes continued to look through him.

There was a long and unpleasant silence.

"I think," said Raynes coldly, "that there is probably a great deal more you could tell me about the circumstances leading up to this murder. It is possible that you do not realize yourself what those circumstances were. They may come to you in the next few days. But I cannot rule out the possibility that the murderer intended to kill you. If he has failed, it may be that he will try again, I think you should be on your guard."

Raynes looked at his watch.

It was nearly 12.00 pm.

He concluded: "I would like you to go back to the farm along with Neil and the boys. I would be very grateful if you could keep our conversation confidential – and, above all, say nothing to the Press."

Graeme nodded.

"I quite understand."

Raynes threw one final question at him: "I don't suppose you have remembered what, if anything, was different about your tent?"

Graeme, who was about to open the door and step out, turned back surprised.

"Why, yes, Inspector, I do. My bottle of orangeade was missing! How did you know?"

Raynes smiled. "There was rather a dark stain on the ground-sheet beside the binoculars. The stain suggested a bottle. The fact that there was no bottle to go with the stain made me wonder. Did you move it?"

Graeme shook his head.

He looked puzzled.

"It was certainly there last night," he said. "But I didn't remove it."

33

"Of course not," said Raynes. "The murderer took it! But what would a murderer want with a bottle of orangeade?"

5 *Munching Mangoes*

"Well, what did you make of all that?"

Raynes and Carlisle were walking across the field towards the row of tents. The mobile incident room had now arrived and the meadow seemed to be full of policemen. Coloured tapes fluttered in the lunchtime breeze, casting a festive atmosphere over the murder scene.

Carlisle shook his head.

"Still waters run deep … Someone trying to get a proficiency badge for making sandcastles seems to have gone a little too far! One of the scout leaders is knocking off his colleague's wife – not to mention every other woman he sees! Another is spying on everyone else – and gets it in the neck! Half the lads are fornicating with Grace the Lace and numerous husbands in Grasshallows are longing to castrate Graeme Wilson. Bottles of orangeade are vanishing mysteriously and Newcastle Brown is being shipped in. Meanwhile, everyone is trying to play it cool … fresh air, healthy exercises, songs round the camp-fire … all the pleasures of country life!"

"Scouting's not changed much over the years, has it?" said Raynes.

"Not really. Except we didn't kill people!"

"Part of the new image!" said Raynes.

* * *

He walked over to the forensic experts who had examined every detail and had filled several bread trays with labelled items and had plastic sackfuls of other bits and pieces all ready for the laboratory.

"Have you found the missing bottle of orangeade?" asked Raynes.

"Yes – it was in the third crate down."

"Anything in it?"

"Just a few dregs – enough for a sample."

"Anything else interesting?"

"Well, I think we've found part of the murder weapon. There's a plastic funnel in the kitchen department." He picked it out of the tray. "You can see it's got teethmarks round the top of the stem. Funny place to have teethmarks!"

"Do they correspond to those of the victim?"

"We'll soon find out."

"Has the body gone yet?"

"No. It's still in the tent. We've taken everything else out. Everything's been dusted for fingerprints."

"I'd like a full report on what you find in his stomach. I fancy you'll find a bit more than orange juice."

"Drugged?"

"I should think so. I can't see how a healthy young man – in top class physical shape – could let someone pour all that sand down his throat – even in the depths of the night. I should think there was a little something added. Drugs or alcohol – or both. So his reactions would be slow. He would be snuggled down deep in his sleeping bag to counter the loss of bodyheat from the alcohol." Raynes looked over towards the heap of kitchen utensils. "Are you still looking for the bottle or container that had the sand in it?"

"We've got every jar, bottle, tin, canister, billy-can or tea-pot that we can lay our hands on! If there's a speck of sand in any of them, we'll find it."

"He – or she – may have thrown it into the river."

"We're looking into that."

Raynes smiled.

"I think you're doing an excellent job. In fact, there seems to be nothing more Carlisle or I can do – so we'll go and have some lunch. Have you got anything to eat?"

"I've got my sandwiches, sir."

"Well, make sure you don't drink any of their orangeade. It does things to people!"

* * *

Raynes and Carlisle drove into the centre of Picton Dale. There was only one pub in the village – *The Carpenter's Arms* – but a sign outside promised 'Real Home Cooking'. The Inspector took the innkeeper at his word and over a generous helping of steak and kidney pudding, he outlined for Carlisle the case as he saw it.

"There are only two alternatives," he said. "Either someone meant to kill Allan. Or they meant to kill Graeme. If they wanted to kill Graeme, they killed Allan by mistake ..."

He paused.

"... If the object was to kill Allan, they must have known somehow that the two lads had switched tents at the last minute. Because it's my belief that if Allan had been sleeping in his normal tent – beside Neil – he would not have been murdered. That means that either they must have made their decision to murder him on the spur of the moment or they must have been watching the camp to see who was sleeping where."

"That seems unlikely," said Carlisle.

"It does," agreed Raynes, "but where you've got murder, anything is possible. My point is ... that the murderer could have had no prior knowledge that Allan would be sleeping in that tent that night. It was only when Graeme gave Allan the dirty book, and Allan decided that he would stay up and read it, that Graeme offered to exchange places. He said: 'Feel free. Use my tent.' Graeme knew that Allan could hardly sit up half the night reading a dirty book in front of Neil."

Carlisle nodded.

"Now, if the decision to switch tents was taken after the other boys had gone to bed, the only two people who would have known where Allan was, would have been Neil and Graeme ..."

"Plus any casual observers."

"If you insist."

Raynes ate two more pieces of delicious kidney before continuing:

"My contention is – casual observers apart – it was only Graeme and Neil who knew for sure that Allan would be alone in Tent No. 3. Therefore, if Allan was to be murdered because he was Allan, then the murderers would have to be Graeme or Neil or the two of them together. Is that fair?"

"So far."

"But if it was Graeme *or* Neil, the murderer would have to have taken a great risk, creeping out without his tent-mate noticing. Had his absence been noted, almost certainly we should have been told that 'X' was out and about during the middle of the night. This we have not been told. Therefore, either 'X' was not noticed ... 'X' did not go out ... or 'X' and 'Y' did it together."

"I can't see Neil murdering anyone. He's too weak!"

"True. It seems highly unlikely. But – remember – a couple of hours ago, we knew nothing about his wife having a fling with Graeme at the Christmas party. His reactions may have been decidedly wimpish but it's often weak people who resort to violence. Graeme is very self-confident, arrogant, contemptuous of people like Neil and Allan. Feeling contempt for such worms, he sees no need to attack them. But sometimes the worm turns. Neil may have tolerated Graeme, but suppose he found Allan doing the same thing on a more permanent basis? It might have led him to violence."

"So Neil is a possibility?"

"So is Graeme. If Allan knew something absolutely devastating about Graeme and was going to reveal it, I can see the possibility that Graeme might strike first. Remember – he comes from a family where fraud and violence are not unknown. The fact that Allan was stuffed with sand seems to suggest that the person who killed him wanted to shut his mouth in a highly dramatic way."

Raynes finished off his gravy and consumed the last, juicy roast potato.

"Now, if Graeme is right – that Allan did have enemies – and if those enemies did want to silence him – then we have to include your casual observers – people prowling round the camp night after night, waiting to catch Allan at a vulnerable moment. Last night, on the tenth night, they learnt that Allan was going to be on his own in Tent No. 3 – and they moved in to strike a deadly blow." Raynes shook his head. "I must say I find it difficult to believe. How could any casual observer tell one scout from another on a pitch-black night lit only by the dying embers of a camp-fire?"

37

"Voices?"

"The voices would have been low so as not to waken the lads. I can't see Graeme suddenly shouting out: 'Allan, take my tent! Take No. 3!' It would be out of character."

Carlisle nodded.

"I agree with you," said Raynes, "that we should not ignore the possibility of a casual observer muscling in – but I find it a little far-fetched."

The barmaid came over to collect their plates. Raynes looked at the menu and ordered peach crumble with plenty of cream. Carlisle ordered a fresh fruit salad.

"So you see," Raynes continued, "in the event of Allan being murdered because he was Allan, the suspects are limited to two. But if we take the other possibility – that Allan was murdered because the murderer thought he was Graeme – the field is wide open! First of all, there are the twelve scouts. Neil said that on the whole they liked Graeme, but there may be one or more who had a secret grudge. Then there are a whole host of women – apparently of all ages – whom Graeme has picked up, used and discarded. Not to mention their husbands and boyfriends thirsting for revenge. Possibly there may even be some enemies of his father. We musn't forget them! Then there is Neil's wife, Jenny. She might see murder as the only way out of an impossible situation. And, finally, of course, we have Grace the Lace – almost living on the doorstep – though why she should want to attack him beats me! Any one of these, trying to attack Graeme, could have killed Allan by mistake. But only Neil and Graeme could have killed Allan deliberately."

"Presumably the young scouts would be more likely to know which was which?"

"Very probably. An irate husband or boyfriend might just crash in regardless and not be quite so careful …" Raynes paused; "… and yet, you know, this case has all the hallmarks of an inside job. The sand was dredged up from the river. The funnel was borrowed from the kitchen … or at least returned to the kitchen. The orangeade must have been laced with some drug and the bottle was most tidily washed and put away. Even if the murderer was not one of the scouts, he or she had a friend at court. And that friend could well have been Graeme. He's such a smooth operator that he could well have briefed an outsider – as well as providing the opportunity for Allan to be alone."

Carlisle finished off his fruit salad.

"Is Graeme your No. 1 suspect?"

"Not yet! If he was the intended victim, he can hardly be suspected of plotting his own death! But it strikes me that Allan may have stirred up a hornet's nest and the hornets have come back to sting him. If that is the case, then I suspect that Graeme might be involved. But if Graeme was the intended victim and Allan was killed by mistake – my fear is that the murderer may strike again. He has been very resourceful the first time. He may spring something nasty on Graeme again."

"Graeme didn't seem very worried about it?"

"No. That surprised me."

Raynes looked at his watch.

"I don't think we've got time for coffee. We've got twelve more people to see this afternoon and some of them are going to be pretty emotional. I'm not looking forward to it."

6 *The Budding Holmes*

Raynes and Carlisle arrived at Bert Sheldon's farm at about 2.00 pm. Mrs Sheldon had very kindly offered them the use of her dining-room, so it was decided that the interviews should be conducted there rather than up at the incident room where the surroundings might prove a distraction.

"Who should we have in first?" asked Carlisle. "Oldest or youngest?"

"I think we'll start with Colin Fisher. After all, he is our only witness."

Carlisle called out to Neil: "Send in Colin!"

Colin turned out to be a small, plump scout with a round pink face, chestnut brown hair and twinkling brown eyes. He seemed to be a little too big for his uniform. On the sleeves of his jumper, he had badges for hobbies, crafts and entertaining.

Raynes treated him kindly.

"How old are you, Colin?"

"Thirteen."

"And how long have you been with the 14th Troop?"

"Eighteen months, sir. I joined after Christmas last year."

"Do you enjoy being a scout?"

"Oh, yes!"

The enthusiasm was genuine.

"And I think you go to Henslea Comprehensive?"

"Yes."

"Is Mr Gray one of your teachers?"

"Yes. He's my form-master – and he teaches us Maths."

"Are you good at Maths?"

"No." A little shame-faced.

"What do you enjoy most?"

"Reading."

"I gather you like reading detective novels?"

"Oh, yes."

"Which ones?"

"Well, I've just finished Sherlock Holmes and now I've started on Agatha Christie. I tried Dorothy Sayers, but I found Lord Peter Wimsey a bit stupid."

"How right you are!" said Raynes. "Can't stand him. Beats me how he solved any murders! You have to be clever for this job!"

He smiled at Colin.

"Now we've got a pretty dreadful murder to solve …"

"Yes, sir."

"… and you seem to be the only person who heard anything?"

"They were all asleep."

"Were you asleep?"

Colin nodded. "Something woke me up."

"At what time would this be?"

Colin's face glowed with enthusiasm.

"2.35 am. I looked at my watch but it was upside down. I thought it was five past eight but I knew it couldn't be break-fast-time. It was so dark."

"No moon?"

"No moon."

40

"So what did you hear?"

"It was a sort of heavy breathing. Like a horse, you know, when it snorts." Colin tried to demonstrate the noise, made a mess over the table and had to borrow a handkerchief.

"Thank you," said Raynes, "I get the idea. And how long did the noises last?"

"Well, they might have been going on for some time, sir. I wouldn't know. But I don't think they lasted longer than a minute or two. There was a sort of sighing – then a rustling – and then I heard footsteps moving over the grass ..."

"Walking or running?"

Colin paused to think.

"Just walking."

"And in what direction did they go?"

"Towards the river."

"Away from you?"

"Yes, sir."

"And you were frightened about this?"

"I didn't know what was happening. I didn't know some-one was killing him."

Tears were starting to well up in Colin's eyes.

Raynes decided to press on.

"Who did you think was in that tent?"

"Graeme, sir."

"You had no idea Graeme and Allan had changed places."

"Not till this morning, sir."

"Do you help in the kitchen?"

"No. I help with the equipment. Ropes and things."

"So what did you think was happening in Graeme's tent?"

"Bad things, sir!"

"What kind of bad things, Colin? Murder?"

"Oh, no, sir. The sort of bad things boys do in toilets."

"Do scouts do things like that?"

Colin was silent. His face went a deeper red.

"Sometimes, sir."

"Well, I'm sorry to have to ask you these things – but it may be that the person who was in Graeme's tent was doing bad things with Allan?"

41

"Oh, no, sir! Allan didn't do bad things."

"Graeme?"

"Oh, never, sir!"

"Then who?"

There was an uncomfortable silence whilst Colin wrestled with his conscience. He obviously did not want to sneak on his fellow scouts, but Raynes was determined to get a full picture of the 14th Grasshallows Troop. He had no intention of letting Colin's conception of Scouts' honour stand in his way.

"I shall have to find out eventually – so you might as well tell me now. Sherlock Holmes had to have all the facts or he could never have been a great detective."

Colin seemed relieved to find that there was an honourable precedent for parting with top-secret information.

"It's Tom, sir."

"Who's Tom?"

"He's one of the leaders, sir. He's not at camp this year. He fell out with Allan. Allan reported him to Neil and there was a terrible row. Allan told me. Tom got a right bollocking. So he said he wouldn't come to camp this year."

"So Tom does bad things?"

"Yes, sir."

"To you?"

"Once, sir. At the Scout hut."

Raynes looked down the list of names.

"To Garry and Stephen?"

"Quite a few times – but they didn't seem to mind."

"Simon and Geoff?"

Colin nodded.

"What about Tony and Harry?"

"They wouldn't let him."

"I see, what about Johnny and Mark?"

"Yes. They're quite proud of it."

"Ian?"

"He ran away. His dad went to see Mr Gray."

"And the twins – Pat and Doug?"

"That's what the big row was all about. Allan caught him doing things to Pat in the shower ..."

42

"I see. And that put an end to 'bad things'?"

"For the moment, sir."

"You don't think he'll be a reformed character from now on?"

Colin shook his head vigorously.

"You don't like him?"

"I hate him."

Colin's face was transformed.

"I can quite understand," said Raynes.

He looked over to Carlisle to see if he was keeping up with the flood of revelations. He turned back to Colin:

"So it sounded as if bad things were happening in Graeme's tent?"

"It sounded like that, sir, but I couldn't believe it."

"And then, I think, you called out to Graeme?"

"Yes, sir."

"And were told to shut up?"

"Yes, sir."

"Did you?"

"No, sir. I woke Ian."

"Was he interested in what you had to say?"

"No, sir."

"So what did you do then?"

"I thought about things, sir. I thought that if Graeme didn't want to say anything, then I shouldn't neither. So I didn't, sir. I went to sleep."

"Very wise," said Raynes, "because if you'd gone outside you might have met the murderer and he might not have been very keen on being spotted by a keen young sleuth like your-self."

"No, sir."

Colin looked thankful he had been spared such a terrifying encounter.

"Well," said Raynes, "what did you think when you woke up this morning?"

"I was glad to see Graeme, sir."

"You could see he was all right?"

"Yes, sir."

43

"You never dreamt that Allan was sleeping in Graeme's tent?"

"No, sir."

"None of the scouts knew that?"

"Mr Gray did."

"Yes, I know. But none of you young ones?"

"No, sir."

Raynes branched out a little further.

"You didn't see anyone digging sand out of the river, Colin? Or putting sand into a bottle or can?"

"No, sir."

Raynes noted a slight hesitation in the reply.

"Well, did you – or didn't you?"

"I saw lots of people doing things in the river, sir. They were building a dam to block up the pool. They were using stones and sand and branches – and they had the pans for the little stones. I think they may have been digging up the sand as well. I'm not sure."

"I see. Did you help them to make the dam?"

"No, sir."

Colin's face displayed a deeper shade of pink.

"You were elsewhere?"

Colin nodded.

"Seeing Grace the Lace?"

Colin's mouth dropped open in amazement. Eventually he breathed: "How did you know, sir?"

"Instinct!" said Raynes.

"You won't tell my mother! Please, sir, don't tell my mother. She'll kill me! Really she will!"

"What about your father? Won't he be angry?"

"No, he's away. He's in Saudi Arabia – on an oil-rig."

"Well," said Raynes. "You're lucky. I shan't say a word to anyone, Colin. But you see how very important it is that you tell me the truth."

"Oh, I have, sir."

Raynes looked at him.

"Yes," he said, "I rather think you have."

44

7 *Punchinello*

After Colin had gone, Raynes turned to Carlisle:

"This case is beginning to develop feet and legs!"

"The Invisible Scout-leader!"

"Another person with every reason to hate Allan …"

"But surely not enough to kill him?"

"I shouldn't think so." Raynes smiled grimly. "Did you get all that on Colin?"

"A District Commissioner's nightmare!"

Raynes laughed. "You know," he said, "sitting here, I feel rather like that famous picture: 'When did you last see your father?'" He mimicked Colin: "'Please sir, he's half-way up an oil-rig in the Red Sea!'"

He looked at his notes.

"I think we'll see Harry Robb next. He seems to be a fiery sort of personality."

Carlisle called out to Neil: "Send in Harry Robb!"

* * *

Harry Robb was a thick-set, rather rough-looking youth, with a pug nose and an aggressive chin. He had mousy brown hair and a very surly look in his eyes.

"How old are you, Harry?"

"Sixteen. Seventeen in November."

"And you're still at school?"

"Just left."

"Have you got a job?"

"I'm part-time at Tesco's. Shelf-filling. But I'm starting an apprenticeship after my birthday."

Raynes discovered that Harry's chief aim in life was to be a cabinet-maker like his father. He noted that the boy had strong, square, capable hands. When he said anything, he spoke in short bursts – rather like a machine gun. He did not call Raynes 'sir', but when he answered a question, he looked the Inspector straight in the eye. Raynes took an instant liking to him.

"How long have you been in the Scouts?" he asked.

"Seven years."

"And before that a Cub?"

Harry nodded.

"And nothing like this has ever happened before?"

"Never."

"I believe that there are fights?"

Harry grinned sheepishly.

"Sometimes."

"And if there's a fight, you're likely to be involved?"

"Sometimes."

"And what was the fight about this time?"

"Garry said things about my sister."

"What did he say?"

"He said she was a whore!"

Raynes raised his eyebrows.

"And why should he say that?"

"Because she'd been going around with Graeme."

"That doesn't make her a whore ..."

"That's what I said. But Graeme's got a bit of a reputation where women are concerned. And when Garry said that, I just saw red. I lashed out – there and then. He won't say things like that again! I told him."

"Had you been drinking when all this happened?"

Harry paused.

"Well, yes. I'd got in a few bottles."

"Strong stuff, Newcastle Brown?"

Harry shrugged his shoulders.

"My dad drinks it. He says it's a real man's drink."

"But it led to a bit of tension?"

"It was all over in five minutes. No hard feelings. But Garry had better watch his tongue – or else! I told him."

Raynes nodded.

"How do you feel about Graeme?"

"All's fair in love and war! That's what my dad says. I warned Betty. I told her what Graeme was like. She's no fool. She can look after herself ..."

"Do you get on well with Graeme?"

46

"He's a bit of a show-off, but on the whole, he's a good lad. I've nothing against him. He likes Scouting. But he likes women better. He's always chatting them up. I can't see why they don't see through him. He's nothing but a big con-man – just like his dad."

"Was it Graeme who introduced you to this lady on the caravan site?"

Again Harry looked embarrassed. Clearly the Inspector had been well-briefed on what had been going on. He looked Raynes squarely in the eye:

"Well, yes. I suppose it was. Graeme told Tony she was up for grabs, so we went along – just for the ride!"

"And which other scouts went along – just for the ride?"

Raynes' voice had a harder edge.

Harry took some time to answer.

"Well, there was me and Tony. Johnny and Mark, Simon and Geoff ... young Colin and Garry. And Graeme, of course."

"But not Ian Mackay?"

"No."

"Stephen Hogg?"

"No."

"Nor the twins?"

"They're too young."

"So's Colin!"

"Sure, but he's into everything! Can't keep his nose out of anything. Anyway, we let him string along. But we made him wait till the end. He didn't seem to mind."

Harry clearly enjoyed his memories of Grace the Lace. Raynes let him ramble on. He was preparing to drop a small boulder into Harry's quiet erotic pool.

"Now, Harry," he said, "you're being very honest with me and I appreciate that. But I wonder if you'd mind telling me why you were seen filling up a jar with sand outside this lady's caravan?"

Harry Robb looked thunderstruck.

For almost a minute, he seemed lost for words.

"Me?"

It was almost a squeak.

"Do you deny that there was a heap of sand near this woman's caravan?"

Harry continued to look amazed. Even hurt.

He stuttered: "There was certainly some sand there. And paving stones. But I didn't touch it. I swear to God I didn't touch it! If anyone said I did that, they're a liar. I'll kill 'em!"

Carlisle was shaken by the violence of the last three words. He looked up at the boy and then over the table to Raynes, who was clearly ignoring his fury.

"Well, if it wasn't you, it must have been one of the other scouts. Perhaps I was misinformed. In that case, did you see any other scouts mucking around with the sand?"

Harry looked slightly happier as the heat was turned off him personally.

"Johnny and Mark were kicking it around whilst they were waiting. And Simon ... he got pushed into the sand by Geoff. I remember he got it all down shorts. It was a bit of a laugh, that! I remember Graeme saying that although Grace wasn't very particular, she might draw the line at sandpaper ...!"

"So that's all you saw?"

"Yes."

"And you didn't see anyone putting any in a jar?"

"No."

"You know why I'm asking that question?"

"Because you think that someone who went to see Grace used that sand on Allan last night?"

"Correct!"

Harry was deep in thought.

Raynes continued:

"I'm sorry my suspicion has fallen on you. After all, you are one of the toughest scouts and it must have taken a tough person to hold Allan down ... So, if it wasn't you, who d'you think was capable of doing such a thing?"

Harry looked tearful.

"I can't think of any of the lads doing a thing like that. Of course, Allan was a bit of a snooper. A big-mouth. But everyone took that with a pinch of salt. I've got nothing against

48

him. He helped me get my mountaineering badge last year. When you're hanging on to a rope half-way down a fifty-foot rock face, you can't help being bloody grateful to the person on the other end of the rope. He saved my life at least three times …"

"Quite so," said Raynes, "but suppose it had been Graeme in the tent – instead of Allan? Suppose the murderer didn't know they'd switched at the last moment? Is there anyone who would have liked to do in Graeme?"

Harry shook his head.

"We all know about Graeme," he laughed. "As I say, all he does is screw around. Perhaps some woman's husband might have it in for him? Revenge, you know? But I should think they'd be far more likely to beat him up and knock that smarmy grin off his stupid face."

"If Graeme had knocked off your sister, Betty – is that what you'd have done?"

Harry Robb looked thoughtful.

"I might have socked him in the eye – or kneed him in the balls. But I wouldn't have killed him."

"And you don't know anyone who would?"

Harry shook his head.

"Not round here. You'd have to be pretty bloody angry to do something like that …"

"So you think we should look further afield?"

"None of the lads'd do a thing like that. Never in a month of Sundays."

Raynes looked over to Carlisle who was still trying to keep up with the conversation.

"One final question … You were in the big tent … the one nearest the river?"

"That's right."

"With Tony and the twins? Did you hear anyone go in or out of your tent during the night?"

"No. But I'm a heavy sleeper."

"You didn't hear Colin shouting out?"

"No."

"You didn't hear anyone telling him to shut up?"

49

"No. I didn't hear anything till breakfast-time. Until Graeme went over to his tent to wake him up, I hadn't the vaguest idea that anything was wrong. None of the lads knew. It was awful. Just awful."

Raynes nodded.

He had got the measure of Harry Robb.

8 *Fire in the Galley*

Raynes looked down his list.

"Now who shall we have next?"

"What about Harry's sparring partner?"

"Good idea!" said Raynes. "Call Garry Hogg."

* * *

Garry was a tall, wiry, nervous-looking youth with lank black hair which did not seem to have been cut for a very long time. Considering his hair-style and his generally uncouth appearance, Raynes could imagine him in later life doing an audition for the part of Adolf Hitler on Channel 4. His eyes were shifty and watchful, but apart from an occasional glance upwards at the detectives' faces, his gaze was set firmly on their hands. He seemed ill at ease.

"How old are you, Garry?"

"Sixteen."

"Same age as Harry?"

He nodded.

"Have you left school as well?"

He shook his head.

"I'm staying on to do my 'A' levels."

"Hoping to go to University?"

"That's what my Dad wants."

"And eventually get a job in the family firm?"

"That's what he hopes."

"But not what you want? What's your ambition?"

"Catering. Something in the food line."

"Are you responsible for the meals at camp?"

Garry nodded.

"Tom and I normally do it together. But he's not here this year."

"In disgrace, I hear?"

Garry looked up with a rather pained expression on his face: "I wouldn't believe everything you're told. Allan's been on his back for months, trying to get him thrown out of the Troop. I know you're not supposed to speak ill of the dead, but Allan had it in for Tom. He was always snooping, sneering and threatening. And then he made a big song and dance about some incident in the shower-room. It was nothing serious … just a bit of horseplay. I was there. But, by the time Allan had spoken to Neil, it had reached crisis proportions. It's a good job Tom's not here at camp. If he was, he'd probably be the No. 1 suspect."

"Where is Tom?"

"Back in town, I should think. He works with the Council. Public works …"

Raynes nodded. Another one with access to sand.

"So you like Tom?"

"He's a hard worker. Works hard; plays hard."

"And he's a homosexual?"

Garry shrugged his shoulders.

"It's difficult to say. He's had one or two girl-friends. I think it's just a phase he's going through."

"But Tom's not got through it yet. How old is he?"

"About twenty, I think."

"Does he get on well with Graeme?"

"Seems to. I think Graeme enjoys his cooking. It's not everyone who can turn up a good meal on a two-ring Calor gas stove."

"And you've been taking his place? How did you get on?"

"No complaints so far."

Garry managed to raise the ghost of a smile.

"And who helps you in the kitchen?"

"Ian Mackay, Simon and Geoff. My brother gives a hand sometimes."

"That's Stephen? How old is he?"

"Thirteen."

51

The same age as Colin. Another of the younger scouts.

Raynes looked at Garry's hang-dog demeanour and decided to be provocative. "Does Harry Robb ever help you?"

"Does he hell!" Garry's reply was cutting and hostile. "He's another of them ..."

"Another of what?"

"Liars and story-tellers. Just like Allan! He spends his time talking about things he knows nothing about. And Neil does nothing to stop him. I think he should. But Neil's too weak. He just lets him get away with it."

"Hold it!" said Raynes. "I thought you and Harry had fallen out over something *you* had said about *his* sister? Something not very nice ..."

Garry looked aggrieved.

"That was nothing! You don't know what he was saying before that! He was saying that my dad was a crook. That he was stealing money from the shop. Fiddling the books. He said that Allan had been looking into it and that my dad was for the high jump when the accountants heard about it ..."

"Allan worked for your father?"

"Well, he's employed by the company – Star Travel – because he's a trainee. My dad was hoping to get him transferred to another firm because he kept putting his nose into things that didn't concern him. My dad's sick and tired of him and that's the truth."

"So when Harry spouted that lot ..."

"I just thought I'd spill the beans about his sister. I know what she's been up to. Tom told me ..."

"And Harry hit you?"

Garry sniffed miserably. "I hit him back. But he's stronger than me."

Raynes looked at Carlisle. "Still waters run deep," he said. To Garry, he said: "Well, I suppose there's one blessing in all this. Your dad won't be having any more trouble with Allan. His stories have perished with him."

Garry sat on his hands and bent so far forwards over the table that Raynes could see down the back of his shirt.

"I hope so," he said miserably. "But what if you lot try to pin the blame on my dad? He could lose his job. And he's spent years building the firm up."

Raynes tried to sound comforting.

"If he has nothing to hide, your dad's got nothing to fear. I'm far more worried about you."

"Me?"

Garry looked up with surprise.

"Yes, you!" said Raynes. "You've told me that you're in charge of the kitchen. And presumably of all the equipment?"

Garry nodded.

"Well, you know how Allan died?"

"Someone stuffed him full of sand."

"Yes. But how did they do it? They used one of your kitchen utensils. We've found the teethmarks on the stem ..."

Garry looked blank.

"The plastic funnel ..."

Garry opened his mouth.

"That would explain it."

"Explain what?"

"I was looking for it yesterday. I wondered where it had gone. We don't use it often except when we're pouring cooking oil back into the tin. I noticed it had gone."

"When was that?"

"Yesterday lunchtime. Just after lunch. I actually thought the twins had taken it. They were busy building dams across the river. I thought they'd probably walked off with it. I didn't bother too much because I wasn't needing it. But I'd seen it was gone. That's the grey one ..."

"Yes," said Raynes. "The grey one. I'm glad you'd noticed, because it's a very important piece of evidence."

"Where did you find it?"

"I'm not sure," said Raynes, "but I believe it was back in the bread tray by noon today."

"I see."

Garry looked glum.

Raynes turned the screw a little tighter.

"I'm also told that you were one of the lads visiting Grace – the lady on the caravan estate?"

Garry went bright red.

"Did Harry tell you that?"

"No. As a matter of fact, he didn't. But he did tell me that there was quite a quantity of sand outside this lady's caravan …"

Garry looked anxious at Raynes' implication.

"It wasn't me," he said. "I didn't touch any of that sand. Well, I did touch it. I put some down Geoff's neck. We were just mucking about. But I didn't do anything to Allan. I wouldn't kill someone …"

Raynes looked at him silently.

Garry continued: "I hated his guts – right enough. He'd done a lot of damage. But I didn't touch him. I never went near his tent that night. Anyway, he wasn't in his tent. He was in Graeme's. None of us knew that."

Raynes looked at him coldly.

"I'm just putting two and two together. You have just told us that you disliked Allan. You had a reason to dislike him. He'd been prying into the business details of your father's firm. He may have uncovered some shady business …"

Garry shook his head.

"You don't know the full story and neither do I – just yet. But he could have discovered something. He tells the other scouts. Harry puts it to you. You are so angry at the allegation, that you end up in a fight. Quite a bloody business, from what I hear. You now know what Allan has been saying. You're very close to your dad. You're very anxious to defend him. You're very concerned about his reputation. As you say, his job depends upon it. You wanted to silence him. Perhaps you went a bit too far?"

Garry looked shocked at the suggestion.

"I never touched him."

"I never said you did. I am merely suggesting that you had a genuine motive. You also had the means. You were able to get sand from this lady's garden. You have a number of con-tainers in your food store – and you have the funnel. You wait your turn till you can get Allan on his own. Last night, you were presented with a golden opportunity. Allan was on his own. Perhaps you overheard the leaders agreeing to switch tents. You were in the third tent from the right – next door to Neil and Allan? You could silence him once and for all. You had access to all the equipment. It would have been quite easy for you to wash it all out and put it back in its place? Couldn't you?"

Raynes waited to see how Garry would respond.

The reaction was more dramatic than he had expected.

Throughout his lengthy description, Garry had sat riveted to his chair, staring at the Inspector with anxious eyes. "It's not true," he screamed. "It wasn't me! I never touched him! It's a lie! It's a filthy lie! I never heard anything! I never set foot in that tent! Never!" His last word was almost a hysterical shriek. He stood up. "You bastards!" he yelled. "You cold-blooded bastards!" Then he burst into tears and ran out of the room, screaming and howling down the passage.

Raynes watched his reaction closely.

How interesting!

He turned to Carlisle:

"Interview closed, I think?"

"He got a nasty shock."

"Too near the bone."

As he spoke, Neil Gray came rushing into the room.

"What's happened to Garry?" he asked. "What have you done to him? He's gone absolutely bananas!"

Raynes tried to calm him down.

"I'm afraid he's very upset. A troubled conscience. He didn't like Allan. He had grounds for wanting to silence him. He had access to the sand and to the funnel ..."

"The funnel ...?"

"They found teethmarks on the stem."

Neil looked distressed.

"Someone used the kitchen funnel?"

Raynes nodded. "Almost certainly."

Neil expressed his total disbelief.

"But Garry would never have killed Allan! Never in a million years! Garry's a coward! A complete coward!"

"That's what worries me," said Raynes. "That attack on Allan was just the sort of attack a coward would make."

"But surely you don't think that Garry did it?"

Raynes shrugged his shoulders.

"You saw what happened. That wasn't a normal reaction. A person that's completely innocent doesn't go hysterical. There's something bugging him. What it is, I don't know. Perhaps you can find out? In the meantime, we'll press on. Send in Johnny Cotton."

9 *Jump down, turn around*

"Did you use the thumbscrews on him then?"

Johnny Cotton grinned.

Raynes shook his head. "Police methods have advanced a little since then! We pull out the odd fingernail or hold a lighted cigarette close to the left eyeball and it's amazing how quickly people confess!"

Johnny looked at the table.

"I don't see any cigarettes!"

"I don't smoke," said Raynes. "Vile habit!"

"So he didn't confess?"

Johnny sounded disappointed.

"No one's confessed. We haven't got that far. People are just telling us what they've seen and heard. It's my job to put the pieces together – like a jigsaw. Until you've got all the pieces together, you can't see the picture. Now what can you tell me?"

"About who?"

"About anyone. Let's start with you."

"I missed it. Sick as two parrots, Mark and me were! Slept through it all. Heard no sounds of choking. Nothing."

"Colin seems to have heard something?"

"He would!"

"Apparently he called out to Graeme and woke you up?"

"To be honest, I don't really remember. I was fast asleep. Mark tells me I told Colin to shut up. But I'm always telling him to shut up."

"Why?"

"Oh, because he's such a bighead. Always bursting with plots and conspiracies. D'you know what he was telling us this morning? He'd heard from Allan that his stepmother had been having it off with Graeme ...!"

Raynes groaned inwardly.

Not another one!

"... Apparently he's been doing her garden for her and when he came in for a cup of tea, she gave him much more!" He giggled. "Allan told him he walked in and caught them at it. Colin's convinced that Allan's stepmother bumped him off because he had threatened to tell his father! That's the sort of stories Colin tells!"

"There might be some truth in it. Graeme seems to have quite an eye for the ladies?"

"But have you seen her? She's really fat! Graeme wouldn't go with someone like that!"

"He seems quite happy to visit Grace!"

Johnny grinned.

"You met Grace?"

"No. She's a treat in store."

"You'll like her. She's great! We go over before tea. I try to get in first. Don't have to queue then. She makes me laugh so much, it puts me off. Really long legs, she's got." Johnny made a sucking sound with his mouth. "Real brown too."

"Not Newcastle Brown, I hope?" said Raynes.

Johnny groaned and shut his eyes.

"That stuff," he said, "it was foul. Mark and me both had the diehorreas for two days. It was piss-awful!"

"Some people like it!"

"They can keep it. Bloody gut rot, if you ask me! Who needs sand?"

Raynes sighed.

"Well, that seems a good moment to get back to the point. If you didn't see anything and you didn't hear anything, all you can offer is circumstantial evidence ...?"

"Circum-what?"

"... a personal picture, shall we say, of why Allan died and who was responsible."

Johnny rolled his eyes. "Well, that's quite simple, isn't it? He was choked to death with sand. Graeme carries sand around in his truck. Stands to reason, he decided to bump Allan off. He gave him that dirty book. He said: 'You use my tent, old fruit.' Allan says: 'Thanks, mate!' And in the depths of the night, Graeme crawls in and duffs him. 'That'll silence you, you grasser!' Or words to that effect. Then he crawls out and skips it back to Allan's own tent before Neil notices he's been and gone. 'Cept Colin who heard him go."

"Is that your theory?"

"One of them."

"Oh, there's more than one?"

"Well, of course, it could be Mr Gray."

"Why should it be Mr Gray?"

"'Cos he was frightened of what Allan'd tell the District Commissioner about Grace! Fancy Colin getting the clap …!"

"He hasn't, has he?"

Raynes was shocked.

"I don't know. But imagine the blow-up! Gee! Mr Gray sacked on the spot. Allan made Scout Master. Tom and Graeme would resign. Half the parents would take their kids away from the 14th. We're sitting on a volcano! Mr Gray's got a lot to lose!"

"Yes. That's a fair point. Do you think Mr Gray knows about all of you going round to see Grace?"

"Sure. Allan would have told him!"

"Didn't Allan ever visit Grace?"

"Not this year, he didn't. But last year, him and Tom and Graeme used to vanish away. We didn't know where they went. But this year we followed Graeme and guess what we found?"

"Why d'you think Allan pulled out?"

"Because he's ambishous! Very ambishous! Doesn't want to blot his copy book. He's hoping to be made Scout Master of the 8th Troop. And, besides that, Mark tells me he's got a girl-friend …"

"Who's that then?"

"Mr Gray's wife's youngest sister. Sheila, I think he said her name was. Sheila – or Shirley. Anyway, if that's true –

it stands to reason, doesn't it? Doesn't want to catch anything! Not that there's anything to catch! Grace is real careful! You'll like Grace!"

"I'm sure I will," said Raynes, winking at Carlisle who was trying not to laugh.

He made a severe effort to keep the interview under control. "So you think Allan was a reformed character?"

"Looks like it," said Johnny, "but it hasn't done him much good, has it?"

"Suppose it wasn't Graeme or Mr Gray who did it? Who else d'you think could have done it?"

Johnny thought deeply – then laughed.

"Why not Colin himself? Committing the perfect crime! He'd like that. Pulling wool over the eyes of Mr Hocule Parrot and Mr Hemlock Sholmes! Except perhaps it's a bit too crude?"

"No finesse," Raynes agreed, "and perhaps there's another reason. Wasn't Allan teaching Colin mountaineering? He'd hardly be likely to murder him before he got his badge?"

Johnny looked disappointed.

"I hadn't thought of that. In that case, it's got to be Tom. Or Garry – he hated Allan's guts. Harry told Garry what Allan had said about his dad. That was a real fight! Blood all over the place! Mm," he chuckled at the memory. "Garry shares a tent with his brother, Steve. So he could have done it. Sworn his brother to silence – or put something in his bedtime cocoa. That'd be in character! And then crept out and did the dirty deed. It wouldn't have taken him long. Honour of the family and all that!"

"So you think anyone could have done it?"

"Not the twins!"

"And not Johnny Cotton?"

"Innocent, your honour!"

Raynes smiled: "Off you go, you rascal – and behave, or else you'll end up like Graeme!"

"Could do worse!"

As Johnny swaggered off down the passage, Carlisle turned to Raynes: "Do you think there might be a grain of truth in all that?"

Raynes smiled.

"A whole container-full, I should say! What a character! And what a collection of red herrings! A witness like that makes me feel like retiring on the spot! Everything so plausible. And yet, so confusing. I think I could do with a cup of tea before I face the next one. Could you ask Mrs Sheldon to wave her magic wand? Two sugars!"

10 *Softly sings the donkey*

After a cup of strong tea, Raynes buckled down to the task of interviewing the remaining scouts.

Ian Mackay was solid and disapproving. He was a dour, cautious boy of fifteen who subjected all Raynes' questions to prolonged reflection before giving an answer. His family, being staunch members of the Baptist Church, did not approve of immoral behaviour by members of the Scout movement. He thought that Tom was a dangerous and wicked pervert who should be drummed out of the Troop immediately. He disapproved of Colin and the other scouts visiting Grace the Lace. He thought it was disgusting and he was very surprised that Neil Gray had not put his foot down firmly and put the caravan site out of bounds to the boys. His father had already spoken to Neil about his failings as a leader, but it didn't seem to have had the slightest effect. In fact, even before this morning's murder, he had been thinking of transferring his allegiance to a decent troop – with a firm accent on the word 'decent'.

Yes, he had been woken up by Colin. He was often woken up by Colin. He was a difficult person to share a tent with because he sat up half the night reading a series of paperback thrillers by torchlight – often exclaiming loudly when clues were found or murderers revealed. He had a great passion for explaining the plot – or parts of the plot – even though you had made it perfectly clear that you did not have the slightest interest in what the book was all about. All Ian wanted to do at night was sleep. He needed at least eight hours a night. But Neil had asked him to look after Colin and, heavy though the cross was to bear, he had done his best. On balance, he thought that perhaps there was some minor improvement.

"Does anyone like Colin?" Raynes asked.

Ian mulled over the question for a lengthy thirty seconds.

"His mother!" he said eventually. "He's very fond of his mother."

"Well, I'm glad someone likes him," said Raynes.

Anyway, Colin had woken him up, declaring dramatically that Graeme was being attacked. He had listened for a moment or two but hadn't heard anything. He wasn't particularly bothered about Graeme because, being one of the leaders, he was quite capable of looking after himself. No, he didn't like Graeme.

The only scout he had liked was Allan. He had admired him as a dedicated scout with high principles and great leadership potential. If Allan had moved to the 8th Grasshallows Troop, he would have gone with him. He had found him a very kind, helpful and enthusiastic leader and Ian had learnt a lot from him. He was very distressed about the murder and the way it had been committed. He did not think that any of the scouts could have done the actual murder, but conceded that it looked like an inside job. Or had been made to look like an inside job. He agreed that there were deep undercurrents of bad feeling between Garry and Allan which might have played a part in all this. However, Ian Mackay had no theories to offer – a pleasant change from Johnny Cotton whose list of homicidal maniacs had included virtually everyone except himself.

Raynes tried out his personal theory that Allan had been killed by mistake and that one of Graeme's many lovers – or their partners – might have engineered his death. But Ian disagreed. He could not see why anyone should wait till they were all at camp. Surely there were many other opportunities back in Grasshallows – cutting the brake pipes on his truck or something equally unpleasant? Ian deplored Colin's tendency to portray everyone as a potential killer. He felt Colin was not being helpful. In fact, Ian was glad that the summer camp had come to an end. It had been an unmitigated disaster from start to finish.

When Raynes asked Ian what career he hoped to follow, he was surprised to hear that Ian had always wanted to be a policeman. He regarded it as a safe, quiet job, with good pay and a free house. Besides all that, he would be enforcing the law of God upon his fellow citizens – something that he felt would combat the wiles of the Devil. Raynes made a mental note that in no way should Ian Mackay ever become a policeman – and certainly not in Grasshallows!

* * *

Mark Todd was a more lively person than Ian – but he enjoyed all the vices which Colin's tent-mate deplored. He admitted to a variety of experiences with Tom and Garry, Simon and Geoff, but he didn't feel morally corrupted or ashamed. He regarded it all as part of life's rich tapestry – just as Grace was.

Mark admitted that he and Johnny Cotton had been using empty orangeade bottles to shoot the rapids in the river till Neil had stopped them. There were plenty of bottles round the camp – full and empty. They had all been bought from the same shop so it would be quite possible to exchange one bottle for another – or to use a bottle full of sand as the murder weapon. In fact, he had seen the twins filling several bottles of sand whilst they were building their dam. The weight of the sand was to act as a foundation in the main structure.

Raynes looked closely at Mark and noted that he had very thin lips and a tongue that shot out – thin and cutting – rather like a snake. In fact, everything about him had a snake-like quality. He had a yellowish complexion, a long neck and sharp black eyes. He was tall and thin and his clothes did not seem to hang well on him. Raynes felt that he was basically a spiteful and vicious character and that with his venom and Johnny's wicked sense of humour, they made rather a dangerous pair.

Mark did not have much to say about the murder. It had come as a surprise and he was sorry he had missed it. If it had been Graeme, he would not have been surprised. But Allan, he thought, was well-liked – except by Garry and Tom. However, knowing both these lads over a number of years, he could not imagine for one minute that they would stoop to murder. If he had to select anyone as the killer, he – like Johnny – would have chosen Graeme. But it was hard to think of any plausible motive. Jealousy, perhaps?

Mark confirmed that Allan was indeed going out with Sheila, Neil's sister-in-law, who was a Sunday School teacher at St Benedict's. A girl at Henslea School had told him that they had been out together a few times, but everything was very platonic. Mark said that he personally liked Allan very much, but he couldn't deny that he talked too much for his own good. He didn't like the way Allan had treated Tom but Tom had over-reacted. For Neil Gray, Mark had a healthy respect. It was not easy being a scout-leader, but he was very fair and did his best. This year's summer camp had been a good one and, unlike Ian, he had enjoyed it to the full.

* * *

Stephen Hogg was to his brother what a pint is to a litre. He too was tall, thin and wiry, with loose black hair. But, in proportion, he was smaller, tidier and seemed less shifty than his brother. He told the detectives that he was thirteen. On the question of the murder, he had little to offer. He was sleeping in the same tent as his brother, but he had been dog-tired on Monday night and had heard nothing. Not even Colin. He had never imagined anything of that kind ever happening at camp and was deeply shocked.

He shared his brother's violent hostility towards Harry Robb for the lies and untruths he had spread about their father. He seemed to think that Harry was the source of the allegations – not Allan. He had nothing against anyone – except Harry Robb. The only thing that concerned him was what Inspector Raynes had said to his brother which had caused him to weep hysterically in Mrs Sheldon's kitchen. The tears and the wailing had clearly unnerved him. Because Neil had been keeping separate those about to be interviewed from those who had already been seen, Stephen had been unable to talk to his brother. He felt the Inspector must have made some damning accusation against him, and Stephen was fierce in defending his family's good name. Raynes explained

63

calmly and carefully that he was looking for a motive for the killing and for someone who had the means. Garry had had both a motive and the means for killing Allan. Raynes said that when he had placed these facts before his brother, Garry had got extremely worked up. He, Raynes, had not accused him of anything. And if he and Garry were innocent, they had nothing to fear. Stephen did not look as if he believed the Inspector and scurried off to find his brother.

* * *

Tony Mason was Harry's friend and it seemed that, except in looks, they had much in common. Tony had close-cropped blonde hair, a square red face and very blue eyes. He too had broad shoulders and well-muscled arms. He looked as if he would be a tough customer if it came to a scrap.

Raynes was immediately impressed by his respectful tone of voice. He spoke softly with a distinct West Country accent. He had been born in Somerset and his father was a technician in the University. Tony had about him the warm glow of a cider apple ripening on a tree.

He shared Harry's view about Graeme being a con-man and a show-off but he could not for one moment accept that he was capable of murder. Graeme was sly, devious and immoral but, in Tony's experience, he always took the easy way in and out of things. Tony told Raynes how, on the first day of camp, he had followed Graeme – tracking him from field to field and then had crept up to Grace's caravan to see what was going on. He had not been surprised by what he had heard. Later that evening, Tony had asked Graeme point-blank who the female was, and Graeme had laughed and said she was the local nympho and might be glad of a little more company. He and Harry had gone to sample the goods and eventually Grace had proved so attractive that some after-noons there had been a small queue.

After the first couple of days, Graeme had kept away from the caravan, but Tony could not imagine for one minute that Graeme was tasting the wine of celibacy. There had to be 'another woman'! He had kept an eye on Graeme, and on Sunday night, twenty-four hours before the murder, he had

64

tracked him down to the *The Carpenter's,* where he had seen him getting into a car with another woman. Not Grace. Graeme had not been away long and he fancied she must have brought him back to the campsite at about 10.00 pm.

Tony was surprised that Neil tolerated Graeme's comings and goings. But he felt that, in some way, Neil was frightened of Graeme. He couldn't see why. Although he himself was only sixteen, he wasn't frightened of Graeme. Or Tom. Or anyone, come to that!

He was sorry he couldn't be more helpful to the Inspector and his team, but if he heard anything from the other boys, he would immediately be in touch. Raynes thanked him for his help.

* * *

Simon Wallace and Geoff Stewart were like two amiable pigs. They were messy, grubby and cheerful. Both had greasy brown hair; both were small; both liked food and drink; both were eager for any excitement life had to offer; both looked as if they had been sliding down haystacks for most of the afternoon, and both were fifteen years old. They looked at Raynes with small piggy eyes.

They worked in the kitchen with Garry – so they shared his views about Allan and Harry Robb. They were convinced that Garry was completely innocent. He would not dream of killing anyone. They thought that Allan was being quite wicked making any allegations against Mr Hogg who was a kind, good-natured man who had often given them a lift home from scout meetings. Now and again, they had been round to Garry's home for a barbecue with Tom and several other scouts, and they thought that perhaps Allan was jealous because he had not been invited.

Food was their chief interest in life. Bangers and mash. Baked beans and hamburgers. Lashings of chips. Mugs of tea. Chocolate biscuits. Large chunks of rich fruit cake. For them, camp had been a gastronomic paradise. They had been up mountains – they had gone canoeing. They had done all the things that scouts usually do at camp. But their heart was in the kitchen, and the longer the interview continued, the more

65

Raynes realized that they had little to offer his investigation. They were not interested in murder. They had no information to offer – no opinions. All they were anxious about was being fed. They kept asking the Inspector when they would be having their evening meal … and where?

* * *

Finally, Raynes saw the Armstrong twins. It was now about 7.00 pm and Pat and Doug had been waiting for over four hours for their interview. Consequently, they were both tired and tearful. They were the youngest scouts at camp – younger even than Colin. They had lived next door to Allan and his father, and had known the victim since childhood. The sight of Allan lying dead in his sleeping bag with his mouth full of sand had clearly distressed the twins and Raynes fancied that they would be having several unpleasant nightmares in the months that lay ahead. Already their eyes were red with crying.

Murder was something entirely beyond their world. They had enjoyed their first camp. They had been at their happiest paddling about in the river, building their dam. Mr Gray had shown them how to weigh down the foundations with bottles full of sand and, together with various rocks and lumps of wood, they had built two impressive dams blocking one tributary of the river and created a small lake. They believed that their bottles of sand were still where they had put them because otherwise the dams would have collapsed. The twins said that they had not seen anyone else filling bottles with sand, but they had seen Johnny and Mark using empty orangeade bottles to shoot the rapids. But Mr Gray had been quite angry with them and warned them about the dangers of broken glass and cut feet.

Raynes asked them for their opinion about Allan's step-mother. Did they like her?

Their first statement was that she was 'bossy' and that 'she shouts a lot', but on balance they agreed that she was 'all right'. They didn't think that Allan liked her. His real mother had died in a road accident and the new Mrs Foster was rather different. They had got the impression that she was always watching people – particularly Allan and his father.

The twins confirmed that Graeme Wilson looked after the Fosters' garden. He also looked after their garden when Mr Armstrong was too busy to do it himself. They thought he did the gardens of several other parents. He had also done Neil's garden in time past – but not since Christmas! They thought there had been some quarrel between Neil and Graeme.

All in all, there was not much that the twins could add to the sum of Raynes' investigations. He gathered that they liked Tom and thought that Allan and Ian Mackay's father had been most unfair. They were sorry that Tom had not been with them at camp this year because Tom cooked popcorn and covered it with syrup and sugar. It was delicious.

Whilst talking about food, Raynes discovered that the twins had been amongst those who succumbed to the Newcastle Brown. They shared the large army tent with Harry Robb and Tony Mason so they had drunk the left-overs. And how they had suffered!

* * *

Raynes thanked them for all their information and also thanked Mr and Mrs Sheldon for looking after the scouts all afternoon. He decided that he now had enough information to be going on with and so he gave Neil Gray permission to organize their return home. The police would return their tents and camping equipment in due course, once the investigation was complete.

Fortunately for Simon and Geoff, Mrs Sheldon had decided to cook a huge cauldron of home-made soup; so whilst Neil was at the telephone arranging for a mini-bus to come and collect them, the boys piled into the kitchen and had one last meal before they returned to Grasshallows.

For Inspector Raynes and Detective-Constable Carlisle, it had been a long day. They refused a bowl of soup and, before returning to Grasshallows, they called in to the incident room to see what was happening. But apart from two constables on duty, the place was deserted. All the information had been taken back to the city for analysis. Feeling that there was nothing more that either of them could do, Raynes and Carlisle decided to call it a day.

11 *Down at the station*

When Raynes arrived at his office at 9.00 on Wednesday morning, he realized that he was in for another busy day. He would have to speak to the Press; he would have to examine a lot of forensic reports and he wanted to read over the notes which Detective-Constable Carlisle had made. Above all, he needed time to think. To record his own impressions. To try and see precisely what the truth was behind all the statements he had received.

However, as he arrived at his desk – a new one, he was pleased to say – the first message that was relayed to him was that a Mr Hogg would like to see him at the earliest possible moment. He was bringing round his accountant and his lawyer and he wanted to silence – once and for all – the completely false allegations which had been made against him and his son.

Raynes pencilled him in for 11.30 am.

Carlisle had arrived half an hour before the Inspector and had already begun the process of dictating his notes. Raynes impressed upon him that he must not elaborate, gloss over or seek to interpolate any of the statements made. He must get down the exact words that were used – even if the final product was rough and bitty. Carlisle assured him that this was already being done, but it would probably take till lunch-time – if not longer.

Raynes said that was fine, but he would like at least three copies made since he expected to be writing all over them and they were bound to get a bit messed up.

By the time the first cup of coffee had been brewed – black with two sugars – the photographs had been delivered in a large brown envelope. Raynes considered them as he sipped his coffee. He noted the position of all the objects in the tent. They were just as he remembered them – including the half-moon stain where the bottle of orangeade had been ... or rather, the invisible bottle of orangeade ...

He looked at the pictures of Allan. Their formal nature reminded him of one of those medieval stone statues that one often finds in Cathedrals. The knight who died in the Crusades. All he needed was a sword. Raynes noted that his mouth was filled to the brim with sand and that some of it had flowed down both sides of his face. There were little heaps of it around his neck and ears. Raynes wondered how much sand had been used. He was still curious to know where it had come from.

He looked at the other pictures taken in the tent. There was a small smattering of sand on the right-hand side of the tent near the foot of the sleeping bag. The murderer had spilt a little as he crawled in. Raynes tried to imagine the scene. The assailant, with the funnel in his left hand, slightly off-balance as he crept forward. Funnel into the mouth with the left hand. The murderer must be right-handed!

It was a simple observation – but it all helped.

By 10.15 am, he had received another urgent message, this time from Allan's stepmother. She too was most distressed. Could she please come and speak to the Inspector and find out what had been happening? Raynes reckoned that there would be quite a number of parents anxious to see him – but at this moment they would be a hindrance rather than a help. He would have to see them – but in his own good time. He picked up the phone and arranged for two policewomen to do the rounds. They were to be as sympathetic as possible and obtain a full picture of the family backgrounds. They must make a list of all the pills kept in each house and ask if any of the boys had been seen doing suspicious things with sand before they set off to camp. However, he excluded the stepmother from the visitation. He would like to see her himself. Raynes pencilled her in for 4.00 pm.

Next to arrive was the report from the police surgeon – a pathologist in the University. He had cut Allan open and examined the contents of his throat and stomach. As expected, the cause of death was asphyxiation, and the time of death was given as between midnight and 3.00 on Tuesday morning. The sand had completely blocked the larynx and obstructed the rear nasal passages. About three-quarters of a pound of rough sand had been used.

The surgeon had also found clear evidence of Allan having been drugged. There were tiny white grains – infinitely small and well-ground down – mixed up with the contents of his stomach. The grains belonged to a common sleeping pill. The surgeon reckoned that as many as eight pills had been used but some had doubtless been absorbed. Corned beef hash had been on the menu on Monday night, followed by peaches, sponge and custard. The victim had also drunk large quantities of orangeade and sweet tea. It was difficult to say in which food or beverage the grains had been administered.

Raynes read the report in full.

The third batch of papers to land on his desk came from the forensic department. They confirmed that the teethmarks on the plastic funnel were those of the victim. As the funnel had been thrust into his open mouth, the victim's muscles must have reacted strongly against this alien object. For a few seconds his teeth were clenched together, gripping the upper part of the tube and had left their mark – so strong had been his reaction. But then the mouth had fallen open again as the sand poured rapidly through the funnel. It was reckoned that within ten seconds the oral cavity would have been completely blocked. Even if Allan had managed to bite through the stem of the funnel, it would not have saved him. The aperture of the funnel was about 1.75 cm. The forensic department had sent the funnel up to Raynes in a plastic bag. He looked at it and sent it back. They were merely confirming what he already knew.

The next paper concerned the bottles of orangeade. All the empty bottles – and the half-empty bottles – had been taken to the lab and tested. The suspect bottle had been found in the third crate down – in the middle of the crate. It had faint traces of the little white grains from the sleeping pills – very faint because someone had tried to wash out the bottle with river water. Two other bottles had traces of river water but only this one had two or three tell-tale white grains stuck to the inside.

Raynes made a mental note that the bottle must have been washed out in the dark – otherwise the murderer would have seen the tell-tale traces. Doubtless he – or she – would not have expected the orangeade bottles to be so carefully examined. After all, he – or she – had taken the trouble to remove the suspect bottle so that no suspicious questions would be asked.

The fingerprints department had not been so successful. It wasn't that there was nothing to go on. Rather, there was a superabundance of evidence – so much as to be completely confusing. Various sticky fingers had held the suspect bottle and Allan's fingerprints were amongst them. Raynes wondered whether he should bother having the scouts in to have their dabs. Almost certainly the murderer would have used a pair of pink plastic gloves – there were no fewer than four pairs in the kitchen tray. He had probably worn the fifth pair, done his dirty work, peeled them off and thrown them into the remains of the camp-fire. They would have been burnt in seconds.

He looked at the list of items found in the pockets of each boy. Sand had been found in the pockets of Johnny Cotton and Mark Todd, Simon and Geoff Wallace and in Garry Hogg's. Neil Gray also had some in his pocket – as did the Armstrong twins. In the case of the first five, the sand was of a reddish colour. In the case of Neil and the twins, it was brown sand from the river. Neither sample matched the sand found in Allan's throat, which was the sort of sand used on building sites. The forensic department noted that it had been dried out – perhaps in an oven – and contained a very low level of water.

Raynes thought this was most interesting. Where could a scout have found an oven in the middle of Picton Dale to dry out his sand? If indeed it was a scout who had prepared the sand? Obviously the sand had not been gathered from the riverbed on the spur of the moment! The crime had been premeditated and the sand specially brought to the campsite! But by whom?

Returning to the pockets, he found a comprehensive list of objects: sweets, knives, handkerchiefs, contraceptives, a cartridge, a packet of tissues, a balloon, two water pistols, a dried conker, a plastic pen top, two corks, a fish hook, a pan scrubber,

71

eight compasses and several bus tickets – together with coins, keys and banknotes.

Raynes looked down the lists for each boy but could not see anything suspicious. What interested him was the absence of any bottle of pills. No traces of the pills had been found on any groundsheet, nor on the blade of any knife. Either the murderer had cut them up and ground them down in the open air – or he had prepared his medicine carefully before he came. Like the sand. How many pills had the murderer had in his possession? And where had he got them from? A friend? From a medicine cabinet at home? How were they transported? In a plastic bag? These were all questions for which he would like an answer.

The forensic department had been unable to say what container the sand had come in. There was a variety of plastic boxes and tubs in the waste bin – and one old salt drum had been found lodged against the riverbank two hundred yards downstream. But there was no evidence to show that it had ever contained sand. If the container had been used, every grain had been washed away. Raynes was not surprised.

For the next half hour, Raynes composed a bland and diplomatic communiqué for the Press. News of the murder had now leaked out and the duty officers at the campsite reported that a small army of photographers had invaded Picton Dale and large sums of money were being offered for first-hand accounts of the murder. Within twenty-four hours, thought Raynes, Colin would be selling his story! He could see it now!

He put together the essential facts: dates, times, the cause of death ... (that was sensational enough) ... But, for the rest, all he wanted to say was: 'The scouts have been interviewed' ... 'No arrests have been made' ... 'Forensic tests are continuing' ... 'Further investigations are being followed up' ... 'The net is being cast more widely' ... And finally, he put in a plea for privacy. (Not that the Press would pay any attention!)

He arranged his news conference for 12 noon and steeled himself to say: 'No comment' to any question which had the slightest relevance or interest. 'Bore the pants off them' was his motto!

12 *There ain't no flies on us!*

By 11.30 am, he was ready to see Mr Hogg.

Garry's father bustled in with a large man with orange hair and orange shoes, whom he described as the company's accountant. With them, they had brought files and papers filling two large brief cases. Bringing up the tail was Raynes' old sparring partner from a previous case – the lawyer, Mr Derek Coates-Smythe, who seemed most unhappy to be seeing the Inspector again – and so soon. His coded gesture was an eyes-to-ceiling look of despair, which indicated to Raynes that Mr Hogg's visit was not to be taken too seriously.

Mr Hogg launched his attack.

He was very angry – in fact, he was very, very angry – to hear that his son had been accused – officially accused – of murdering Allan Foster. He believed that this accusation was based on completely unfounded allegations made by the deceased to another young gossip named Harry Robb, who had had the audacity to suggest that there were some irregularities in the business affairs of Star Travel.

First of all, there were no irregularities of any kind. And, secondly, he had brought his accountant along to prove it. He had all the figures for the past ten years during which time he had been responsible for auditing all their accounts. His company's headquarters in London had always gone through his accounts with a fine toothcomb and they had never raised the slightest complaint – as his accountant would confirm. He was prepared to go through his books with the Inspector, page-by-page if necessary, and leave them with him for official scrutiny. He had nothing to hide.

Raynes made faint murmuring noises about being very busy already. He said that such substantial corroborative detail was hardly necessary. He was more than happy to take Mr Hogg's word for it.

But once Mr Hogg was in full flow, there was no stopping him. Serious accusations had been made against his son, Garry, and repeated to his younger son, Stephen. These must be with-drawn. Immediately! Otherwise, his lawyer, Mr Coates-Smythe, Grasshallows' most distinguished lawyer, would be taking legal action in court to restrain the police from repeating the allegations publicly. He had been told that there was to be a news conference at 12 noon. Time was short.

When the torrent had eased up sufficiently for Raynes to speak, the Inspector explained that the allegations made about Star Travel had not been made by him. They had been made by one of his own trusted employees. In normal circumstances, one would naturally regard such allegations as idle chit-chat, but Allan had been suddenly struck down and silenced in a particularly brutal way.

He, Raynes, was obliged to question suspects and search for motives. When he had been told by several scouts that these allegations had been made – and that a serious fight had already taken place over the issue – then he was duty-bound to take them seriously. If they were untrue, then no one had any reason to be upset. But, if they were true, then obviously they could constitute a substantial and serious motive for murder.

He pointed out that Mr Hogg's son, Garry, had freely admitted to being in a place where sand was copiously available. Sand had been found in his pockets. And, working in the kitchen, he had had access to both the funnel and the container which had been used in the murder. All he, Raynes, had done was to put two and two together and invite Garry to come clean. He had not done so. He had in fact stormed out of the room – giving every appearance of guilt. In the absence of any clear denial, what was he, Raynes, to think?

Whilst he was speaking, Raynes withdrew from the brown envelope the most horrible photograph of Allan's face – taken in close-up – showing the staring eyes and the pool of sand within the lips. He put the picture in front of Mr Hogg.

"This is what I'm worried about, Mr Hogg! This young man. Someone has killed him – and at the moment, suspicion points to one of these scouts. Until I know who killed Allan, I shall leave no stone unturned. In return, I require from each of these lads the most complete honesty and their fullest co-operation. I must say that, apart from Garry – and to a lesser extent, Stephen – I got a very helpful response."

Raynes eyed the travel agent coldly.

"You may be quite sure," he continued, "that I shall say nothing publicly until I am sure my case is cast-iron and final. Mr Coates-Smythe will be able to tell you that I shall not be hamstrung by any legal restraints whatsoever. I am the servant of the court and my duty is to find the murderer who did this. If it was your son, I shall be very sorry … very sorry indeed … but until I have more information, no one is being excluded from my investigations. And the position of your son is far from satisfactory. I shall certainly have to see him again …"

"He didn't do it. He told me."

Mr Hogg sounded a little more amenable to reason.

"Well, I wish he'd told me."

"You upset him terribly."

"I upset a lot of people."

Raynes put the photograph back in its envelope.

He smiled apologetically.

"Thank you for your visit. I understand your concern. You will appreciate that I have this news conference in about two minutes' time." He looked at Mr Hogg. "However, to set your mind completely at rest, I shall be quite happy for you to leave your company's accounts with me. I'll have the Fraud Squad give them the once-over. If they give you a clean bill of health, it'll certainly clear the air! Good day, gentlemen!"

* * *

"So they went off with their tails between their legs?"

Carlisle was amused.

"They hadn't a leg to stand on – and that photograph finished them off! I thought Mr Hogg was going to be sick all over my lovely new desk!"

"Are you really going to turn their accounts over to the Fraud Squad?"

"Why not?" said Raynes. "They wanted to make trouble. I've simply taken them up on their offer. There's probably

75

some fiddle going on. The expense accounts, I should think. We'll get the Squad to have a look at Mr Hogg's expense accounts, his bonuses and commission, free holidays and gifts in kind. If that doesn't produce one or two skeletons, I shall be most surprised. I hardly think Allan would have said what he did without there being some truth in it. No smoke without fire! Who knows? It may turn out to be the key to the whole case. We can't afford to ignore it."

"I bet Mr Derek Coates-Smythe wished he'd never come!"

Raynes shook his head sadly. "As far as I'm concerned, that man's a broken reed. He was no help to his client. He never said a word. But I expect he'll charge him a hefty fee. In fact, I'm sure he will."

13 *Ten sticks of dynamite*

The news conference was now over and Raynes and Carlisle were having a snack lunch in Raynes' office, eating steak and kidney pies from the police canteen.

"These things are bloody awful!" said Raynes.

"Nothing like those pies we had yesterday at *The Carpenter's*. They were delicious."

"I should think they've carved this steak off some prehistoric woolly mammoth in Grasshallows Museum! It tastes like Granny's knitting!"

He got up, opened the window and threw out the remains of the offending pie. Carlisle wrapped up the rest of his pie and put it in the bin.

"We'll let forensic take it up to the lab. Perhaps they'll be able to tell us what it was?"

Raynes phoned through for a jug of coffee.

"Now," he said more cheerfully. "Let's see what we caught yesterday."

* * *

Raynes and Carlisle pored over the transcripts of all the interviews they had conducted in Picton Dale the previous day. Raynes underlined certain remarks in blue ink and put circles round others.

"It's quite a marathon, isn't it?" he said. "Fourteen interviews in one day!" He looked at some of the statements and admissions made by the scouts. "You know," he said, "Johnny Cotton was right. This little lot could sink Neil Gray. If the District Commissioner were to see this document, Neil would be finished!"

"It's pretty damning," said Carlisle, "but where does it leave your theory about Graeme being the intended victim?"

"I don't know. At the moment, all the money seems to be on Allan. According to Graeme, Mr Hogg might have had it in for him – or, failing that, his stepmother ... By the way, she's coming in at 4.00 pm ... Mark Todd and Johnny Cotton both suggested that Graeme did it ... Not entirely seriously, I think ... Johnny and I both had doubts about Garry. And events this morning haven't exactly removed them – reinforced them, if anything – Johnny also opted for the stepmother, for Colin and for Neil Gray. Colin didn't suggest anyone ..."

"Wasn't it he who suggested the stepmother?"

Raynes shuffled through the papers.

"Yes, so it was. But Neil didn't suggest anyone. Nor did Ian Mackay. And the last lot were worse than useless ..."

"All they could think about was food."

"Perhaps we ought to get them back in? They must know something!"

"Are we going to look at Grace?"

Raynes smiled.

"Of course we're going to look at Grace! She's the one bright spot in this whole miserable business! I've booked her in for tomorrow morning. I think that if we go in the afternoon, we might have to queue ...!"

"I can't see why she would have wanted to murder Allan."

"No. But she might have wanted to murder Graeme! Fancy him bringing all that tribe along to her caravan for free rides! She must be absolutely boiling with resentment. Hell hath no fury like a woman scorned ... Who knows? Even though we know the sand didn't come from her caravan site, there is still a distinctly feminine touch to this crime. It's all very homely – what with the kitchen funnel ..."

"You said yesterday that it was cowardly too?"

"It is. A very sneaky, cowardly crime. That's why I wonder about Tom."

"The Invisible Scout ... Colin hated him. Ian Mackay was frightened of him and Allan reported him ..."

"But he seems to have quite a few friends?"

"We'll have to see him tomorrow."

There was a long silence whilst each of them read through the conflicting statements.

"Neil told us a lie!"

"Yes. I noticed that. He said he'd never seen anyone putting sand into a bottle. And yet the twins said that he showed them how to use bottles to ballast their dam."

"And yet he was shouting off to Johnny and Mark ..."

"He's a mass of inconsistencies."

"He certainly doesn't know how to handle Graeme."

"His private life's too bound up in it."

"I think he's going to have an even harder job now that Allan's gone. He seems to have been the one person who held the whole thing together."

"Undoubtedly," said Raynes. "Allan was the king-pin. Remove him – and the whole thing falls to pieces. Anyone who wanted to destroy the 14th Grasshallows Troop only needed to destroy Allan. You're quite right."

"But he was going anyway? Or, at least, he was hoping to?"

"Yes," said Raynes reflectively. "So why not let him go?"

"Neil had nothing to gain by losing him?"

"No. But perhaps Tom and Graeme did? Graeme is rising slowly to the top. But if he keeps on screwing Neil's wife, Jenny, he's skating on thin ice. Neil has only to open his mouth ..."

"But would he?"

Raynes shook his head.

"I'm getting worried about this case. I thought the murderer would stick out like a sore thumb. But he doesn't. Apart from Garry's dad, I'm hard pressed to see any motive. Most of the lads seemed to like Allan and I didn't pick up any obvious lies. Did you?"

78

"No. I thought they were a nice bunch."

"So – either the murderer was being extremely clever ... or perhaps," said Raynes, shoving the papers away, "... perhaps he or she isn't here at all. Perhaps these interviews were a complete waste of time and the motive is something completely different that we know nothing about?"

"But if the murderer wasn't one of the scouts, he wouldn't know that Allan and Graeme had switched tents at the last moment. So we come back to your theory ..."

"Which seems even more dubious! All the scouts seemed to like Graeme. Except for Neil, of course. Not forgetting the people that Graeme seems to have used ..."

"Or abused ..."

"Most of whom are off the campsite as far as we know."

"What about the mysterious woman Graeme saw on Sunday night? The one Tony Mason tracked down? She might be in on it?"

Raynes sighed deeply.

"When I was at school," he said, "I remember one night when the school prefects went off to raid the junior school's summer camp. They cycled out there at the dead of night and had quite a bit of fun, loosening the guy ropes and letting the tents collapse. In the confusion, they made their escape and cycled home. But it didn't take the camp leaders long to put two and two together and within minutes they had got to a telephone and were phoning back to the school. Consequently, the moment the prefects crawled back through the dormitory window, they were caught."

"I wish this case was as simple as that."

"It is simple," said Raynes, "very simple. If we knew the motive, we'd find the answer in a second. But where's the motive?"

"Perhaps his stepmother'll give us a clue?"

"Perhaps." Raynes did not sound hopeful. "I still think I'll ask Graeme to give me a list of his conquests ... if only to eliminate one element in the equation ..."

Carlisle's mind moved on to other things.

"When are we going to release the body?"

79

"They can have it now. We don't need it."

Raynes passed over all the other documents and envelopes. "You can file this lot," he said. "I've got it all in my head. But make sure you're back by 4.00 pm. I'd like you to take notes on what this lady says. It may be interesting."

14 *Better far is Woad!*

Mrs Foster was ushered into Raynes' office shortly after 4.00 pm. She was not fat, but she was certainly on the plump side. She had thick, bushy, chestnut-brown hair immaculately waved. Her eyes were also deep brown, but they and her nose were tinged with pink – showing signs of recent tears. She was wearing a smart white linen suit over a pale apricot-coloured blouse. Raynes reckoned that she was in her early forties.

He greeted her courteously.

"It's not often we have ladies in our office. Carlisle, get Mrs Foster a cup of something. Or perhaps you'd prefer a glass of sherry?"

"Sherry'd do nicely!"

"A glass of sherry then."

Mrs Foster settled herself to the left of Raynes so that the light from the window was on his face – not on hers. She put her white leather handbag on his desk and crossed her legs.

"Call me Ellie," she said. "Everybody does."

"Is that short for Ellen?"

"Jacqueline."

"And what do you do for a living, Ellie?"

"I'm a staff nurse at Grasshallows Royal."

"And you've been married to Mr Foster for …"

"Arthur and I've been married for five years."

"And what does he do?"

"He's a travelling salesman. Not in this country. He goes abroad selling pharmaceuticals …"

It seemed a large word, but, after all, Ellie was a nurse.

"Does he know about Allan yet?"

"No. That's half the trouble. His company is trying to find him. I just wondered if the police could do anything to help?"

"We'll do our best."

Raynes wrote down: 'Find Arthur' on his pad.

Ellie watched him.

"I also think that I might have been told a little earlier that Allan had died. I didn't hear till after 7.00 last night when Neil's wife came round to tell me. I think that's dreadful! His relatives should have been told immediately."

Raynes tapped his pencil softly on his pad.

"I have no intention of going into every detail of police procedure, Mrs Foster, but for the sake of the boys themselves, I put on a news blackout till 6.00 pm. No one was to be informed till I had completed my first round of questions. I didn't want to be surrounded by hysterical parents or besieged by the Press. But you are quite right. You had a duty to be informed. After all, you are his stepmother!"

Ellie looked slightly happier at Raynes' apology.

The Inspector continued: "So you've known Allan for the past five years?"

"Longer than that. Arthur and I were going out for three or four years before that."

"After his first wife died?"

"Just about."

It was amazing what a wealth of information could be conveyed in just two words.

Raynes smiled.

But Ellie had another surprise in store.

"Of course you know that Allan wasn't her son – or Arthur's?"

"No," said Raynes. "I didn't know that."

"I thought the police knew everything! Allan was adopted. She couldn't have any children of her own so they got him through the adoption."

"The way you speak, it doesn't sound as if you think they got a very good bargain?"

"I've got nothing against Allan." Ellie's eyes looked guarded. "He was always a hard worker. Very healthy and fit. He got on well with people. He was clean. Always kept his things tidy ..."

81

Raynes could see that these things would be great virtues in Mrs Foster's eyes.

"But …?"

"But he talked too much. His tongue always let him down. If he could just have kept things to himself, that would have been fine – but no! He's always had to spout. I said it would be the death of him. And now it has."

Raynes nodded thoughtfully.

"And who d'you think had most to lose by his 'spouting'? Star Travel?"

Ellie snorted. "They're a fine crowd – according to Allan. A bunch of crooks, if you ask me! 'Ghost payrolling' I think it's called. They'd employ temporary staff and then claim they were still paying them for a month after they left …"

Raynes looked at Carlisle.

"… At least, that's what Allan said."

"And what about Tom?"

"Well, there's another one! Allan would have been much better going to see the District Commissioner privately and telling him what was going on. But he didn't. Instead, he went and told Neil and then he let everyone know he'd spoken to Neil. So the whole Troop was talking about it – and taking sides. Some supported Tom – though how they could, I just don't know! The rest supported Allan and Neil. But it made Neil's job so much harder. If Allan could just have curbed his tongue! But of course he didn't."

"D'you think Tom could have been involved in his murder?"

"Who else? If you knew the bad feeling there's been in that Scout Troop these past two months! Something had to give! The tension. The gossip. Complaints from parents. Scandal and shame. That's why half the troop didn't go to camp this year. They said it was a question of money – but it wasn't. They were frightened of moral corruption."

"But Tom didn't go to camp?"

"He was told not to. Neil told him he wasn't to come. But it's the first time he's missed. He's the one that always does the cooking. He's a good cook – I'll say that for him. But everything else about him stinks. He can't keep his hands off the younger boys. In the showers. In dark corners. He's disgusting! They should have thrown him out of the Scouts years ago! He's the sort of person who gives the movement a bad name."

"So Allan was the one who brought all this up?"

"Yes. But in completely the wrong way. He should have been discreet. Said what he had to – in the right ears. But, instead, he had to let everyone know he had told Neil. He told them one by one but, in a small community, gossip spreads like wildfire and within a week, everyone heard ..."

Raynes thought that perhaps he could understand why Allan had done what he had. Adopted children have a great need to be loved and accepted. By sharing information and secrets, Allan was subconsciously seeking support and acceptance. Underneath the surface of physical prowess and adventure, Allan was deeply insecure.

"How did Tom react to all this?"

"Well, of course, he was extremely bitter. He said that Allan had been lying and exaggerating. He got Allan round the neck one night and threatened to strangle him ... Tom's quite strong. He said to Allan: 'If I catch you alone on a dark night, don't complain! And don't expect any mercy 'cos you won't get it!'"

"So you think Tom had a good motive?"

"Better than most! He's a strange person is Tom. Very much a loner. He reads all those occult magazines, and Allan caught him teaching the boys to read Tarot cards. I wouldn't be surprised to hear he was a warlock and took part in Satanic rites."

"The Devil Incarnate?" Raynes smiled in polite disbelief. "You paint a formidable picture of this young man, Mrs Foster. But how can we be sure he was up in Picton Dale at 2.30 on Tuesday morning? And how can we be sure he knew which tent Allan was in?"

"He was in Graeme's tent."

"Who told you that?"

Ellie thought for a minute.

"Jenny, I suppose."

"And how did she know?"

"I expect Neil told her."

"So you are suggesting that Tom was lurking in the darkness near the camp, watching what was going on?"

"It would be quite in character."

Raynes smiled grimly. She was determined to blacken Tom. And she was doing a splendid job of it. But what would happen if he accused her? He decided to see.

"That's all very interesting, Mrs Foster, but what would you say if I told you that no less than two people have named you as a possible suspect?"

"I've been accused of many things in my life – but never murder."

"But you may have had something to hide? Something which Allan knew? Something that worried him? Something that he might have 'spouted' to a whole number of people which could have done you enormous damage?"

Ellie returned the service with a superb backhander.

She looked Raynes straight in the eye.

"We've all got skeletons in our cupboards, haven't we, Inspector? Or did my eyes deceive me? In a little restaurant outside Grasshallows – about three weeks ago? Didn't I see you with a lady of very ill-repute? A certain Mrs Debbie May if that's what her name still is?" She laughed contemptuously. "People only want one thing from Mrs May and she makes them pay through the nose for it! But perhaps it was a professional meeting, Inspector? Your profession, I mean, not hers. Not that it looked that way from where I was sitting!"

Carlisle dared not lift his eyes from his notepad. What would Raynes say in reply to that?

Raynes smiled coldly.

"Next time I go on one of these moral improvement courses, I shall have to wear a wig and dark glasses!" He laughed, but there was no doubt that he was embarrassed. Ellie had scored a superb hit.

She opened her handbag and lit a cigarette. The extent of her victory was that Raynes said nothing. Usually he hated people smoking, and an edict had been passed that his office was to be a non-smoking area.

Ellie took a couple of drags on her foul-smelling weed and looked at Raynes with humorous contempt.

"So you get my point, Inspector? We all have little things we would rather not be made public." She looked at Raynes through a cloud of cheap tobacco smoke: "If you're accusing me of having a little on the side, I'll not deny it. But I don't see how that makes me a murder suspect."

"Because you might have wanted to hide it from your husband, Arthur? You might have wanted to silence the gossiping mouth once and for all?"

"Are you accusing me?"

"No. I'm merely suggesting you might have had a motive."

"And what am I supposed to be hiding from my husband?" She looked calm and unconcerned. "Do you have an ash-tray round here?"

Raynes suggested she might use her empty sherry glass.

"I think," he said, "that you might be wanting to hide an affair with Graeme?"

"Oh, Graeme? He just does my garden."

"He has quite a reputation with the ladies?"

"Not with me, he doesn't! I've heard him boasting about his conquests. I think you should take his evidence with a pinch of salt, Inspector. I'm old enough to be his mother!"

"I think that's what worried Allan."

Raynes waited to see what Ellie would say in reply. She said nothing. She ground out the remains of her cigarette and looked the Inspector in the face.

"Is that the extent of your case against me?"

"There is no case against anyone – yet. We're simply hearing evidence from every possible source. Later on, we have to make up our minds who is telling the truth. I think you've told me at least one lie. Probably several more. Unless you are covering something up, there's no need to lie."

"What difference would it make if I said I was having it off with Graeme? What good would that do?"

"It would confirm what two people have already said; that you were having an affair with your gardener. That Allan discovered it – and was going to tell his father. What then more

85

natural that you should want to save your skin and seek to silence him? That you and Graeme should get together and do the deed?"

Ellie shook her head.

Raynes continued: "Graeme was able to provide the means. He suggested Allan should use his tent. He could easily have told you which tent it was. I'm told he was seeing some woman on Sunday night. At that meeting, the final details could have been arranged. Once you knew which tent Allan was in – the whole thing was quite simple." Raynes spoke quietly. "But, doubtless, you have an alibi for Sunday night?"

"I was working."

"And Monday night – Tuesday morning?"

Ellie said nothing.

"You don't like the picture, do you?"

"Would you?" she said. "I've already told you who I think it is. I didn't come here expecting you to accuse me! I came in here to help."

"You've been most helpful," said Raynes, "but not quite in the way you think." He looked at her through half-closed eyes. "I notice that you're right-handed?"

"Most people are."

"That's true. Even the murderer was right-handed. But Tom – dear Tom – whose name you've tried so hard to blacken – he's left-handed. So where does that leave your evidence?"

Ellie looked dismayed.

"There's nothing more I can say. You've told me that I'm a liar and a bitch; I commit adultery with my gardener and now I've murdered my step-son. Is there anything else?"

"You tell me!" said Raynes.

Mrs Foster stood up. She was clearly preparing her final onslaught. Her cheeks were bright red. She leant forward over Raynes' desk and delivered her attack with venom.

"You're the sort of detective that gives the police force a bad name! You're a bully – and a coward! And there's just one other thing I want to say to you, Inspector. You deserve Mrs May. I hope she screws you down to your last penny! And I hope she gives you the clap!"

Raynes took the onslaught with good humour.

"That's very charitable of you, Ellie. I shall pass on your good wishes." He raised his hand. "But, before you go – there is still one little piece of business. The police surgeon is ready to release Allan's body. As you are his next of kin, I think you should get in touch with an undertaker and he will collect the body. I'm afraid it's not in very good shape. I would recommend a funeral by Saturday – at the latest. As you asked me, we shall do our best to find your husband, Arthur. I expect we shall find him within the next twenty-four hours. If not, you may have to go ahead with the funeral without him."

Ellie looked grim.

"Thank you for your help, Inspector."

Her voice was cold and sarcastic and she stomped out of the room without a single backward glance.

Carlisle saw her out to reception and came back to find Raynes emptying the cigarette ash into an envelope and putting it into his waste-paper basket.

"What a character!" said Carlisle.

"Une femme formidable!" said Raynes. "Imagine her in court!"

"Do you think she could have done the murder?"

"Not on her own. She would have needed someone to tell her where Allan was sleeping. But if you are asking me whether she was capable of pouring sand down his throat, the answer is 'Yes'. She is a highly organized and ruthless woman. She would stop at nothing."

"She used to be a Guide captain. My wife was in her Troop. So was Jenny – Jenny Gray. My wife said she ran a very tight ship."

Raynes smiled.

"She doesn't seem to think much of my friends!"

"I presume you don't want that bit minuted?"

"Well, we could always do her for slander!" Raynes looked thoughtful. "No, I suppose you're right. Leave my skeletons hidden in their cupboard!" He grinned. "It's quite a nice skeleton though!"

Carlisle was the perfect courtier.

"I know the lady, Inspector – and I think she was much maligned."

"Thank you," said Raynes.

He looked down at his desk.

"Well, I think that's all for today. There's nothing else on the agenda. Could you put out a search call for Arthur? After that, we'll call it a day."

"There's just one thing," said Carlisle. "How did you know that Tom was left-handed? I can't remember anyone telling us that. Did you have some private information on that point?"

"None whatsoever," said Raynes. "I don't know whether Tom's left-handed or right-handed. I just wanted to undermine her case. She came in here determined to do the dirty on Tom. I'm sure Tom's no saint, but I don't see why he deserves a hatchet job from her. I thought I'd just clobber her in return. When she finds out that Tom's right-handed after all, then she'll really fizz!"

15 *Boeuf Wellington*

Raynes walked back to *The Green Man*. It was a splendid, soporific August afternoon. Even though it was now the height of the summer vacation, the number of students hardly seemed to have diminished. There were bicycles everywhere, weaving in and out of the traffic. On the pavement, there seemed to be people from every nation under heaven – judging by the babel of languages which caught his ear. Many of them were of course attending the various summer schools laid on by the University to increase its income. But there was also a superabundance of tourists soaking up the sun and bathing in the nostalgia of an old-fashioned English town whose quaint streets and buildings had scarcely changed in the past two hundred years.

Appearances were of course deceptive. Behind the traditional frontages, enormous alterations had been made. *The Green Man* was a case in point. To the outward eye, little had changed. There was still the great archway through which the London coach had rattled in, its scarlet wheels pounding over the cobbles, the six post-horses steaming with sweat, and the postillion blowing his horn. There was still the charming black and white Elizabethan exterior and the curious bow windows bellying out over the street. But within, the whole structure had been completely gutted. Breeze blocks and reinforced concrete had created new floors and new walls. Miles of electric cable had been laid and air-conditioning ducted to every conceivable corner. Each bedroom had its own en suite bathroom and every luxury that sophisticated customers might expect. There were three lifts and a marble fountain in reception.

Only two things remained unchanged within. The service and the food. Despite the pressures of inflation and the demands for productivity, *The Green Man* had retained a high ratio of staff to guests. Employees were close at hand to answer every call. In the dining-room, each waiter felt a seigneurial responsibility for his own. Traditional English roasts were the backbone of every menu. But, being a University town since medieval times, Grasshallows had long ago acquired a taste for continental cooking, and the sauces and soups offered by *The Green Man* were regarded, not so much as a gourmet's treat, but rather as a natural part of any civilized meal.

As he sat down at his customary table beside the window, Raynes was aware of both of these superlative traditions. The waiter, who had been looking after him for the past five weeks, complimented him on the picture which had appeared in the evening paper.

"Nice seeing your picture in the paper, sir."

Raynes said that he hadn't seen it.

"A good likeness, I said to myself when I saw it. Bet the parents are glad too, sir, to have you handling this case. Soon catch the little swine that did it! ... Would you like to see the paper?"

"Indeed I would," said Raynes, who had almost completely forgotten the Press conference. For him it was a non-event.

But the *Evening Echo* had had a field day. 'Crimebuster Leads Inquiry into Savage Death' was the headline. And a grim-faced Inspector Raynes was shown facing the cameras.

His statement was printed in thick black type, and the most optimistic interpretation placed on his words. The leading article ended with the ominous prediction: 'An arrest is likely at any moment'. Raynes raised his eyebrows in amazement. This was not how he liked things to be handled.

But for the *Echo,* this was a scoop. Pages two, three and four were also devoted to the murder. There were pictures of the campsite from every conceivable angle – even from the air. There were photographs of individual scouts. Raynes looked at them closely. It seemed that they had been culled from their school photographs, taken several years before. There was a nice picture of Allan; a photograph of weeping staff at Star Travel, and a statement from Mr Hogg saying what a good, hard-working and trustworthy assistant Allan had been. There was a paragraph about his father being in the Middle East – 'Tragic Hunt for Victim's Father' – and a statement from the District Commissioner saying that it was over twenty years since any scout had been seriously injured at camp. Never before had anyone been murdered. It was a tragedy for the Scouting movement. He praised Allan as a most promising young leader, and offered all the families involved his deepest sympathy.

The sheer magnitude of the coverage made Raynes almost ashamed that he had stopped work for a meal. It seemed positively indecent to be gorging himself on fine food whilst the murder remained unsolved. How could he spend the evening in the lounge watching Inspector Morse on television whilst the population of Grasshallows were slavering for justice?

Raynes decided that they would have to wait.

After that diabolical snack lunch, his innards were crying out for a decent meal. And on his way home, he had decided what he would choose. It was too early for grouse so it would have to be *boeuf wellington* with all the trimmings – and avocado with prawns to start with. A half bottle of claret would garnish it nicely.

He ate his meal slowly – and thoughtfully.

He had not abandoned his theory that Allan had been killed by mistake – and that Graeme had been the intended victim.

90

He still felt that this was the logical deduction. But throughout the past two days, he had received a flood of evidence suggesting many reasons why Allan might have been killed in his own right. And all this evidence had to be considered.

Tom was perhaps the most obvious suspect. He had borne a bitter grudge towards Allan for exposing his indecent behaviour. He had threatened him with violence on a dark night – and violence had been done – on a dark night. Tom had access to sand and earth. He knew where the kitchen things were kept. He was apparently well-built. He would have been strong enough to overpower Allan whilst thrusting the funnel into his mouth. According to Ellie, he was the sort of person who crept around, spying on people, keeping his dirty deeds out of the limelight. If he was right-handed, he would become the prime suspect.

Or would he?

Inspector Raynes had come to the conclusion that Ellie, too, was under suspicion. Until their meeting that afternoon, he had discounted her. But she had shown herself to be a very forceful and unscrupulous person. Raynes had little doubt that she had been having some sort of affair with Graeme. Doubtless she had always been a bit of a girl, but how would Arthur react to his middle-aged wife carrying on behind his back? It would have been all right if everyone kept mum. But if Allan opened his big mouth, Ellie could have been heading for divorce in a very juicy scandal. It seemed quite in character for Ellie – with Graeme's help – to have silenced Allan once and for all.

And what about Garry Hogg – defending his father? Defending the reputation of the family firm? Apparently Star Travel was doing some shady business and Allan had rumbled them. Would it not have been possible for Garry to have gone over the top in a fit of anger? He was clearly a lad who burnt on a very short fuse. Raynes had seen that for himself.

All these were reasonable possibilities. But Inspector Raynes could not see why any of the other boys should have wanted to murder Allan.

He was therefore forced to conclude that there were really only three main suspects. Ellie, whom he had seen. Garry, who would have to be interviewed again – more carefully. And Tom.

As time went by, Tom appeared increasingly important as a witness. He must be seen as soon as possible. Tomorrow's diary was already getting booked up. He must strike whilst the iron was still hot. Whilst the sand was still wet. He could not spend a quiet night with his mind still churning through the case. The people of Grasshallows would expect him to be hard at it. Not putting his feet up or taking an evening off. Both conscience and a sense of duty demanded that he see Tom right away.

To the waiter's surprise, Raynes declined both the dessert and coffee. With a distant look in his eye, he rose from his table and headed for the nearest telephone.

The waiter watched him leave the dining-room. He wondered. Had the Inspector had a flash of inspiration? Or had the evening newspaper given him the vital clue?

He might have been a little disappointed to know that Raynes was simply phoning Neil Gray to ask: "Where can I find Tom?"

16 *The Artful Groper*

Tom Hayward lived on a council estate near Henslea Comprehensive School on the outskirts of Grasshallows. His home was a semi-detached, two-storey dwelling in a long row of similar semi-detached, two-storey dwellings erected in the early 1950s when the chief political aim was quantity rather than quality. However, it was clear that Tom's parents were – as the phrase has it – upwardly mobile artisans, for they had bought their semi, added a porch and a garage, double-glazed the windows and built an extension over the garage.

Raynes arrived at the house shortly before 8.00 pm.

He knocked at the door.

It was opened by a tired-looking woman wearing an apron and a pair of pink plastic gloves. There was a strong smell of stew.

Raynes introduced himself.

"I'm Detective-Inspector Raynes of the Grasshallows Police."

A gleam of recognition dawned in the woman's eyes.

"You're the man in the paper!"

Raynes smiled. "That's right. I'm pursuing the inquiry into the death of young Allan out at Picton Dale ..."

"Come in," she said. "You're most welcome."

Raynes was ushered into the sitting-room.

"... and I was wondering if I could see your son, Tom?"

"He wasn't there."

"No, I know he wasn't. But I'm trying to visit all the scouts in the 14th Grasshallows Troop to see if they can shed any light on this unfortunate business."

Mrs Hayward resumed her tired, worried look.

"It's upset him terribly. He didn't go to his work this morning. He's hardly eaten a thing. He's just been sitting up there in his room playing loud music. He's locked the door so I can't go in. I just don't know what to do ..."

Tears came into her eyes.

"... He's just going through a difficult age. That's what I say – but it doesn't make it any easier. His dad's fed up with him. The two of them don't speak to each other. It's like living in an asylum. One's as bad as the other. It's high time someone knocked a bit of sense into him. The past year's been one long disaster."

"In what way?"

Mrs Hayward looked at the Inspector anxiously.

"You've heard about the accusations?"

Raynes nodded.

"Well, it's been terrible. Really terrible. People have been stopping me in the street, telling me my son's a ... a pervert ... saying that he ought to be locked up. That he should be ... castrated! What an awful thing to say! To his mother! You've no idea how hurtful, how cruel people can be ... Of course, Tom won't speak to me about it. Keeps himself to himself does Tom. He just shuts off. Slams the door. Goes upstairs to his room. Sits alone for hours up there. He's very bitter, Inspector. All these stories! I'm sure they're exaggerated. Tom wouldn't do things like that. He's a good boy. He always was ..."

Mrs Hayward sobbed uncontrollably.

Raynes did not think he was going to get much information out of her so he put a kindly arm around her shoulder.

"Let me have a word with Tom and I'll do my best," he said.

Mrs Hayward calmed down, but still shook with emotion.

"He's in his den. That's the room over the garage. You go upstairs and it's the end door on the right."

Raynes climbed the steep staircase lined with imitation pine panelling. He did not have much difficulty in identifying Tom's room. Sounds of heavy rock reverberated down the passage and a strong smell of incense or joss-sticks filled the air. Raynes knocked brusquely on the door. "Police!" he said loudly.

The door opened very quickly.

Tom was a stocky, well-built youth with a longish body and short legs. He had brown curly hair and the face of a spoilt child. His eyes were surly; he had a snub nose, freckles and a sullen mouth. He was wearing a grey tracksuit and white trainers.

He did not look pleased to see Raynes.

The Inspector cast a quick eye over the contents of the room. To his left was a large music centre with several racks of albums and a loudspeaker attached to the wall. Then there was a small desk with a home computer and a television. Cassettes were neatly stacked against the wall, which sported two huge posters of Godfather-type figures wearing suits and dark glasses. On the end wall, there was a white wardrobe covered in stickers promoting Grasshallows Athletic and Manchester United. A bookcase showing a curious collection of tastes and a small table-lamp. To the right, under the window, was a bed-settee covered in a tartan rug and another very powerful speaker like its fellow blasting out Fleetwood Mac. The room was slightly misty with the fumes rising from an orange joss-stick burning on the bookcase beside his bed. Raynes detected the tell-tale odour of marijuana.

There was a small chair beside the desk. Raynes sat down on it. Tom turned off the music. Suddenly, everything was terribly quiet.

"I'm Detective-Inspector Raynes ..."

"I know. I saw your picture in the paper."

Raynes nodded. "When did you first hear about all this?"

"Last night ... Graeme phoned me at about 9.00 pm. Just after he got back from camp."

"And how d'you feel about it?"

Tom seemed genuinely upset.

"Shattered ... just shattered. It's an awful thing to happen to anyone. I can't really believe it. You don't expect things like that to happen at camp."

"Was Allan a friend of yours?"

"Not lately. You've probably heard ... he's caused a lot of trouble amongst the boys. Spreading gossip. Stirring up trouble. The past two months have been pretty foul."

"Was there any truth in his allegations?"

Tom looked uncertain.

"Depends which way you look at it, Inspector. To me, they were just harmless romps – a bit of horseplay – the sort of things lads have always done. Now and again, it might have got a bit out of hand – but it was really just larking about. Nothing serious. I don't think anyone's suffered because of it."

Raynes noted that Tom was willing to talk. He had been worried that he might be the strong, silent type from whom every detail would have to be prised out with a knife. But perhaps, having had twenty-four hours to chew over the facts, he was glad to talk to someone. Perhaps the marijuana had also loosened his tongue.

"It may not have been serious to you," said Raynes, "but other people saw things in a different light. Ian Mackay ..."

"He's a religious fanatic! Very narrow-minded!"

"... Nonetheless, he told his dad and his dad reported the matter to Neil. Just as Allan did."

"Allan was out for promotion. He's been hoping to get a troop of his own. He just wanted to appear whiter than white. To get into the Commissioner's good books. I could tell you a few things about Allan ..."

"I'm sure you could," said Raynes quickly. "But the point is, Tom, that, given your hostility to Allan, many people think you may be responsible for his murder."

"Me?"

Tom looked thunderstruck.

"I wasn't even at camp this year!"

"I know – but that doesn't really help. People think you chose this moment to get your own back. You knew where the camp was being held. You knew the habits and customs. Times and programmes. You knew your way around the kitchen tent. You knew where to get your hands on the funnel ... the plastic funnel which was used to pour sand down Allan's throat ... You could have been watching and waiting for your moment to strike Allan down. No fewer than three people have said to me that they think you are the No. 1 suspect."

Tom had gone completely white.

He could hardly speak.

He swallowed twice.

"It's a lie, Inspector! Another dirty lie! Who's saying these things?" Tears came to his eyes. "They've been trying to drive me out of the Scouts for the past year. Now they're trying to drive me out of Grasshallows!"

Raynes spoke as gently as he knew how.

"The simplest thing to do, Tom, is to tell me where you were on Monday night and early Tuesday morning. If you have a sound alibi, you can silence these allegations once and for all. Where were you?"

"I was in bed."

He looked shifty.

"What time did you go to bed?"

"About 1.00 am."

"Can you be sure of that?"

"Not really. But it was well after midnight."

"And you have a motor-bike, I believe? How long would it have taken you to get back from Picton Dale?"

"I wasn't there!"

"But if you had been there?"

Tom showed the utmost reluctance in answering the question. "About ten or twelve minutes, I should think ... but I wasn't there, Inspector! I swear to you!"

Tom's eyes were very like his mother's. Raynes could see that he was on the threshold of tears. Raynes offered him a handkerchief. Tom sniffed and snuffled.

"It wasn't me," he said lamely. "I wouldn't have thought of such a thing. I couldn't murder anyone."

Raynes looked at him doubtfully.

"That's not really true is it? I've been told that you threatened Allan with extreme violence. You got him round the neck and told him that you would strangle him ... You said something like: 'I'll get you on a dark night and don't expect any mercy 'cos you won't get any ...' You said that, didn't you?"

Red flecks of embarrassment appeared on Tom's cheeks.

"I was just joking!"

"You admit that you said it?"

Tom bit his lip.

"Yes, I said it. He really got my goat. The self-righteous prick! I couldn't control myself! I was so angry!"

Raynes persisted with his question: "You threatened him?"

"I did. But it was just words, Inspector. Words spoken in the heat of the moment."

Raynes sighed.

"But it's those sort of things that people remember. And when something like this happens, they put two and two together." He looked at Tom's large capable hands. "Are you right-handed or left-handed?" he asked.

Tom looked at his hands as if they contained some deadly secret.

"Right-handed ... why?"

"I was just wondering ... Someone said you were left-handed."

Tom shook his head. He didn't see the point of the question.

"Be a bit difficult cooking if you were left-handed. Most of the pots are made for right-handed people. Pour on the left ..."

Raynes moved the questioning forward. "You've been cooking at the Scout camp for a number of years, I believe?"

"For the last four. This was the first year I've missed."

"Where did you learn to cook?"

"My mum. She taught me."

"Graeme likes your cooking. He told me."

Tom smiled.

"Graeme's been a good friend. He's the only one who hasn't turned against me. He's kept in touch. In fact, I think it was him who spoke to Neil – to stop him throwing me out of the Troop."

Raynes nodded.

"Graeme's got his own vices. He can afford to be tolerant."

Tom looked aggrieved.

"That's the point, Inspector. There's one law for him and one law for me! Graeme spends his life screwing one woman after another and no one complains. He knocks off Neil's wife at the Christmas party – and what does Neil do? Nothing! What does he say? 'Don't do it again!' But Graeme's still at it. Perhaps I shouldn't be saying this … but Graeme's trying to get Jenny to leave Neil and live with him. He likes Jenny. Thinks she's great. But it doesn't stop him knocking off any other woman that crosses his path. But no one reports him to the District Commissioner – and certainly not Neil!"

"Do you like Neil?"

"I used to. He used to teach me Maths at school. I wasn't very good. I left school at sixteen …"

"But you don't like him now?"

"Well, I wouldn't say I dislike him. I just think he's wishy-washy. Spineless. Two-faced."

"And you think he should get rid of Graeme as well as you?"

"Well, he can't have it both ways. Allan knew what Graeme was up to with his stepmother. He told Neil – but Neil did nothing. I think he's frightened of Graeme. Frightened of losing Jenny. They've got two kids. He'd lose them too."

"What's Graeme been doing with Mrs Foster?"

"Just his usual. He does her gardening. She admires his rippling muscles." Tom grinned. "She invited him in for a little light refreshment. He said he had her brown corduroy dungarees off in about ten minutes. He's a fast worker is Graeme. Can charm the birds off the trees. But Allan caught them at it."

Raynes smiled.

"Doesn't it make you wish you were doing a spot of private gardening rather than working for the Council?"

"I'm not that way inclined."

"But you used to be?"

Tom looked confused.

"You went along with Graeme and Allan to visit Grace last year?"

"Just once or twice. I didn't really like it. In fact, that was the thing that put me off. She was old enough to be my mother. So's Mrs Foster. It seems sordid ... disgusting." Tom was full of moral indignation.

Raynes said quietly: "But, Tom, can't you see? Other people find your behaviour equally disgusting. At least Grace and Mrs Foster are adults. They know what's right and wrong. If they do wrong, they know what they're doing. People are against you because you are corrupting children. People who are innocent till you get your hands on them ... People like the twins – or Colin ..."

"Colin's a little shit! A conceited little shit!"

"He didn't like what you did to him!"

"And now he's accusing me of murder?"

Raynes did a mental re-run of the evidence he had received. It had been so voluminous, and some of it so contradictory, that he was hard pressed to remember who had said what. But Colin had suggested Ellie ... at least Johnny Cotton had said so ... what a mix-up! Detective-Constable Carlisle would have remembered.

Raynes returned to Tom.

"As a matter of fact, he didn't."

Tom shrugged his shoulders. "But the others did. I don't think there's any future for me here in Grasshallows. When all this comes out, I shall probably lose my job. I'll be kicked out of the Scouts. People will be staring at me. My mother's told me what they've been saying to her. It's an impossible situation. I'd be better away!"

"You may be right," said Raynes slowly, "but you're not going anywhere yet. You're not going anywhere till I get to the bottom of this murder and we find out who's done it."

"Well, it certainly wasn't me!"

Raynes' voice developed a harder edge. "But how can I be sure that what you're saying is true? All you've told me so far is that you were in bed some time after midnight – perhaps 1.00 am? Perhaps? You're not sure. Could your mother vouch for that? Or your father?"

Tom shook his head.

"No."

"Where were you earlier in the evening? Before you came home?"

Tom's face began to look tense and drawn.

"I'd rather not say. But it's got nothing to do with Allan."

Raynes raised his eyebrows.

"Let me be the one who decides whether or not it's got anything to do with Allan. You just tell me your movements on Monday night!"

Tom shook his head again.

"I can't. I'd get into terrible trouble if I told you."

"You're in deep trouble as it is!"

Tom was tight-lipped. He was saying nothing.

"A drugs party?" suggested Raynes. "It's no use pretending. I could smell it when I came in."

Tom looked helpless. He buried his head in his arms, bowed himself over his knees and started moaning. Raynes waited patiently.

As he waited, he heard steps in the passage outside. He leapt to his feet and opened the door. Outside was Mrs Hayward with two mugs of milky coffee.

"I thought you might like a little refreshment, Inspector. I've put in one sugar." She looked down at her son.

"I hope the Inspector's giving you a good talking-to. You need it. It's about time someone knocked some sense into you. We've had just about enough of you and your stupidities round here. It's time you grew up!"

Tom's face emerged from his arms – bright red. Tears were pouring down his face. His knuckles were tight with rage.

"Shut up!" he screamed. "Shut up – you old bag! Get out of my room! Get out!" He sounded hysterical. Raynes put down his mug of coffee in case he had to be restrained.

His mother turned to Raynes.

"You see what I have to put up with!"

Tom leapt to his feet.

"Get out before I kick you out!"

"I'm going," she said. "Don't worry. I'm going! I'm not going to listen to my own son abusing me. After all that Bob and I have done for him. It's like having a wild animal in a cage ..."

The Inspector encouraged Tom to sit down and put a hand on Mrs Hayward's arm. "Enough's enough," he said. "Tom's under great strain. In fact, we all are. Let's not make it worse. Now, before you go, Mrs Hayward, could I ask you just one thing? Did you by any chance notice what time Tom came home on Monday night – or rather, on Tuesday morning? He says it was after midnight. Could you by any chance tell me when?"

Mrs Hayward raised her eyebrows.

"He says 'midnight', does he?"

"After midnight."

Mrs Hayward shook her head.

"He wasn't home at all on Monday night. He didn't come back till half past seven on Tuesday morning – and a fine mess he was in! Dark rings under his eyes! Looked as if he had come through a hedge backwards! He only came back to get his breakfast and his working clothes! Even then he was late at the depot!" She looked down on her son with withering contempt before she delivered her final blow. "They'll not put up with that, you know. They'll give you the sack. You mark my words, son, they'll sack you!"

Tom said nothing. Once again, his head was in his lap and he was crying bitterly. Raynes ushered Mrs Hayward out of the room and made sure she went downstairs and left them in peace.

With a mother like that, it went some way towards explaining Tom's preference for the other sex. For people he could dominate in his own right. He felt rather sorry for the young man. Tom needed a true friend. Someone to whom he could really pour out his heart. He would be better leaving home and moving elsewhere.

But for the moment, certain important questions had to be answered. Raynes sipped his coffee slowly and waited for the emotional storm to abate.

"Well ...?" he said eventually.

"I was with another bloke. All the night."

"You can give me his name and address?"

"I'd rather not."

Raynes took a deep breath.

"Tom, if you won't come clean with me, I shall have no alternative. I'll have to take you into custody – on suspicion. If you have anything to say, you might as well say it now. There are no witnesses here ... no tape-recorders. If you have anything to say, this is the place to say it. Once we get you down to the police station, we shall have to drag it out of you the hard way. I can't think of anything worse! For heaven's sake, be sensible!"

It was blackmail. Raynes knew it was blackmail. So probably did Tom. But it worked. Slowly, painfully, the story emerged.

Whilst the boys had been away at camp, Tom had decided to compensate for his loss by doing a little 'slumming'. That was the word he used. If he could not enter Heaven, he would at least enjoy Hell. He had decided to sell his soul to the devil and be as wicked as possible. He would live up to his reputation. He knew a pub in Grasshallows where people were always pushing drugs ...

"The Red Dragon?" said Raynes.

"Yes?" Tom seemed surprised that Raynes should know such things.

Well, he had hung around at *The Red Dragon*; had a few pints; got chatting with a couple of mates from the Public Works who decided that they would all go on a blinder with the help of a little hash. Tom had got quite a good deal out of the pusher and they had retired to Joe's flat where, with the help of a few more cans of 80/- ale, they had had an ecstatic night. The other blokes were a bit wild (which Raynes took to mean gay) and they had had a bit of an orgy. In fact, at the height of the evening, they had thought of applying to become the Grasshallows branch of Hell's Angels! This had excited Tom enormously because he was into witchcraft, and the thought of a secret coven had been very tempting. However, nothing had come of it.

On Saturday night, they had had a repeat performance at Joe's flat with a couple of really hard-core videos which had got them all going. Tom had told them about some of his exploits with the young scouts and Joe had arranged to get a kiddie-porn video for Monday night which they would all enjoy. In fact, Joe had gone one step further. He had obtained an American snuff-video – where a real bloke had actually been killed as part of the film. It had been pretty disgusting and Tom had been sick – probably as a result of drinking too much 80/- ale. Anyway, he had left at that point and gone home with Doug – whom he had been seeing a lot during the past week. They had gone back to Doug's flat and bedded down at about 1.00 am. He had blacked out and remembered nothing more till about 6.00 am. Feeling very much the worse for wear, he had staggered back across Grasshallows to get his working clothes and his breakfast. He was not surprised that his mother had described him as a mess. He had felt completely shagged out.

That was Tom's story. Not a pretty one – but it had a certain ring of truth. Tom was obviously terrified lest his revelations should lead to Joe and his pals being arrested. He was very fearful that the pusher and the person who had supplied the videos might be taken into custody. They would all know who had shopped them to the police and they would 'get him' at work – or on some dark night down some quiet back street. They were tough blokes. They would make mincemeat of him. He didn't want to get his head kicked in or lose an eye. He begged Raynes to keep the information to himself. He would never have told the Inspector anything except to save his own skin.

Raynes murmured some comforting words of assurance. They meant nothing to him. He would respect Tom's confidence only so far as it suited his book. He had to consider the possibility that Tom's story was a cover. One horror to cover another.

Was it not possible that after watching the child porn video, they could all have decided to go up to Picton Dale and raid the camp? Alternatively, perhaps just Tom on his own? Excited by the snuff video, he could have decided to crown his wickedness by killing Allan whom he did not like, and against whom he had threatened revenge. High on drugs, he was only a ten-minute ride away from Picton Dale. His story about being sick could have been a lie. He could have gone home early with Doug, doped him up and left him to sleep it off. At any time after 1.00 am Tom could have been on his way – on his bike. With his knowledge of the camp, he could easily have collected what he wanted and done the dirty on Allan.

Two things, only, were in Tom's favour. He could not have drugged the orangeade in advance, nor could he have known in which tent Allan was sleeping. But perhaps the times he had given were false? Perhaps he had left Grasshallows much earlier and had been lurking in the darkness round the camp? Perhaps Ellie was right?

Raynes sighed.

It was always the same.

The more he knew – the more he needed to know.

"You'll have to give me Doug's name and address," he said, "so that he can at least confirm that you were with him that night. We can ignore the videos and the … party, but we have to be sure that you're telling the truth about your movements."

Tom continued to agonize for several more minutes and then gave Raynes the information he needed.

"It'd better be true!" Raynes said ominously. "Because if it isn't …"

He decided to leave the rest to Tom's imagination.

The Inspector looked at his watch. It was now nearly 10.00 pm and the interview had been very difficult and very emotional.

Tom was a pervert; he was also a coward. He had certainly sold his soul to the devil – but at a very high price. Once this case was over, Raynes did not think there would be much future for Tom in Grasshallows. He would probably go to Amsterdam, drown himself in drugs and sex, and come back in a plain wooden box. His mother would never understand.

Raynes left Tom crumpled and still crying. He avoided any further contact with Mrs Hayward and left as swiftly and as silently as he could. The jingle for 'News at Ten' sounded through the living-room door as he passed by.

He drove back to *The Green Man* feeling exhausted. He reckoned that the taxpayers and the Police Committee had had their pound of flesh from him that day. Let him now relax! Let him now find some pleasant consolation! He phoned Debbie, but she was out. The hotel was like a morgue. The cocktail bar was deserted. Raynes' sole consolation was a glass of whisky and a packet of peanuts! Semi-sober – but with a clear conscience – he went to bed.

17 *Amazing Grace*

Carlisle and Raynes made their way across the fields – as they had been directed. Half a mile up the river from the Scout camp, they came upon the Picton Dale Country Caravan Park – a small encampment of twenty vans settled on a grassy knoll, protected from the northern and westerly winds by a substantial belt of trees.

The caravan they were looking for was on the south side of the encampment and was easily recognizable because of the nearby heap of sand and paving stones which seemed to have been dumped there quite some time ago.

Raynes picked up a handful of the sand and let it run through his fingers. It was deep reddish-orange stuff – quite unlike the sand which had been poured down Allan's throat. Raynes shook his head: "Pity he didn't use some of this. It would have made our job much easier!"

He turned his attention to the caravan which was painted chocolate brown top and bottom with a faded band of cream around the windows. Clearly, it had seen better days. In two places, the glass was cracked but the curtains hanging at the windows seemed bright and cheerful. Wild flowers grew on all sides of the caravan, covering the wheels and flanking the wooden steps.

The top half of the door was open.

"Is anyone at home?" Raynes called.

There was a sound of little feet scurrying across the floor and a woman appeared at the hatch. She had dyed blonde hair drawn back tightly into a sort of pony-tail. It looked as if it had been quite some time since the dyeing process had taken place for there were long dark streaks of brown amid the gold. Most of her face was taken up with an enormous pair of sunglasses with orange frames, but what there was to see was brown, smiling and cheerful. Carlisle noted that she had good teeth but a scraggy neck. Mutton indeed dressed up as lamb!

She opened the other half of the door and Raynes could see that she was wearing a loose black top over a black lace bra, black shorts and gold sandals. Her finger-nails and toe-nails were painted bright red. She had long, slim legs tanned deep brown in the sun. He reckoned that she was in her late thirties or early forties.

"Hello, boys!" she said. "You're a bit early. But it's never too early to entertain a couple of really mature men!"

"We're from the police," said Raynes.

"No need to apologize! I've nothing against the police. Some of my happiest moments have been with the boys in blue! Well, don't just stand there! Come in and have a gin!"

Raynes and Carlisle followed her up the steps and into the caravan. Inside it seemed quite clean and comfortable. There were lots of colourful rugs and pictures. A coffee percolator was steaming on the stove and a copy of the *Sun* was lying open on the table. Raynes noticed that she had been reading the piece about the murder: 'Dead Scout in Tent Mystery'.

Grace bustled about getting glasses, gin and tonic. Her birdlike swooping movements displayed a supple body, splendid haunches and an aroma of cheap perfume. She poured out the liquor and snuggled in beside Carlisle on the narrow benchtype seat and gave Raynes a smile of radiant welcome.

"Cheers!" she said. "Down the hatch!"

She consumed her gin in a single gulp.

Raynes, more conservatively, took a small sip.

"I believe you're called Grace," he said. "Grace what?"

"Grace Turner to start with. Grace Buchanan after the first marriage; Grace King after the second; Grace Lawrence after the third. After that, I gave up marriage! So it's back to plain Grace …"

"Have you been living here long?"

"For the past four years. I used to live in Grasshallows. Lived there for almost forty years. But now I prefer the country life. The country air. So much more natural. No more gossiping neighbours. You can do what you want." She smiled.

"Do you do anything for a living?"

"Why should I? I get £4000 a year in alimony. That keeps me in gin. When things get a bit tight, I help behind the bar at *The Carpenter's*. Most of the time, I'm 100% Romany."

"Good for you," said Raynes. "But I'm sorry the real world has to intrude. I see you've been reading the paper – about this murder …"

"Tragic," said Grace, adjusting her bra strap.

"Did you recognize his picture?"

"Not really. It's a lousy photo."

Raynes produced a recent photograph of the whole 14th Grasshallows Scout Troop. "Would this help?" he asked.

Grace smiled.

"This is a real trip down memory lane!" she said. "Which one's Allan?"

Raynes pointed to a smiling face sitting in the front row.

Grace shook her head.

"He's not one of mine! But I recognize quite a few of the others." She ran her eyes over the photograph. "Don't they look cute in their uniforms?"

"Which ones can you identify?"

"Well, there's big Graeme in the front row. He's a character. Just like his father. He can charm the birds off the trees … His father had me when I was still at school." She giggled at the memory. "And there's Johnny … he's a scream … and his friend …"

"Mark."

"He's got a cruel mouth. Look at it. Then there's Harry with his funny nose. He's the only one who's been circumcised! And those two – they're like pigs at a trough …"

"Simon and Geoff."

"I don't know what they're called but they certainly deserve the Duke of Edinburgh's award for carpentry … or something!" Her finger traced along the front row. "He was here last year. He's a bit weird …"

"That's Tom. He's gay."

"Doesn't surprise me. And there's that shifty one. He can't look you in the face …"

"Garry Hogg."

"Hogg? Yes, that's right. I know his Dad. He runs the Travel Agency in the High Street … He was a shit … I wouldn't trust him an inch … Now that one's a gentleman …" She pointed to Tony.

Raynes looked over to see which one she was referring to. As he lifted his eyes, he found himself looking right down her cleavage. He found the sight highly distracting.

Grace looked up.

"They're real," she said.

"So I see," said Raynes.

Grace turned to Carlisle. "Are you married?"

Carlisle nodded.

"What a pity!" she said. "What a waste! Something goes out of a man when he gets married!" She returned to the photograph. "Which one was I looking at?"

"The gentleman."

"Oh, yes, he's so sweet. So considerate. A perfect bedside manner. Always says 'please' and 'thank you'. I like him." She sighed. "And there's young Colin. So serious! So anxious to do the right thing. A great passion to experiment. Wants to cram a lifetime's experience into quarter of an hour!"

"You've got them all taped," said Raynes.

"Oh, I can read them like a book," said Grace. "They're all thrusting for adventure. I do what I can for them. I always think it's so sad the way young people learn about sex. Books, films, groping each other in dark corners. I try to show them how it should be done. 'Don't forget the aperitifs', I say. (Sounds better than *hors d'oeuvre,* don't you think?) 'Make the woman happy', I tell them. Of course, they all want to rush the first time. It's understandable. But once they've been here once or twice, they begin to develop a little finesse."

"Even Graeme?"

Grace's lips narrowed.

"He knows too much, that lad! He gets everything he wants. He despises women. He only comes here because he can't get away into town. If you ask me, that landscaping business of his is just a cover for philandery ..."

"How do you spell 'philandery'?" asked Carlisle, whose shorthand had a limited range and whose nervous system was rapidly being overwhelmed by wave after wave of *Rive Gauche*.

"Two 'f's," said Raynes. "As in burffday suit!"

"You don't spell it," said Grace, "you do it!"

"I'm afraid Detective-Constable Carlisle had a very sheltered upbringing," said Raynes maliciously. "He was in the 3rd Grasshallows Troop."

"I was in the Guides till I got engaged," said Grace. "They taught me everything I ever knew."

"Well, I'm glad to see it's still coming in handy," said Raynes, finishing off his gin and tonic.

"Do you want another one?"

"No thanks." He tried to see her eyes through the dark glass of her spectacles. "What I'm really wanting is your help in trying to find the person who murdered this chap, Allan Foster. I'm not sure if it was one of the scouts, but if it was, you might have entertained a murderer unawares ..."

"What a horrible thought!" said Grace. "Still, there's safety in numbers!"

"What I want to know," Raynes continued, "is whether you were anywhere near their campsite early on Tuesday at about 2.30 am?"

Grace looked surprised.

"I've never been near their camp. They come here."

"So I understand. And whilst they're here, they muck about with that sand?"

"The younger ones do. The older ones listen at the door or make vulgar jokes. Or pinch my gin or my sleeping tablets.

109

Do you know, Inspector, last year, one of them pinched a pair of my knickers! I expect he wanted a trophy to show off to his friends! But what his mother would have made of it, I just don't know!"

Suddenly the message got through to her.

"This sand? You don't mean that he was choked to death with sand from my garden?"

Raynes nodded.

"It's quite possible."

"Oh, how terrible! The poor creature!"

She fell silent. Raynes could see tears running down her cheeks.

Raynes was at his most gentle. "It could have been one of them. I can't be sure. Not yet anyway. I was just wondering whether your Romany instincts could give me a little enlightenment?"

Grace managed a smile. "I've only got one talent, Inspector, and that's not second sight! But my instincts as a woman tell me it must have been someone with a tremendous grudge against ... against Allan. Someone whose life had been shattered or put at risk. Someone who is trying to cover up some horrible secret or exacting a hideous revenge. It shouldn't be difficult to find out what Allan has done. Once you have found the deed, you'll have found your man!"

"Or woman?"

"I don't think it could have been a woman ..."

"Why not?"

"It doesn't sound like the sort of thing a woman would do. Too brutal. A woman would deal with it in a different way. Probably get some other man to do it for her. More subtle like ..."

Raynes looked at her thoughtfully.

How much should he say?

He decided there was more to be gained by being open with her – even though she would probably blab. He looked at her red finger-nails and thought of all the young bodies those fingers had caressed.

"It isn't quite as easy as that," he said. "Allan was sleeping alone in Graeme's tent. They switched tents at the last moment.

110

To me, it looks far more likely that someone was trying to kill Graeme – but got the wrong man."

Grace took off her sunglasses.

She had the makings of a rather nasty bruise around her right eye.

"Graeme Wilson?"

She nodded.

"When he doesn't get what he wants, he can be violent. Just like his father. He's too much of a coward to hit a man – but when it's a woman, it's a different story! 'Treat 'em rough and they'll come running'. That's his motto. It may work for some women but it doesn't work for me …" Grace put back her sunglasses. Raynes suspected that she was close to tears. "… If you're looking for people who want to get their own back on Graeme," she said, "you'll have a very long list, Inspector. Rejected lovers. Vengeful husbands. Angry wives. *Cherchez la femme!* I'd say. But I don't think it would be a *femme* who did the deed … She'd get someone else to do the dirty. If it was Graeme …"

Raynes nodded. "Unfortunately, if it was Graeme they were after, they got the wrong man."

"So you think they might try again?"

"That's what frightens me. So perhaps you see why I came here this morning. Not for a little horizontal levitation …!" He smiled. "Although I'm sure I should have enjoyed it! … But to find out a bit more about these young rovers and what makes them tick."

"Have I helped you at all?"

"You have. But not perhaps in quite the way you might have expected!" He rose to his feet. "And if I need any more help, I shall come back and ask for more."

Grace's spirits had clearly revived.

"Well, Inspector, you know where to come – and at least you know it's free!"

"You are a generous woman," said Raynes. "I wish there were more like you!" But then, looking at her dyed hair and her scraggy neck, he thought to himself: "No, perhaps not!"

111

18 *Beside still waters*

Raynes and Carlisle walked back across the fields.

"A character?"

"Very much so."

"And a victim?"

"I'm afraid so. That Graeme Wilson's got a lot to answer for … That black eye!"

"Done about two or three days ago, I should think. Monday or Tuesday." Raynes paused to climb over a gate. "I wonder how it happened? And why? What did Grace say or do to provoke him? And was there any connection between that blow and the murder?"

"Why didn't you ask her?"

"I didn't want to frighten her. She's the sort of person – if you put pressure on her – she might do something stupid. Attempt suicide … or even run away. That would be most inconvenient. I wanted to establish a rapport …"

Carlisle smiled.

"Is that what you call it?"

Raynes laughed.

"I wanted to encourage her to talk to us. To treat us as friends. I don't think she's the sort of person who would be involved in murder. She's too scatty … too jumpy … too nervous. As she said, she's only good at one thing and that's not murder. I can't see her creeping across these fields at the dead of night … Of course, I may be wrong."

"But she was holding out on you. She's bound to have known Allan. It wasn't a very good picture in her paper but our photograph was a good one. And she recognized the rest. She knew all their names. Allan may not have been to see her this year – but neither has Tom – but she recognized him."

Raynes was thinking deeply.

"Yes," he said. "She was definitely lying. But the question is why. Who is she covering up for? Graeme? Has he threatened her with violence? What does Grace know that we don't?"

Carlisle chuckled.

"She certainly knows all the scouts! She said she could read them like a book. I would say that she was a very good judge of character. She knew Tom was weird ... and she got Graeme down to a tee."

"She didn't mention Neil?"

"No. But I was wondering why she should point us towards a woman? A woman with a grudge? But a man who would carry out the deed? Do you think it could be Mrs Foster – or Neil's wife, Jenny?"

"Does she know them?"

"Probably not."

There was a long, thoughtful silence as they trudged back to the campsite. But Carlisle was curious:

"Why did you say to Grace that she'd helped you?"

"Because she confirmed almost exactly everything Graeme said."

"And what does that show?"

"It shows that they are very close. Bruise or no bruise. Graeme is undoubtedly using her and she is also protecting him. It might involve money. It might involve sex. Graeme doesn't seem very particular in his choice of lady friends. But Allan has fallen by the wayside. She doesn't want to know him. Perhaps Allan said something to her – or did something? Perhaps he was the one who took her knickers?" Raynes laughed. "It would be in character. I think Allan liked to boast of his achievements. He liked to talk and show off. Perhaps he knew something about Grace that Graeme didn't want him to know? Perhaps that was why he was killed?"

"We keep coming back to Graeme."

"I'm afraid we do. He was destined to be either villain or victim – but now the net has been cast a little wider, there are some equally interesting fish ..."

"Ellie?"

"Ellie, Tom, Jenny. Perhaps one of the scout parents? You can't rule them out. Many of them must have had a deep grudge against Graeme. Grace was right about that. In fact, she was right about quite a lot of things. But my instincts say that she wouldn't murder anyone."

"Not even if she was desperate?"

"Any middle-aged woman who goes round seducing scouts must be pretty desperate! But I can't see her hurting anyone. Her attitude towards the scouts seemed almost motherly – not vicious …"

"Some mother!" said Carlisle.

"I know," said Raynes.

By now, they had reached the site of the camp. During their absence, all the tents had been struck and the groundsheets rolled up. All that was left was a number of green and muddy patches on the grass where the tents had been. The orange tapes had gone. The mobile incident room was being hitched on to the tow-bar of a police van. Two patrolmen were hanging around.

"Did you find anything else?" asked Raynes.

"Just a bottle of Newcastle Brown! Empty of course!"

19 *Lady in Red*

On Thursday evening, Raynes suddenly realized that it was rather a long time since he had seen his female friend – Mrs Debbie May. In fact, it must be all of ten days! He phoned her from his hotel, remembering that the police switchboard had ears.

"Is that Debbie?"

"Sure! Who's that?"

"Richard Raynes."

There was a pregnant pause.

"Never heard of him! There's no Raynes in my book!"

She was being ridiculous.

"Oh, come!"

"Now you're talking," said Debbie. "As long as it's a question of business, we do have a few spare bookings."

Raynes grovelled nobly. "I'm sorry I haven't phoned you before now, but I've been busy with this wretched murder. You've probably read about it in the paper …"

"I thought he only died on Tuesday morning? What happened to last week? I didn't read about any murders then!"

114

Raynes continued to be apologetic.

"I didn't think you'd miss me ... you being so busy!"

Touché.

But Debbie was never lost for words.

"A girl's got to know where she is with a man, Inspector!"

"A chap's got to get his pay cheque before he plays in Monaco!"

"I should have thought vingt-et-un was a bit beyond you – at your age!"

Raynes could not let that insult pass.

"I shall say to you what the elderly French count said to his mistress: 'Double or quits!'"

"That suits me," said Debbie. "Provided I get paid for the doubles!"

"You're nothing but a bloody little gold-digger! Utterly shameless! Would *The Carpenter's Arms* suit you? It's a little pub up Picton Dale? They serve meals in baskets."

Debbie considered. Any booking was better than none. "It's a bit beneath my usual standard," she said, "but if you insist, I'll be there."

* * *

Raynes' relationship with Debbie was a delicate matter – and he was feeling even more sensitive after his interview with Mrs Foster. It would not be very diplomatic to be seen out and about with her in Grasshallows so they had to meet either at her flat late at night or at some hostelry well out of town. Over the past six weeks or so, they had been out for meals two or three times but, as Debbie had said, *The Carpenter's Arms* was a little rough. Put another way, it lacked finesse.

For a start, she appeared somewhat over-dressed. She was wearing a tight-fitting, low-cut, red velvet dress which seemed to magnify an already generous cleavage.

The entire company of dart-players, pin-ball fanatics, domino deadbeats, 80/- drinkers and village idiots turned to look at her as she came in. Debbie was not the sort of person to pass unnoticed.

"So this is your latest gastronomic Mecca?" she said, with a sweep of the hand.

115

"When you've been out in the fields all day, it seems positively palatial! And, besides, they do a very good steak and
kidney pudding."

Debbie looked heavenward.

Steak and kidney pudding!

"Don't they do anything else?"

"I'll get the menu." He caught her eye. "And a nice gin and
tonic."

"A double!" said Debbie, "and two bottles of tonic!"

The publican at *The Carpenter's Arms* recognized the Inspector and said that he thought his wife could probably knock up
a nice piece of lemon sole or a cold salmon salad for the Inspector's wife.

Debbie chose the salad.

Raynes looked at her figure-hugging dress with a critical
eye.

"Our aim is to please, Inspector!"

"Not to say – dazzle."

Debbie smiled sweetly over her glass. "Well, it must certainly make a change from looking at boy scouts!"

Raynes groaned. "Don't mention it. I've had quite enough
for one week!"

"But this is the scene of your latest triumph," said Debbie.
"Tents full of dead scouts! The river flowing with blood! Where
did it happen?"

"Just up the road. About half-a-mile away."

"How exciting! Shall I be shown the murder spot by torchlight?"

"If you insist."

"Is his tent still erect?" She grinned. "If you know what I
mean?"

"I know what you mean and I think the answer is 'no'. It
was taken away this afternoon."

"What a pity!" She leant conspiratorially across the table.
"You and me could have gone up there and done naughty
things! Terribly spooky! Just you, me and his ghost! Really
kinky! Oh, it makes me feel all excited just to think about it."

Raynes shook his head.

"There's been quite enough of that going on as it is. More than half the lads were visiting a woman on a caravan estate. Grace – she's called. Even fourteen-year-olds were going up to see her ..."

Debbie looked thoughtful.

"I knew someone called Grace. I wonder if it's the same person? Grace ... Lawrence. She used to work at *The King's Head*. It must be about eight years ago. She must be well into her forties by now. Slim, blonde, quite racy ..."

Raynes nodded.

"Sounds like her."

"She had two husbands ..."

"Three."

"She led them quite a dance!" Debbie smiled. "Well, well! What a turn-up for the book! I wonder if I'll be entertaining scouts when I'm forty?" She turned to Raynes. "Richard," she said, "say you'll never let me sink so low!"

"I'll never let you sink so low."

"Thank you. I shall hold you to that."

There was a brief interruption as the salmon salad and the steak and kidney pudding arrived. Debbie looked with mock horror at Raynes' plate.

"Richard, you are not going to eat all those chips!" Then she relaxed. "But speaking of sinking ... my new jacuzzi was fitted last Friday. Would you like to come and try it? It's terribly exciting! We could try it together!"

Whether naked in the jacuzzi or simply talking in a public bar, Raynes always found Debbie irresistible; she was always bubbling with wickedness and laughter. He knew that it was all an act – and that he was paying for the act – but the act had become so much second nature that once Debbie had turned on the switch, the record could run and run. However, after about an hour of sparkle, gossip and innuendo, she settled down and it was almost possible to conduct a sensible conversation with her.

Although Raynes should really have kept the details to himself, he found himself telling her about the different scouts

117

and their stories and how it was quite impossible to find any plausible motive for the killing. Raynes said that he was sure Allan had been murdered by mistake. How else would anyone know Allan was in *that* tent – *that* night? No one knew – except Neil and Graeme – and, just possibly, the murderer ...

Mrs May listened with at least half an ear, thinking how easy men were to entertain. You just let them talk about themselves and they were perfectly happy. Richard was no exception. Now and again you asked a question or two to show that you were taking it all in – and on they went. And, because you listened to them, they thought you were wonderful! So sweet, so understanding, so caring! So unlike their wives and girlfriends!

But that was really what she was paid for! She spent most of her professional life listening to people. People talking about their fantasies. Doing them only took minutes – seconds even! But the pleasure lay in the talking. And if you could make them think you were really interested in their fantasies – really turned on by their egos – then bingo! You struck it rich!

But then, when you thought about it, you'd heard it all before. Very little was new – or sensational. Even murder was a bit old hat. She remembered a man who had spent a whole evening with her telling her how he was going to murder his wife. Later, she read in the paper that his wife had murdered him. Good for her!

But back to present company ...

Whilst the Inspector was banging on about his boys, a small, sneaking memory – the size of a man's ... hand – had begun to focus in the depths of Debbie's mind. Grace Lawrence? What was it that she had heard about Grace? She broke into Raynes' monologue:

"How old did you say Allan was?"

"Twenty-one. Why?"

"And was he adopted?"

"How did you know?"

"Just put the usual two and two together, Inspector! Just like you do every day. Grace was Allan's mother!"

Raynes was amazed.

"Are you sure?"

"A little arithmetic. Twenty-one years ago. That's when she left Kenny Buchanan. She didn't want the responsibility and neither did he. She passed him over to the adoption agency. It was still going then. I remember someone asking her what had happened to the baby (I didn't know she'd had a baby), but I heard her say it'd been adopted. Yes, that'll be it. Grace was Allan's mother."

Raynes was over the moon.

"Of course! That'll explain everything!"

It explained why she wouldn't admit that Allan had been to her caravan. Of course not! Not if he was her own son. That was why she had lied. Said she didn't know him. Of course, she didn't know – not to start with. But Graeme must have told her! Graeme must have got it from Ellie? Yes, that was it. Ellie had told Graeme – and Graeme was blackmailing Grace. Threatening to ruin Allan's career unless she did what he said. And had he told Allan? Well, yes, he must have done, because Allan, Tom and Graeme had gone over to see Grace last year – but, this year, Allan had kept away! He had disapproved of the boys going round to see her. But what could he say? Graeme had got him where he wanted him. Incest was a very nasty blackmailing weapon. Poor, poor Grace!

Raynes leant over the table and kissed Debbie.

"You're an angel. You've solved half my problem."

"All you have to do is ask. I'm ready and willing!"

Raynes smiled. "I know that."

"And I'm thinking about my jacuzzi."

"I thought you were. I saw the distant look in your eyes."

"Richard, it *is* fantastic. What it does to your body! Something no man could ever do!"

"Are you trying to discourage me?"

She smiled wickedly.

"No. Just trying to stimulate the competition!"

"Perhaps we should let the jacuzzi take second place? So that I shan't be an anti-climax?"

Debbie raised her eyebrows.

119

"Richard," she said mockingly, "no one could ever accuse you of that." She stood up and stretched out her arms. "The time has come," she said, "to take this scarlet woman home!"

* * *

Raynes continued to count his good fortune even after breakfast the following morning. By then he had emerged as the clear winner over the jacuzzi. At least, that's what Debbie had said!

"I'm so grateful for what you told me last night," he said. "It really makes all the difference to my investigations. It might even provide a key which could unlock other doors."

Mrs May sat perched on a stool, wearing a white satin house coat, her feet bare, drinking white milky coffee. She smiled at Raynes.

"Inspector," she said. "All you want me for is my mind!"

Raynes looked at her.

"It's cheaper!" he said.

20 *Two, two, the lily-white boys*

Whilst Detective-Inspector Raynes was exploring the unfathomable depths of Debbie's new jacuzzi, Graeme Wilson found himself paddling in a much shallower pool. With the camp ending so abruptly – four days early – he was, for once, at an extremely loose end. He had no work to do and many of the people he had phoned, seemed to be away. He could not contact Jenny because Neil was at home and he would not be seeing his father till Saturday. He thought of going round to see Ellie, but he knew that he couldn't expect much sympathy from her. She would have a lot of hard questions seeking answers and she would probably blame him for Allan's death. She would be vicious and emotional; and, to be honest, he could not face another weeping woman! So there was no one to talk to. Not even Betty – Harry Robb's sister – so often a last resort! She had put him off till Sunday night. It seemed that he was condemned to his own dreary company.

For being at home was no joy. He simply encountered all the problems he had shelved or postponed when he went away. There was a load of washing to be done. The fridge-freezer needed defrosting. The garden was full of weeds and the pick-up truck needed a change of oil and some adjustment to the brakes. The house smelt stale and fusty and the windows needed cleaning. The larder was empty. There was no food – and no beer. All he had found on his return was a heap of junk mail, a few bills and ten bottles of sour milk, which the milkman had continued to deliver even though he was obviously away. He could hardly blame the milkman because he had forgotten to cancel … but you would have thought people would have the sense to see …!

Graeme spent most of Wednesday and Thursday putting things right. He cleaned the house from top to bottom, mended his truck and told the milkman what he thought of him. He had paid the bills, weeded the garden and gone shopping. Now, with a pleasant feeling of achievement, he was sitting with his feet up in the living-room, drinking his second can of chilled beer and watching a wrestling match from New York City on satellite TV, when the door-bell rang.

The sound cheered him up. Suddenly, he felt happy. Somebody wanted to see him! He hoped it wasn't that bloody policeman again! He'd seen quite enough of him!

It was Tom.

Graeme gave him a warm welcome. He poured out another can of chilled beer and settled back in his recliner to hear how the world had been treating Tom since they had last met.

"How's things?" he asked.

Tom looked subdued.

"I had that detective round last night."

"What? Raynes, the super sleuth, and his ever-faithful poodle, Detective-Constable Carlisle?" Graeme managed to pack a fair measure of contempt into the word 'constable'. Carlisle had been one of the officers involved in putting his father away.

"Just one of them. It was quite enough."

"What was he seeing you about?"

"About Allan."

Graeme was surprised.

"But you weren't even there!"

"No, I know I wasn't. But he seemed to think I might have crept up to Picton Dale on Monday night and done the dirty. He seemed to think I had a thing against Allan ..."

"There's no denying it. You did! You told me that you were out for revenge. That you'd wait for some dark night and duff him."

"I know. But it was only words. I wouldn't have done anything to Allan. I just wanted to frighten him."

"And now you're a suspect like the rest of us?"

"I suppose so. I just wonder who told him?"

"Neil, probably, They grilled him for about forty-five minutes. He'd have blabbed ... sure as eggs!"

Graeme had not forgotten the story he had told the police, but it seemed better to blame someone else. He looked at Tom with deep concern: "Those bastards will latch on to anything!"

"But what I said had got nothing to do with the murder!"

"Of course not. But if they can pin anything on you, they will. Look what they did to my dad. Forced a confession out of him. Wouldn't even let him see a lawyer till they'd broken him down. They could do the same to you."

"Well, he did threaten to take me down to the police station."

Graeme took a long swig of beer.

"Told you!"

"They don't give you much option."

"What'd he want to know?"

"What I was doing on Monday night."

"What were you doing?"

"Just slumming around. I met a friend of mine at *The Dragon* – a workmate. He had some of those blue movies, so we went round to his place and got blootered."

"You didn't tell him that!"

Tom looked despairing.

"What else could I do? If I hadn't told him, he was going to arrest me. He said so."

"Will the bloke back you up?"

"I hope so. I spoke to him this morning and told him what was brewing." Tom sniffed. "Trouble is that I don't know what time it was I came home. He was freaked out so he wouldn't remember. That detective seemed to think I could still have gone out there on my bike, murdered Allan and then come home for breakfast."

"I suppose you could," said Graeme, rather enjoying Tom's discomfort.

"Don't you start. I've had it up to here from my mother. I can't stand it! I'm going to move out next week."

"I told you to move out long ago."

"I know you did. But it's difficult. You've no idea of the constant scenes – and tears. She's either accusing me – or grovelling. Frankly, it's driving me up the bloody wall. There's only so much a person can take."

"Have another beer?" said Graeme.

"Thanks!" said Tom.

Graeme went through to the kitchen and came back with a couple of cans and a bag of peanuts he had bought at the local supermarket.

"Have the police got anything on you?" Tom asked.

"Shouldn't think so. Raynes is convinced that I was the intended victim – not Allan. He's worrying himself sick that the enemy'll strike again!" He laughed. "Some hope!"

Tom was surprised at Graeme's self-confidence.

"He could be right?"

Graeme shook his head.

"It was Allan they were after. Not a shadow of doubt! I didn't like to say too much to Raynes, but it's obvious! Allan had stirred things up at work something dreadful. His mother told me. He'd uncovered some pretty embarrassing things about his boss. Quite enough to interest the tax people. Mr Hogg would have been for the high jump and no mistake!"

"Really?"

Tom was relieved that Graeme seemed to know the full story.

"The whole family have had it in for Allan for weeks. I believe he was just about to get the sack when he came back from camp. Stephen told me last week. And then there was a big fight about it ..."

123

"A fight?"

"They probably didn't tell you. Last Friday, it was. Neil was away, knocking off Grace, when Harry Robb spouted off about what Allan had been saying. Garry laid into him, but Harry's a tough nut. He smashed his nose in – there was blood everywhere ..."

Tom was more interested in the news about Neil than about the fight.

"Neil – and Grace?"

Graeme looked man-of-the-worldish.

"So I'm told."

"Hell's teeth! Poor Jenny!"

"I know, it's terrible. She'd be better away from him. I've offered her the chance of a decent life, if she'd like to take it. She's making up her mind."

"I didn't think Neil'd do a thing like that!"

"Frustration! Does things to you!"

Tom grinned.

"That's one thing I don't suffer from!"

"Nor me!" Graeme laughed. "But you can see it's breaking him up. He's not the Neil he used to be. He's lost all his sparkle. All his sense of fun."

"Does he know about all this travel agency stuff?"

"Bound to. Allan couldn't keep his mouth shut."

"Would he have told the detective?"

"I don't know. It wouldn't look good. One of the lads bumping off a leader. Could lose his job ... Mark you!" he said, waving an empty can in Tom's direction, "He's probably lost it anyway. He's on the slippery slope. Things have already gone too far. He's terrified your business comes out."

"I thought it had."

"It hasn't reached the District Commissioner yet. But this murder'll be the last straw!" He looked at the row of empty cans littering the surface of the newly-polished coffee-table. "Another couple?"

Tom did not say no.

The succession of cans had begun to activate his brain. He found that he could see things more clearly. He wished he had some crack to illuminate his mind that little bit more. Working in the Public Works Department did not exactly encourage independent thought or reflection. But, now that Graeme had spelt out the sequence of events so clearly, Tom could see it for himself. He felt happier already. A deep burden had been lifted from his shoulders. But he was surprised that Detective Inspector Raynes had failed to draw the obvious conclusion – but had instead come round to his house to persecute him. It was too bad!

As Graeme returned with a fresh pack, he said:

"So you think Garry did it?"

"No doubt about it! He was thirsting for revenge all week-end. Waiting for the ideal moment to strike. When he heard me offering Allan my tent – he wanted to stay up and read – he saw his chance. He and Stephen were in the next tent to Neil's. I thought they were asleep but they could easily have heard me. And then, of course, it was just a question of waiting till everything had settled down. He used things from the cooking tent. Sand from the river. No problem! Silenced Allan once and for all!"

Tom shook his head.

"That's dreadful! Didn't you say anything to him?"

"Couldn't. Just couldn't." He wiped his mouth with his hand. "It was just too sick for words." Graeme proceeded to give Tom a lurid picture of what Allan's body had looked like when he found it.

"I'm surprised Garry didn't show any guilt?"

"Oh, but he did! When Raynes was questioning him, he completely broke down. In fact, he went berserk. Ran away down the passage screaming ..."

"So the detective must know?"

"I think he does."

"And yet he still thinks you were the intended victim?"

"He did yesterday. You'll never guess what he's asked me to do!"

"Go on!"

"He's asked me to draw up a list of all my birds ..."

"That'll be a long list!"

125

"... Just in case any of them should have wanted to take their revenge!"

"Have you done it yet?"

"No. I'm going to do it tonight. That's the best time. I shall sit in bed and rake through all my memories. It's a pointless exercise – but, as you say, when the police put the screws on you, there's not much you can do but co-operate."

"Do you think you'll reach the ton?"

Graeme shook his head.

"Forty or fifty at the most. And some of those were just one-night stands. They don't really count. I don't think I even knew their names!" He drank deeply. "I think the time has come to settle down ... just one woman ..."

"Jenny?"

"I hope so."

He bent forward and tore open the rest of the cardboard pack. "Come on!" he said. "We might as well finish this lot!"

* * *

Not surprisingly, the list was not composed until the following morning. Tom had stayed till nearly 1.00 am and they had rounded off the evening with a delicious fry-up – pork sausages, black pudding, bacon and eggs. When Graeme reached his bed, he just put his head to the pillow and fell into a deep, dreamless sleep.

He was woken by the milkman, slamming the gate.

He looked at his watch.

7.55 am.

Normally, he would have been up by 7.15 am but today there was nothing to do – except that stupid list. The Inspector had said he would be around some time after 10.00 am. So he had two hours to get it done.

He rolled out of bed, had a shower, drank two cups of coffee, read the paper and then retrieved a large white envelope from some insurance company – and started remembering.

Where should he start?

Billy. She was the first.

Funny, starting off with someone called Billy! But her real name was Georgina. His father had called her Billy – just as a

126

joke. But Billy had got tired of Ron Wilson and transferred her affections briefly to his son. He had happy memories of Billy which he had no intention of sharing with Inspector Raynes. All he wanted was a name. He wrote down: 'Georgina (Billy)' and put down the year of their association. Good heavens! Had he only been thirteen?

There followed a number of schoolgirls that had passed through his hands: Liz, with the black hair; Pauline, who had refused to travel on the back of his motor-bike; Helen, who had been no more than a ten-minute romp in the bike shed; and Ann. She had lasted longer. He wondered where Ann was now?

Then there was Miss Fitzgerald – Fitz, as everyone called her. A student teacher – very pretty – who had tried to discipline him, making him stay behind after 4.00 pm. A stupid thing to do. He had instinctively turned the situation to his advantage. Fitz had been the first woman he had deliberately blackmailed. He had told her that he would report her to the headmaster for indecent behaviour – unless she agreed to kiss him. Fitz had stared at him for a full minute, weighing up the pros and cons of Graeme's threat – and decided that discretion was the better part of valour. That first kiss had taken her much further than she had intended. Graeme had exploited his advantage shamelessly. Within a week, he had booked himself in to look after her small garden and, within a fortnight, he was tending more than flower beds! Miss Fitzgerald had left Henslea Comprehensive a wiser and more experienced teacher! Dear old Fitz! One moment, cool as a cucumber; the next, red hot like a volcano. Looking back, he felt sure she had enjoyed it as much as he. Fitz would never have wanted to murder him!

There followed a number of nameless, faceless couplings which he could recall only by the places where they had met, the colour of the underwear worn, the funny things they had said and the turn-offs he had received.

There was the blonde with a large appendix scar. The redhead who wanted to do it standing on her head. The one with the pony-tail who wouldn't speak to him afterwards. The

French au pair who had almost laid him out with the over-powering smell of garlic. Was that Giselle or Catherine? It was difficult to cast one's mind back so far! He would not forget the middle-aged dolly bird who had surprised him by dialling 999 and asking for the fire brigade. (That had been very embarrassing!) Nor would he forget the one with black beady eyes and a Mercedes who had ordered him out of her car and left him to walk the eight miles back to Grasshallows!

But the bad trips were far outweighed by the good. That lovely, baby-faced American girl with red, white and blue stockings and large white leather boots. He wished he'd kept in touch with her. Then there was Marion – the one who kept falling asleep. And Linda, a flushed barmaid at the University Students' Union, who had abandoned her post at the pressure pumps to minister to his needs … Like Maurice Chevalier, he remembered them all – but he doubted whether Inspector Raynes would find his list of much interest.

He totalled up the list and found that it amounted to only twenty-seven. He racked his brain and after much thought, added two more. But, try as he might, he could not go beyond twenty-nine. Divided over a period of seven years, it did not look quite so impressive as he had led Tom and others to believe. As he had said, many of them were no more than casual encounters – one night stands – some even less than that. Looking at the more recent names on the list, he could see that he was getting more 'constant' in his affections. They were lasting longer. For instance, he had now known Grace for three years, Ellie for over twelve months and Jenny since Christmas. Looking at the list, he could see himself settling down and becoming a respectable married man. It was something that he secretly yearned for.

He got out a clean sheet of paper and drew up his list in a neater and more orderly fashion. Then he washed up the breakfast dishes and cleared away all the cans from the living-room. Finally, he had another shower and put on a deep pink shirt and a pair of white linen trousers and settled back to wait for the Inspector.

* * *

Raynes arrived late.

He had been preparing a report for the Coroner's inquest later that afternoon and he had visited Doug, Tom's alibi. He had had great difficulty finding him and the interview had taken longer than he had expected. However, at 11.20 am, the police Granada drew up outside Graeme's home.

Raynes looked at the large red Japanese pick-up truck and noticed that it was well-maintained and in very good condition. He looked at the garden and noticed that the lawn was well-trimmed and the flower-beds properly tended.

He turned to Carlisle.

"Graeme may be a playboy, but he's certainly not frightened of hard work."

"Must get it from his mother's side of the family!" said Carlisle, who had an extremely low opinion of Ron Wilson.

Once inside, Raynes settled down in Graeme's comfortable recliner and asked for the list. Graeme handed it over.

"Is it absolutely complete and up-to-date?"

Graeme nodded.

Raynes ran his experienced eye down the list of names, raising his eyebrows at the large number of females identified only by the word 'blonde' or 'Students' Union'. He eliminated all the obvious 'casuals' and asked:

"Who's Miss Fitzpatrick?"

"She was one of my teachers. A student teacher in Henslea."

"Is she still in Grasshallows?"

"I don't think so. I think she left about four years ago. I used to do her garden."

'Yes,' said Raynes to himself, 'you did her garden. That's your technique. You do their gardens. You worm your way in. Then you knock them off.'

He looked at the most recent names with greater care, wondering how many secrets lay hidden behind the simple record of names and dates.

'Grace Turner, 1985 –' suggested that Graeme had first met up with Grace at the scout camp three years before. He had been visiting her ever since.

"Where did you first meet Grace?"

"At *The Carpenter's*. She was working behind the bar."

"You were at camp?"

"Yes. We go every year to Picton Dale. She invited me to visit her at her caravan …"

"Did you give her money?"

Graeme looked shocked.

"Good heavens, no! Grace has a very generous disposition."

Raynes looked at him coldly.

"So that's why you gave her a black eye?"

"We had a private disagreement. She got on my wick."

"Nothing that would lead to murder?"

"Hardly!"

Graeme's reply was crisp and contemptuous.

Raynes returned to the list.

"Mrs Foster?"

"We became friendly last summer. Nothing serious! It's just been an occasional encounter. Now and again."

"But Allan caught you?"

"He said he did, but he didn't really. It just looked suspicious. Ellie had forgotten to put her shoes on and I was a bit flushed. I suppose we both looked guilty …"

"And what did Allan say?"

Graeme thought the matter over.

"Nothing much at the time. He just shook his head and walked out. Later he said to me: 'I'm not blaming you. She's just as much to blame. She leads my dad a terrible dance. I don't know why she married him …'"

Raynes looked thoughtful.

"But you like Mrs Foster?"

"Ellie's good fun. A bit bossy – but quite racy for a woman of her age."

"You seem to like women of her age?"

Graeme shrugged his shoulders.

"They're all the same to me."

Raynes reflected that Graeme's affection for the older woman was perhaps a compensation for the absence of his own mother, who had left Ron Wilson when Graeme was just a child. Had it been Ellie who had been murdered, Graeme would have been a prime suspect. Oedipus and all that …

He returned to the list in front of him.

"Wendy Armstrong?"

"She lives next door to Ellie."

"The mother of the twins, Pat and Doug?"

Graeme nodded.

"And what does Mr Armstrong say about this?"

"He doesn't know anything. It was only a couple of times. She wasn't much fun …"

Raynes noted that the date was 1986.

Two years ago.

Surely the urge for revenge would long since have passed?

"How d'you get on with Mrs Armstrong now?"

"All right. She's a bit cagey but I still do her garden."

"Has there been any change in Mr Armstrong's – or Mr Foster's – attitude to you of late?"

Graeme could see exactly how the Inspector's mind was working. As he had said to Tom, he was quite sure Raynes was barking up the wrong tree.

"I can't see why you're so sure that someone's out to get me? Allan was killed for what *he* had done."

"Was he?"

"Of course he was. That business in the travel agency. Everyone knew that Mr Hogg was out to get him. Garry was just waiting to get his revenge. That was what the fight was all about."

"I know about the fight," said Raynes. "But I can't see how Garry knew you and Allan were going to exchange tents?"

"Oh, that's quite simple! He must have overheard me and Allan speaking. We weren't speaking loudly – but he must have heard us. Once he knew Allan was in my tent, he saw his chance."

Raynes looked at Graeme with surprise.

"I thought we had only one detective at camp! Now I see we had two! You're telling me that you are quite sure Garry killed Allan Foster?"

"I'm 98% certain. Remember how he broke down when you were interviewing him?"

"I remember that extremely well."

"He was obviously guilty!"

Raynes looked at Graeme even more thoughtfully. Was Graeme being serious – or was rather an ancient red herring being redrawn across his path? He chose his words carefully.

"You think that Garry came to camp this year intent upon revenge ... You think that he was waiting for an opportunity to murder him ... When he heard you and Allan agreeing to exchange tents, he realized that his moment had come. He then got the sand, the funnel and all the rest and nipped into Allan's tent in the depths of the night?"

Graeme looked quite sure of himself.

"Sounds perfectly straightforward to me."

"I think you're forgetting one thing," said Raynes. "You forgot it on Tuesday. You're forgetting it now. Someone put those sleeping tablets into your orangeade. At the time when that orangeade was put into your tent, neither Garry nor any-one else – except you – could have had the slightest expectation that Allan would be sleeping in your tent that night. Only you could know. So, either you put the pills into the bottle to make Allan sleep or someone else did it – *for you*."

Raynes was so forceful in his explanation that even Graeme was obliged to agree that it made sense. The Inspector continued: "It's therefore quite simple. Either I arrest you now. Or I look for someone with a grievance against you. That's why I'm going through this list. Most of the boys seem to like you. But if you have any enemies, I think we may find them here."

He tapped the list.

Graeme said nothing.

"Doreen Wallace?"

"She's on her own. Divorced."

"Geoff's mother?"

"She's quite nice. Our paths cross occasionally ..."

"... when you do her garden?"

Graeme nodded.

"This gardening business seems to provide you with an open door to all these ladies?"

Graeme smiled.

132

"I think they're lonely. They like a little romance. Makes life more exciting for them!"

'Must be bloody desperate!' thought Raynes.

He moved on.

"Frances Cotton? Johnny's mum?"

"Another divorcée! I can't get away from them!"

"You do her garden as well?"

"I do all their gardens."

"So they all pay you for work done and then sometimes give you a little personal bonus on the side?"

"That's it."

Graeme seemed completely unabashed.

Raynes asked: "Do the boys know about any of this?"

Graeme shook his head.

"I wouldn't say anything to the lads. It's nothing to do with them."

Raynes explored the remaining two names on the list which he did not recognize: Wetherall and Brown. It turned out that they were the mothers of two other boys in the 14th Grass-hallows Troop, but neither had been at the summer camp this year. Mrs Wetherall and Mrs Brown were apparently still entertaining Graeme from time to time. Raynes asked for their addresses. He then turned to the few fortunate mothers who seemed to have escaped Graeme's clutches.

"What about Mrs Mackay?"

Graeme laughed.

"You must be joking! She's a staunch bible Christian! Wouldn't drop her drawers for anyone! Not even Mr Mackay, I shouldn't think! She's pretty. I'll give you that. But she'd never lay her hands on me – never in a million years! Too many principles!"

"Mrs Fisher?"

Graeme grimaced.

"There's another one. A complete snob! She keeps watching you from her sitting-room window to make sure you don't slack! Only opens the door to give you your money! Ellie tells me that she calls me 'her charming young man', but she's tucked firmly into her Playtex! Not much fun there!"

133

Raynes tried not to smile.

"Mrs Hogg?"

"She's dead."

"So Mr Hogg's a widower?"

Graeme nodded.

"... I hadn't realized." He looked down his own list. "That leaves only Mrs Robb and Mrs Stewart?"

"Mrs Stewart's husband's a free-lance artist. He works at home. And Mrs Robb's a bit too old – even for me!"

"I thought you were friendly with her daughter, Betty?"

"Just friends!"

"So far."

Graeme looked thoughtful.

"Harry's keeping an eye on her. I don't want to upset him. Not after what Garry said. She's good company. Laughs a lot. But she's not all that romantic. I think we'll just stay good friends."

Raynes thought it was the most sensible thing Graeme had said all morning. He thought he knew the reason why Betty was sitting pretty. He put his finger on the final name on Graeme's list.

"And Jenny? What about Jenny?"

"I told you about her last time."

"I know you did."

"There's nothing more to say!"

"Nothing?"

Graeme leant forward in his chair.

"I told you on Tuesday. It was just a harmless little romp at Christmas. We'd both been drinking. She was in need of a bit of a cuddle. It just happened!"

"Is it still happening?"

Raynes' question was rapier-sharp.

Graeme hesitated for a long time before answering.

"At this precise moment, no."

It hurt his personal pride to admit it.

"Is it likely to be happening again in the future?"

Graeme shrugged his shoulders.

"I just don't know. I'd rather not talk about it."

134

Jenny seemed to be the only woman about whom Graeme was not prepared to speak. That in itself was extremely interesting – and told the Inspector a great deal.

Raynes decided that Graeme had been sufficiently forthcoming and that he would not probe any deeper into his private life. The picture he had received was clear enough.

He said: "With your permission, I shall keep this list. No one else will see it except myself and Detective-Constable Carlisle. When this case is over, I shall return it to you."

He folded the sheet of paper and put it away in an inside pocket.

"Now," he said, "I would like to ask you one final favour? I should like to look over your house – all the rooms."

"Do you have a search warrant?"

"No. That's why I'm asking you – as a personal favour."

Graeme shook his head in disgust.

"I don't have much option, do I? If I say: 'No', you'll simply go and get one."

"Correct!" said Raynes. "That's why it's so much better to get your permission. Saves time and unpleasantness all round."

"Well, if you want to, I'm not going to stop you. But it sounds like blackmail to me!"

Raynes could not resist getting in a personal dig.

"Well, Graeme," he said cheerfully, "that's something you seem to know quite a lot about!"

Graeme ignored the dig. He said coldly:

"I've nothing to hide."

Raynes left Carlisle with the young man in the living-room and explored the upper regions of the house. He examined all the wardrobes, the bedside cabinets, all drawers and bathroom cupboards. He came down the stairs and worked his way through the kitchen, dining-room and scullery, leaving the living-room till last. In his hand, he had a small brown medicine bottle which he had picked up in the kitchen.

"Those are my dad's!"

"So I see," said Raynes. He looked at Carlisle. "When did Ron Wilson get put away?"

"May or June."

Raynes looked at the date on the bottle.

"Must have got them just before he went away. Used quite a lot though in a short time." He rattled the bottle. "Only six left!" He looked at Graeme. "D'you use them?"

"Sometimes."

Raynes looked at the surly young man in front of him.

"You know what these pills are?"

"Sleeping pills. But they're not the ones you think they are!"

Raynes' eyes were cold and hard.

"For your sake, I hope they're not. But if they are, we shall soon find out." He went to the door. "We shall see you tomorrow – or perhaps even sooner!"

He walked down the drive to the police car. He was conscious of being watched – not only by Graeme at the front door – but also by a host of neighbours skulking behind their net curtains.

"What a 'charming young man'!" he said sarcastically.

"A wolf in sheep's clothing!" said Carlisle.

"Certainly a wolf," said Raynes. "But did the wolf have the guts to kill? That is the question!"

21 *Abide with me*

The funeral took place on Saturday morning in the Methodist chapel in Riverside Road. The entire Scouting community in Grasshallows turned out for the occasion, all in full-dress uniform. The scouts sat in the left-hand aisle of the church and in the gallery. The parents, teachers and other friends sat on the right.

Raynes and Carlisle arrived early and got a seat four rows from the front where they could watch the 14th Grasshallows Troop, who were to occupy the front three rows on the left. It was a beautiful sunny morning and golden rays of light poured into the building.

Allan's coffin lay in state at the front of the church beneath the pulpit. It was a simple oak coffin with imitation brass handles. Allan's scouting trophies were laid out on top of his coffin and there were two massive wreaths, together with many other smaller bunches and sprays. Raynes looked at it and felt like crying. It all seemed so pointless, so sad and so unreal. A young man cut down – probably accidentally – in the prime of his life. Raynes had no children of his own but he knew just how Mr Foster must feel.

Raynes tried to put such thoughts behind him. 'After all,' he said to himself, 'I am here on duty. I am not here as a simple mourner. I am here to find Allan's murderer. And if justice is to be done, it depends on me. All these people are expecting me to deliver the goods.' Raynes wished that he could be more hopeful about the outcome of the case but at that moment he felt far from confident.

Whilst he was waiting, he listened to the music. The organist played a selection of music ranging from Bach to Elgar – all of it soft, slow and emotional. It tugged at the heart-strings. As he played, the mourners flowed steadily in. By 10.15 am, the right-hand aisle was packed solid. By 10.20 am, the scouts began to process in, company by company. Last to arrive were the 14th Troop following their standard-bearers carrying the company's flags – dark green and gold and the Union Jack – processing in slow march, step by step – most impressive. The congregation instinctively stood.

The minister appeared a few minutes later, standing silently in his pulpit, wearing his dark robes. He reminded Raynes of some High Court Judge presiding over a murder trial. His voice was suitably sombre. He announced the first hymn: 'O God, our help in ages past ...'

The congregation joined in with gusto, glad to do something to break the emotional tension which was building up. Raynes did not sing. He ran his eyes back and forward along the lines of the 14th Troop to see what reactions there were amongst the boys. Simon and Geoff, he could see, were just staring down at their service sheets, not singing at all. Neil was crying. Tears were running down his cheeks; he did not bother to wipe them away. Graeme was trying to set a good example. Tom had his head down. Ian Mackay was singing with deep feeling, his eyes raised towards the east window. Harry Robb and Tony Mason were bellowing away. Johnny

137

Cotton and Mark Todd were whispering to each other. Inspector Raynes could not see the others. He was reminded that today twenty-three scouts from the 14th Troop were present – the full company – not just those who had been at camp. Many of the faces were unfamiliar.

Now they were sitting down again. The Minister began his address:

"My dear friends, this is a tragic occasion … a young life suddenly taken away from us … cut down by an unknown hand … taken away from the land of the living … away from those he loved …"

It was not exactly Demosthenes nor Mark Anthony – but then, Raynes had not been expecting great oratory. What irritated him was that the minister uttered every predictable cliché.

"Allan was a great Scout … a faithful son to his family … an example to us all … No evil was found in him … He obeyed the words of the commandment: 'Honour thy father and mother …'"

But Raynes noted that he omitted the second half of the commandment: 'that thy days may be long in the land which the Lord thy God giveth thee'. Allan hadn't lived long; but in that short time, he must have broken the ninth commandment many thousands of times. He had committed adultery and had had sex with his own mother! But Raynes didn't expect the minister to say anything about that.

"There will for ever be an empty space beside the camp-fire … an empty place in our hearts … an empty corner in the office where he worked – an office where he was loved and trusted by all his colleagues …"

Except for those on the ghost payroll! Raynes wondered if Mr Hogg and his accountant were present. As he listened, he began to have serious doubts as to whether the minister actually knew Allan at all. If he did, then his address was blatantly false. If he didn't, it was little short of an insult. Raynes felt that he could have done better himself.

"Would that the evil hand which struck him down, had heeded the word of the Lord: 'Thou shalt not kill ...' Oh, the sins that are wrought by the sons of disobedience! ... Let the head of him who did this foul crime be bowed in shame ..."

Raynes expected every head in the building to jerk upright but over fifty per cent of the heads remained bowed. Surely they couldn't all have done it, thought Raynes? (Though one always had to remember the murder on the Orient Express where about three hundred people had stabbed the poor victim without anyone noticing that he had been stabbed already! Heavens above! The things these lady crime-writers sold to the public!) Raynes concluded that after fifteen minutes, people just weren't listening – and neither was he!

The next hymn was 'Onward Christian Soldiers' – good rousing stuff! It was a hymn Raynes had always enjoyed so he joined in with such enthusiasm that Carlisle was surprised. Carlisle wondered whether the minister might not have been more tactful by excluding the last verse. He noted a sudden faltering in the singing as the congregation sang: "Onward, then, ye people, join our happy throng ..." Surely there was some mistake?

Then there were the interminable prayers:

"O Almighty God, we ask thee to take to thyself the soul of this thy servant, Allan, that dying unto us, he may live unto thee ..."

Five minutes of bilge without a single Amen! And finally some words from the book of Ecclesiastes:

"There is a time to live – and a time to die.
A time to laugh – and a time to cry.
A time to kiss – and a time to refrain from kissing.
A time to love – and a time to hate ..."

Inspector Raynes wondered which of them it was that Colin Fisher had heard at 2.35 am. A time to kill! A time to be heard – but not to be seen. Raynes looked in vain for any sign of remorse from any of the scouts; but saw none. Perhaps he was looking in the wrong direction?

But now the congregation was on its feet again and 'Jerusalem' was blaring out on the organ:

"And did those feet in ancient time
Walk upon England's mountains green?"

A group of the most senior Scout-leaders came forward to act as pall-bearers. They moved Allan's trophies on to the communion table and then lifted up the coffin – their faces grim, their eyes suffused with tears.

"We shall not cease from mental strife,
Nor shall our sword sleep in our hand,
Till we have built Jerusalem
In England's green and pleasant land."

It was a fine sentiment – nobly expressed and splendidly sung. But never for a moment did Raynes forget that it was he who must not cease from mental strife. Nor must the sword sleep in his hand ... till he had found the murderer in Grasshallow's 14th Troop. It was amazing how these new words seemed to fit the tune. He pointed it out to Carlisle and proceeded to sing and whistle them several times on the way to the cemetery.

* * *

Only a limited number of people were present at the interment – mostly immediate family. Ellie and Arthur; Neil and Jenny; the Armstrongs, who were next-door neighbours; Sheila, his girlfriend; the pall-bearers, various aunts and uncles – and Grace.

Raynes and Carlisle stood beside her whilst the coffin was lowered into the ground. Raynes put his arm round her. He could feel her shoulders shaking underneath her thin coat. Grief for a son she had hardly known – a son she had given away as an infant – who had now been murdered. Possibly by one of her other lovers. It had all the hallmarks of a Greek tragedy.

The service at the graveside was mercifully brief.

140

Raynes waited till the board with all the flowers had been laid in position and the mourners had begun to drift away. Then he turned to Grace:

"Why didn't you tell me that Allan was your son?"

"I didn't know till Graeme told me."

"But Graeme told you before this year's camp?"

"He told me on the first day of the camp. I asked him what had happened to Allan. He said: 'I told him.' 'Told him what?' I asked. 'That you were his mother.'"

"What did you think about that?"

"I thought he was joking! I said: 'Don't be stupid! I haven't got a son that age.' But he said: 'Oh yes, you have; but you got him adopted.' To be quite honest, I'd forgotten all about it. Put the whole thing at the back of my mind. You don't want to think about such things; it only hurts you. But Graeme said he'd got this friend who was a nurse. She knew Allan had been adopted. She made enquiries and found out who his mother was. And she told Graeme."

"That wasn't very nice."

"It was a horrible thing to do. Last year, when Allan came over to the caravan, he didn't know I was his mother and I didn't know he was my son. He reminded me of someone but I couldn't think who. It didn't dawn on me – not after all these years. But Graeme told Allan and he was very upset. He came to see me ... we both cried ... He was a nice lad. It was a horrible thing to do."

"Ruining two lives," murmured Raynes.

"And more!" said Grace. "More than you will ever know." Her eyes narrowed bitterly. "Graeme came to me and said that if I didn't do what he wanted, he'd spread it round the whole of Grasshallows – what Allan had done – and that'd ruin his career. That's what he said."

Raynes looked at Carlisle and shook his head.

"And what did he want you to do?" he asked.

"Something not very nice. I don't want to talk about it."

Grace shivered a little.

"I think you've got to," said Raynes. "For all you know, it might hold the key to this murder."

"I doubt it." Grace looked at Raynes sadly. "Well, he's dead now. I don't suppose anything matters very much. Not now anyway. The fact is that Graeme wanted me to seduce Neil."

"Neil?"

"Yes. The Scout-leader. That one – over there!"

She pointed to Neil who was walking slowly with Jenny towards the gate.

"Yes. That's Neil."

"He showed me his photograph and everything. He was trying hard to coax Neil into coming over to my caravan. He wanted me to give him the works ..."

"Ah, yes. I begin to see ..." said Raynes. "And then he'd have the whole scout troop as witnesses?"

"I don't know about that. But the idea was that when he told Jenny, she'd leave him ... divorce him ..."

"And he'd get Jenny?"

"Yes. It was a nasty business. He's got a horrible, rotten mind. He'll use any woman he can lay his hands on. He's not particular. He's probably blackmailing that nurse who told him about Allan. If he gets his claws into you, you've had it!"

"But Neil didn't come over, did he?"

"No. Neil's a good lad. Faithful to his wife. More than she's been to him. She's a stupid creature. Graeme's been leading her up the garden path these past six months ..."

Raynes nodded encouragingly.

This was the best news he had had for days.

"... So last Sunday night, Graeme got me down to *The Carpenter's Arms*. He didn't tell me what he was going to do – but he told me I'd got to say my piece or else Allan would suffer."

"And what did you have to say?"

Although he had asked the question, Raynes could easily guess the answer.

"He told me I'd got to say that all the scouts had been coming to my caravan and having it off with me. That Neil had heard about this and had come over to my caravan to read the riot act. That was what was in the original plan. I was to give him a drink – a couple of drinks – sit on his knee, drop my drawers

142

and give him the works. But Neil didn't rise to the bait. I suspect he had an idea of what Graeme was up to. He did nothing.
But I was to say that he had."

Grace paused for breath.

"Graeme said that I'd got to lie. To say that he'd been over
to see me a couple of times and that we'd done some pretty
way-out things – the sort of things which he'd never dream of
doing with his wife. Graeme made me promise that I would
stick to the story we had arranged. If I didn't, he said that he
would wreck Allan's life. He'd never hear the end of it."

"So you had little option?"

"None whatsoever. But the trouble was I had to say it to
Jenny. It was her he brought up to *The Carpenter's* that night.
He brought her in for a drink and the plan was that when they'd
had a couple, I would saunter over to their table and say: 'Hi,
Graeme.' He'd invite me to have a drink and I'd get introduced
to Jenny. Graeme would say: 'This is Jenny, Neil's wife,' and
I was to say: 'Not the Neil who's with all the scouts camping
in Picton Dale? He's a bit of a cracker …'"

"Graeme was watching me like a hawk so I said my piece.
Not very convincingly, because I don't like telling lies. And
she looked horrified. Absolutely horrified. I'm not surprised.
It was pretty erotic stuff. But Graeme just kept nodding his
head, saying what a bad business it was – and she was in tears.
It was terrible. She was completely shattered. The trouble is –
I couldn't keep it up. I couldn't keep lying – seeing her so
upset. The moment Graeme went to the bar to get me a drink,
I told her it was all lies. I'd been blackmailed into telling her
that story. It was completely untrue. Neil had never been near
me. He'd been totally faithful."

"Well, of course, that put the cat among the pigeons! When
Graeme came back with the drinks, she exploded. She really
let him have it. What was he doing setting up such a rotten
trick? 'What rotten trick?' He claimed it was all true. Neil had
been to my caravan. I said it wasn't true. He looked like
thunder. I said: 'I'm going. I'm not staying to listen to any
more lies.' I ran out of the pub. Graeme came after me and
when he caught me, he punched me, he kicked me and he

gave me that black eye. And then he said: 'On your own head be it! You've landed me in it! Just wait till I've finished with Allan! He'll never lift up his head again! I'll break him!' And that was it. The next thing I knew – Allan was murdered and it was all over the papers."

"And you think Graeme did it?"

"I can't see that anyone else had such a grudge against him. Graeme made the threat. I assumed he would carry it out. But I never thought it would lead to murder. To all this …"

She looked miserably across the cemetery to the grave where the council workmen were now beginning their work, moving the flowers and shovelling in the earth.

"… Perhaps it would have been better to lie?"

Raynes shook his head.

"It's always better to tell the truth."

"Well, I can tell you this," said Grace. "If I ever have a chance to get my revenge, I'll kill him. If I ever see him on the edge of a cliff, I'll push him over. If I ever see him in his truck, I'll do something to his brakes. He's a bastard and he deserves to be punished. He shouldn't be allowed to get away with such things! How many more women is he going to twist and screw?"

Raynes calmed her down.

"We've had enough murder for one week," he said. "Just leave it to the police. We'll straighten things out – and if there are any charges to be made against Graeme, we'll deal with it in our way. After what's happened, I don't think Graeme will dare lift a finger against you. I think he's probably learnt his lesson the hard way."

"I doubt it," said Grace.

Raynes sighed. "Well, we've got to go back to the reception. To see the parents and things – we can't spend all day out here. D'you want a lift back into town?"

Grace accepted the offer.

But it was clear that her mind was elsewhere. There was a distant look in her eyes. A look which spelt trouble. Gone was the easy-going nympho. In its place there was a look of cruel determination and suppressed rage. Raynes looked at her

144

anxiously and remembered the words of the old proverb: 'Hell hath no fury like a woman scorned.' He hoped she would do nothing stupid.

22 *I've got that B.P. Spirit*

The reception was held in the small hall occupied by the 1st Grasshallows Troop. The hall was used for Gang shows, amateur dramatics, coffee mornings and other worthy ventures. There was a stage with dark red velvet curtains, rather tatty walls, battered doors and a general atmosphere of seediness – of faded splendour – which so often surrounds such places.

Reception was perhaps the best word to describe proceedings. It was not a party; nor was it a wake. Rather, it was a gracious opportunity for civilized people to come together to say how shocked they were at what had happened, to comfort each other in a moment of adversity, and to show the world that even though Allan was dead, normal life could still go on. It was a cheering example of British stoicism that, no matter how great the tragedy, no matter how deep the sorrow, the show must go on.

And go on, it did.

The boys of the 14th Troop helpfully intermingled with the guests, bearing sandwiches, biscuits, cups of tea and coffee – polite, smiling, well-scrubbed faces that shone with serenity and goodness. It was rather like a cocktail soirée on the *Titanic*. There was about the proceedings an air of unreality, rather like the Mad Hatter's tea party – where everyone was terribly reasonable and polite, even though the circumstances were bizarre in the extreme.

Raynes and Carlisle were the last to arrive. In point of fact, Carlisle was not even sure if they had been invited. Raynes looked round the hall trying to decide who best to approach. He noticed Graeme speaking courteously to the minister and Jenny and Neil listening respectfully to the District Commissioner. Simon and Geoff, who were circulating busily with the egg and salmon sandwiches, suddenly appeared before them and offered them the choice of four plates.

"The egg ones are best!"

"He's eaten eight of them!"

"The salmon ones are horrible!" Geoff made a face. "Paste! Salmon paste! Mrs Todd made them."

Simon was more direct.

"Have you found the murderer yet?"

Raynes decided to be perfectly honest.

"We're still looking. At the moment, there are about seventeen suspects but we're narrowing them down, one by one."

"Are we in the seventeen?"

"Of course you are!"

"And Pat and Doug?"

"All of you."

"Gosh! It's great being a suspect!"

"Especially if they serve you with unlimited egg sandwiches!" Geoff grinned.

"I hope you won't taste the arsenic, Inspector!"

Raynes smiled and shooed them away.

He and Carlisle decided to divide the hall between them. Raynes took the left-hand side, Carlisle the right.

Raynes noticed that Mr and Mrs Robb were standing on their own. He knew it must be them because Mr Robb was so like his son – thick-set with a pug-nose and an aggressive chin. He went over and introduced himself.

"This is a bad business, Mr Raynes ..." Mr Robb.

"... Nothing like this has ever happened to us before ..." Mrs Robb.

"... And we sincerely hope it will never happen again!"

Mr Robb drew himself up to his full height of five feet five and sniffed contemptuously. "I'm surprised you haven't caught the murderer yet!"

Raynes was at his most emollient.

"We've only had four days, Mr Robb. As investigations go, that's not long. We've had a hard time discovering the motive. I'm a great believer in looking for the motive. When you've got the motive, you've got the man."

"Jealousy!" said Mrs Robb. "There's a lot of it about."

"From what I hear," said Raynes provocatively, "there seems to have been a certain amount of trouble in the Troop of late?"

"Harry can take care of himself," said Mr Robb proudly.

"Yes. He's a fine lad," said Raynes. "You must be very proud of him."

Mrs Robb was in a world of her own. "You can't trust anyone these days. Not with all these maniacs about."

A whiff of strong perfume preceded Ellie as she butted into the conversation, dragging a tubby little man in her wake. The little man was almost bald and had red cheeks with rather sensuous lips.

"This is Arthur," said Ellie. "Say thank you to Mr Raynes. It was him who found you."

"Well, actually it was Interpol," said Raynes modestly. "Where did they find you?"

"In Paris," said Arthur, looking sheepish. "I was on my way home."

"I suppose they need pharmaceuticals in France – just as much as Turkey," said Raynes, keeping a straight face. "Now we're in the European Community, we've got to sell everywhere we can. Spend too …"

Ellie was about to say something rude to the Inspector but, at that moment, the minister appeared at Raynes' elbow – with Graeme still hovering in the background.

Mrs Robb was the first to grovel.

"Oh, Mr Bonham, thank you so much for your kind words about Allan. It was most inspiring to us all."

"That's true," said a tall man who had joined the group with two fashionable-looking ladies. "Young Pat's been talking about becoming a padre. I tell him he'll have to work hard if he's going to make the grade. Too much messing around these days. Not enough parental guidance. Don't you think so, Mr Raynes?"

Raynes nodded.

He was feeling swamped – surrounded by too many people. He felt a little bit lost – out of control; but there was no obvious way of escape.

The minister was unction itself.

"Well, despite the tragedy, life has to go on. Doesn't it, Mrs Foster? Allan wouldn't have wanted it any other way. We've all got to put our backs into things and try to forget …"

"I don't think I shall ever forget …" said Arthur sadly.

"No, no, of course not!" The minister suddenly realized that he might have said the wrong thing. "It's just that – well – life does have to go on."

Mr Robb agreed.

"Well, our Harry'll be back at work on Monday."

"Where does he work?" asked Mr Bonham.

"At Tesco's," said Mrs Robb. "It's just part-time. He's filling in till he's old enough to do his apprenticeship."

The tall man's wife now intervened.

(She must be Mrs Armstrong, thought Raynes).

"Well," she said, "I'm taking the twins down to London on Monday. They want to spend their birthday money in a big way. That'll take their minds off things." She turned to the woman on her left: "What are you doing about Colin?"

Mrs Fisher was wearing a black and white check suit. She had dark hair and long jet ear-rings touched with gold.

"Oh, that's all arranged," she said. "He's been pestering me to let him go and stay with his uncle and aunt in King's Lynn. They've no children of their own. They spoil him completely."

The minister turned to Graeme.

"And is it business as usual for you?"

Graeme scratched his head.

"I suppose so. I haven't really thought about it."

"Well," said Mr Armstrong, "my lawn's in a bad way. It's over a month since you last cut it. I know you've been away at camp and things … but it's beginning to look a bit like a jungle round at the back. If you're doing nothing else on Monday, you can make a start on mine."

Ellie was not to be left out.

"Well, if you're going to be next door," she said, "you could perhaps spare a few minutes chopping down a tree for me …"

Arthur was distressed.

"Not the pear tree?"

148

"Yes. It's had it."

"We still get a few pears from it …"

"It's going!" said Ellie firmly. "On Monday."

Mr Armstrong turned to Mrs Fisher.

"Is there anything you need doing?"

Mrs Fisher looked thoughtful.

"Well, there's that small hedge that needs trimming. It's not a big job – but it's looking very ragged. You know – the one beside the garage."

Raynes was profoundly irritated at finding himself in the middle of such domestic problems as lawns and hedges. Time was passing and people were beginning to drift away. He had not been able to quiz anyone. He was boxed in by this insufferable minister who seemed to dispense nothing but treacle. As far as he could see, no one wanted to talk about the murder. It was as if the funeral service had washed the stain away. People were looking ahead – making fresh plans. The past was too painful.

Raynes kept looking at Arthur. He seemed to be very much under Ellie's thumb. But what was he doing in Paris? He was supposed to have been in Turkey. Caught in the act! But, to give him some credit, he appeared to be the only person still affected by the tragedy. Tears kept welling up in his eyes and his handkerchief was in frequent use.

Eventually Raynes managed to break away and have a private word with Ellie and Arthur, giving them some idea of how the case was going. But Ellie fixed Raynes with a beady eye.

"Did you visit that person I told you about?"

"Yes."

"Why didn't you arrest him?"

"He had an alibi. We're checking it at the moment."

She looked very accusing.

"He's right-handed!"

"I know."

* * *

Carlisle, it appeared, had fared little better. He had been buttonholed by Mr Hogg, who had complained loud and long about

the heavy-handed methods the police used to conduct interviews. "Intimidation!" he declared. "Pure intimidation!" He
had also tried to pump Carlisle for information about what
had happened to his accounts. Carlisle had not liked to say
publicly that they were being sent to the Fraud Squad. Instead,
he said simply: "We're still looking at them."

This had raised the wrath of Mrs Todd, the lady who had
prepared the salmon paste sandwiches which no one had eaten.

"That's the trouble with the police today," she said loudly.
"They'll spend any amount of time on paperwork. But where
they're wanted is out in the field. Out on the streets. That's
where things happen. They should be out and about hunting
for clues …"

Carlisle felt like shouting back:

"Why the hell d'you think we're here?"

Inwardly, he fumed, but to the outward eye, he was as
gracious as Raynes himself: "We're doing our best," he said.
"Just give us time." He sounded more hopeful than he felt.

* * *

When Raynes returned to the police car, he agreed with
Carlisle that the whole reception had been a thundering waste
of time.

"I didn't even have a chance to speak to Arthur. He's been
up to something! Even Ellie was wondering what he was doing
in Paris."

"He's a sly bugger," said Carlisle. "Like father – like son."

"Allan was adopted."

"Sorry. I keep forgetting."

Carlisle laughed.

"What's so funny?" asked Raynes.

"Oh, just something Johnny Cotton said to me. He kept
winking at me whilst he was handing out the teas. Trying to
catch my attention. Eventually I went over to see what he had
to say."

"And what was that?"

"He says that Colin now thinks it was Neil and Jenny who
did the murder. Neil wouldn't have had the guts to do it himself, but he fed her with all the information. She did the deed.

Unfortunately, Neil was unable to tell her that Allan and Graeme had switched tents. Hence the tragedy."

Raynes nodded approvingly.

"Our young sleuth's getting warmer. Jenny's the one person we haven't seen. And yet, as Grace said, she's right in it! We shall have to hear what she says."

Carlisle looked apprehensive.

"I just hope Ellie doesn't get in first."

23 *Jailhouse Rock*

Later on Saturday afternoon, Graeme changed into some more casual clothes, got into his pick-up truck and drove the fifty-five miles that separated Grasshallows from the open prison where his father was detained. His father had been given six months for receiving stolen property, but had earned full remission for good behaviour, and was hoping to be released in the next fortnight. Graeme visited his father every Saturday afternoon to keep him in touch with what was happening in the business and in the city.

"It's not been a very good week," he told his father.

"I read about it in the paper. It's not the sort of thing you expect to happen at camp. It's a good job it wasn't you, son."

"The detective who's conducting the case seems to think it was me they were gunning for."

"Who is this detective? I've never heard of him. Raynes? It was old Parkinson who put me away."

"Raynes has just come to Grasshallows ... Been here a couple of months. He's a tough bastard. Sarcastic. Mean as hell. He's working hand in glove with Carlisle. You remember Carlisle?"

"Don't I half! Ambitious little creep!" Ron Wilson was bitter. "Anyway, what's this sod Raynes doing?"

"Nothing so far – but you feel he's watching everything. Waiting for someone to make a false move. He was at Allan's funeral this morning and at the reception afterwards. I didn't speak to him."

"Does he suspect you?"

"I thought he did at first. Because of the sand, you know. He seemed to think it might have come from some building site we'd been working on. I couldn't say one way or the other ... For all I know, somebody might've set me up."

"What actually happened to the poor bugger?"

"They just filled up his throat with sand – so he couldn't breathe. It was quick. I'll say that. He couldn't have suffered much. It must have been over in a matter of seconds. They drugged his orangeade so that he wouldn't be in any fit state to resist. It was horrible."

"Did you see him?"

"I was the one that found him. He was using my tent. I thought he'd overslept so I went in to wake him. It made me really sick. Not so much the sand – but his eyes. They were staring – just staring. I thought he'd choked on his own vomit. But it was those eyes."

He started crying.

Ron Wilson looked at his son with amazement and a sense of helplessness. He'd never seen Graeme cry for years. Graeme was used to taking life's hard knocks – like he was. It must have been bloody awful if this was what it was doing to the lad.

He patted his arm. "I wish I was home, son. So as we could go and have a drink and laugh about it." (Ron Wilson always thought laughter was the best medicine for life's sorrows.)

"I've tried laughing," said Graeme. "It helped a bit. Especially with the boys. But it's really lonely at home. You can't help sitting and thinking about things. Gets on your nerves, it does."

"Wondering who did it?"

"That and other things. I've been seeing quite a bit of Jenny lately. Trying to persuade her to leave Neil and move in with us ..."

Ron Wilson nodded his head with enthusiasm. "It'd be useful to have a woman around the place. Hasn't been the same since your mother left. House never looks tidy without a woman's touch."

"I was talking to her last Sunday night in the pub up the Dale."

"The Carpenter's?"

"Yes. We had a long chat — but that bloody Grace Turner mucked it up. You remember Grace — the nympho?"

"Grace King? I wouldn't have anything to do with her, son. You don't know where she's been." He laughed sourly. "What happened?"

"I was talking to Jenny. I'd just about talked her round. Told her her marriage to Neil was on the rocks. I said to her that when he found out we'd been carrying on, he'd throw her out ... You remember that bust-up after the Christmas party? That was bad enough! But it'd be nothing to what he'd say if he knew I'd been knocking her off for the past six months! He'd go absolutely spare. He'd throw her out. I know he would."

Graeme licked his lips at the prospect.

"Well, I was telling her all this. It was no use staying. No use pretending. If I told Neil what we'd been up to, she'd have to leave anyway. Better to make the move now. Move into our place. It's big enough. Plenty of money coming in. She's a secretary at the University, so there'd be another seven or eight thousand coming in. And it's a nicer place for her kids too. Bigger garden to play in ..."

"She's got kids, has she?"

"Two. Boy of five, girl of three. They're OK. Wouldn't be any trouble. But she doesn't think Neil'll let 'em go. She thinks that he'll insist on them staying with him. But I don't see how he could look after them on his own ..."

"I've never liked Neil."

"No. He's a bit spineless. Anyway, as I was saying, we were having this talk — over a couple of pints — when Grace turns up ..."

"What's she doing up there?"

"She's got a caravan up the Dale."

"Has she now?"

"Yeah. I've been encouraging the lads to go round and shag her. She didn't take much persuading. They're quite enjoying it. Hoping to get proficiency badges for screwing!" Graeme laughed heartily. "But if Neil says anything, I can report him to the District Commissioner for letting the boys

153

get out of control. So, if anyone gets chucked out of the Scouts, it'd be him – not me!"

"Good thinking, son!"

"Well, I thought I ought to take one or two precautions. You never know what Neil might do! It's spineless buggers like him that turn to violence. I wouldn't want Jenny to get hurt. She's a doll." His eyes lit up as he talked about her. Then darkened as he returned to the events of Sunday night. "Anyway, as I was saying, Grace came barging into the snug, just as Jenny and I were talking – private-like – and she made a right scene! Poured out a whole load of lies! Told Jenny I was completely untrustworthy! A two-timing bastard! That's what she said."

"Show her your fist, son! Show her your fist! It's the only thing these bitches understand!"

"That's what I did."

"Good lad."

"I belted her in the eye good and hard. She started howling and yelling so we got out quick. I told the publican she'd attacked Jenny and by the time she'd come round, we were out in the car park and finding somewhere quieter to talk."

"So when's Jenny moving in?"

"I don't know that she is. I think bloody Grace has put her off. She hasn't spoken to me since Sunday night. She hasn't phoned. When I've tried to phone her, she puts the phone down. I saw her after the funeral this morning, but she cut me dead."

"You don't think …?"

Ron Wilson suddenly saw the connection.

"You don't think Jenny was behind the attack? That she was trying to kill you?"

Graeme stared into nothingness.

"I can't see why she would want to do that. I was offering her a new life. A better life for her and the kids. She's got no life with Neil. But she knows that I sleep on my own at camp. She would recognize my tent. If I hadn't switched tents at the last moment so that Allan could stay up and read a book, I'd have been there – and they'd have got me."

"They?"

"I keep thinking Grace's behind it too."

"Well, go and see her, lad! Put it to her straight."

"That policeman's been seeing her. I think he knows that she was Allan's mother and that I'd been blackmailing her. He hasn't said anything yet, but I got the message when he came round on Friday. It set me wondering if Grace had said anything to Jenny and Neil and whether they'd got together to do me in."

"You don't think it could be any of the boys?"

"Good God, no! They haven't got the guts to do a thing like that. It was obviously an adult. It could have been Tom … he didn't like Allan. Neither did Ellie, his step-mum. But if it was Grace, she'd have had to have help. She couldn't have done it all on her own. What I'm frightened of, is that she's poisoned Jenny against me."

"But I can't understand why she'd want to kill you. A good-looking lad like you!"

"I wish I could speak to her … I'm sure she'd be able to explain."

"TIME'S UP!" shouted the prison officer, who'd already given Graeme an extra five minutes.

Graeme got up. "I'll be back next Saturday, Dad!"

"Look after yourself, son! Good to see you!"

"Roll on a week on Saturday!"

"Make sure you get in plenty of booze!"

Graeme laughed.

Once his dad was back, things would be all right.

* * *

But Graeme was more worried than he had admitted to his father. For, in truth, things had gone very far wrong. A week ago, he was on the crest of a wave. Things had been running very smoothly his way. Jenny had been on the verge of saying 'Yes'. She was the one woman he found really attractive. She wasn't a cow – like the rest. Jenny had real class. An excellent figure. Lovely, shoulder-length corn-blonde hair. Really blue eyes which looked deep into his. A voice that was rich and sweet. If Graeme was capable of loving anyone except himself,

155

that person was Jenny. At the beginning, he had regarded it as a bit of harmless fun, knocking her off at the Christmas party – right under Neil's very nose. But since then, he had found himself falling in love with her.

His only problem was Neil.

That was the ridiculous thing! He had pointed out to her again and again that her marriage was finished. She and Neil could never be the same again. It was all going to end in tears and separation. The sooner she left Neil, the less painful it would be. She could speak to her husband – or Graeme could do it for her. But either way, the writing was on the wall. She could see the logic of his remarks, but she kept hanging on as if she was not sure.

Last Sunday night, he felt sure that he had just about won. She had agreed ... well, at least, he'd forced her to promise him ... that she would speak to Neil the moment the summer camp was over. Even despite the awful embarrassment of Grace coming in and saying all the wrong things, Graeme was convinced that Jenny would do what she had promised. But then, the following night, Allan had been murdered – in *his* tent. Was there any connection between these two events?

In his conversations with Tom Hayward and Inspector Raynes, Graeme had suggested that the obvious murderer was Garry Hogg. The detective had shot that suggestion down in flames. But if it was not Garry, who could it be?

Suppose that Jenny had indeed spoken to Neil? Told him some time on Monday what Graeme was proposing – and what Grace had said. Suppose Jenny had been to see Grace? Or, even worse, to see Ellie, who had been her Guide captain? Might Ellie have told Jenny what he had been doing with her? Proved that Grace was right? That he was indeed a two-timing bastard? Might Jenny's love have turned to hate? Might she have been determined to get her revenge? To punish him in some unpleasant way? Might she have crept into the camp on Monday night to give him his just deserts? Everyone had said that sand was a cowardly weapon. Women were cowards. Therefore it was all too possible that a woman's brain was behind the attack.

He didn't want to believe it, but he was hard put to see any alternative. Jenny would have known his tent. Grace would not. Nor would Ellie. The attack had focused on his tent – so it must have been Jenny. Because of the last minute switch of tents, Neil would have had no way of letting her know. Perhaps she had not told Neil of her plans? Graeme felt that if Neil had known, he might have shown a bit more anxiety about Allan and Graeme doing the switch. But, on Monday night, he'd been his usual, dreary, laid-back self.

If it had been Jenny, her plans had gone sadly wrong. She had killed Allan by mistake. Now she was lying low. No wonder she did not want to talk to him. That was quite understandable. Because if anyone said anything, Jenny would go to jail. It was in everyone's interests to keep quiet and say nothing. He wasn't going to betray Jenny – not even now. She needed his support and silence. He would keep her secret. He would not blab.

The only sad thing was that all this would make it even more unlikely that Jenny would leave Neil. He could only hope that once the hue and cry had died down, things would turn his way again. All he could do was wait – and hope.

24 *In an English country garden*

Graeme, therefore, did not have a very nice weekend.

He might have been even more unhappy if he could have heard a conversation between Jenny and Ellie on Sunday afternoon.

Ellie had come over for a cup of tea – mainly to get away from Arthur who was doing nothing but mope around the house. He had been very restrained on Friday morning when he came home to find his son murdered. He had been very calm and collected at the funeral. But, after that, he had gone to pieces.

He had retired to bed and cried most of Saturday afternoon. Then he had started drinking. He had been drinking all evening – mostly spirits. Ellie had tried to keep him company, but after the fifth vodka and coke, she had pulled out. But Arthur had ploughed on. He had got out all the family albums show-ing Allan as a small boy. He had wept over them – rather like King David weeping over Absalom: 'My son ... My son ...!' Ellie had found this almost unbearable and, after two hours of sentimentality and weeping, she had gone to bed.

Arthur had fallen asleep downstairs. Naturally, he had had a massive hangover and had spent most of Sunday morning in bed sleeping it off. At lunchtime, after she had prepared a beautiful roast, he had appeared at the kitchen door to say that he was going off to Skipper's Hill to play a round of golf. He would be having a few drinks with his friends. Ellie was not to worry about him. He would be back at 9.00 pm.

For Ellie, who was always well-organized, this was the last straw. So she had come round to see Jenny to tell her exactly what she thought about 'men'.

Jenny was sitting on the patio, knitting. She was not knit-ting anything special – just a plain jumper for the Scout Fayre in November. She knitted about one per week.

The children were playing in the sandpit. Neil was at the Scout hut with Garry and Stephen Hogg, putting away all the tents and equipment which had now been released by the police. It was a beautiful sunny afternoon. Jenny and Ellie sat under a coloured parasol and discussed their common problem.

"Neil just won't say anything," said Jenny. "He's keeping it all bottled up inside. I keep trying to speak to him but all he says is: 'Just leave it!' He was bad enough before he went away to camp. But now that Allan's dead, it's even worse."

"Arthur's taking it very bad as well. He's behaving like a spoilt child. Crying all the time. Drinking. Being sentimental. Now he's gone off to play golf with his cronies. I know what that means. He'll come home smashed!"

"Neil doesn't drink ..."

"Might be better if he did!"

"And there's another two weeks of the school holiday ..."

"I think men are better if they're working. The sooner Arthur gets back to work, the happier I shall be."

"Don't you want to be with him?"

"Not when he's like this."

"I don't feel that way about Neil. I want to be with him. The trouble is that it's like living with a brick wall. He doesn't seem to be the same man that I married. I know that I've changed over the past seven years but I feel that – basically – I'm still the same person. But Neil's shut off completely."

"Is something troubling him?"

"Well, I don't think he's forgiven me for having that little fling with Graeme last Christmas …"

Ellie nodded understandingly.

"… I don't think he trusts me any more." She looked at Ellie. "Of course he's right really."

"In what way?"

"I'm not really playing him fair. I'm still seeing Graeme. Did you know?"

"I'm not blind."

"Well, I hope Neil is. I don't think he knows. But he suspects. I've tried to talk to him. About us, I mean; not about Graeme. The less he says, the more I find myself being drawn towards Graeme. Graeme at least talks to you!"

"Is it getting serious?"

Jenny nodded.

"Last Sunday night, Graeme and I were discussing whether I should leave Neil. I mean – leave him for good."

Ellie was horrified.

"Surely you don't want to do that?"

"I don't, really. But I don't see what else I can do. It's bad enough now. But once he finds out I've been seeing Graeme, he's going to blow up sky-high. We had a terrible row at Christmas. This time it'll be far worse."

"But breaking up your family would be awful. Leaving your home … Where would you go?"

"Well, Graeme suggested that I should move in with him and his father …"

"What a ridiculous idea! His father's a complete crook! An absolute swine! It's unthinkable!"

"Well, I didn't like the idea all that much myself, but I don't see what else I can do. Neil wouldn't tolerate me having an affair. Certainly not with Graeme! And I can't bear any more of this unpleasantness between us."

159

"But who's going to tell him?"

"Graeme said he would – if I didn't."

"That sounds like blackmail to me. 'If you don't, I will.' What sort of love is that?"

"Well, it's very difficult living a lie. I don't particularly want to go and live with Graeme. I know what he's like."

"I don't think you know the half! He'd break your heart. He has a terrible reputation! I should think he's had over a hundred women in this city alone."

Jenny stopped her knitting.

"How can you be so sure?"

"Allan told me."

This was not the moment for Ellie to make her confession.

"Allan told everybody everything!"

Ellie looked sad.

"I think that's why he died."

"You mean that someone was trying to silence him – before he said something he shouldn't?"

Ellie nodded.

"I was wondering if he was about to say something to Neil. Perhaps he was going to tell him about you and Graeme. It would have been quite in character. I can easily imagine him doing it."

"That would have been terrible!"

"Allan had no control over his tongue. It was his worst enemy. Ever since Tuesday, it's been in my mind that Graeme might have killed Allan himself."

"Oh, don't say that!"

"Graeme can be very violent."

"I know that." She looked at Ellie. "Last Sunday night, when we were talking about Neil, he beat up this woman. Up in Picton Dale."

"What woman?"

"I don't know who she is. She lives on a caravan site. Grace …"

"Oh, Grace Turner?"

"You know her?"

"Not to speak to."

160

"Well, she came in while we were talking and said some terrible things about Neil. What he'd been doing to her in her caravan ..."

"Neil?"

"... I couldn't believe her. It was the most dreadful load of rubbish. And Graeme was lapping it up. I felt quite shattered. And then Graeme went off to get us some drinks. Then she told me it was all a lie. Graeme had been blackmailing her. All about Allan. If she didn't say these things about Neil, he was going to blacken Allan's reputation for life. Make it impossible for him to stay in Grasshallows ..."

Ellie looked grim.

"The bastard! Blackmailing bloody everybody!"

"That's what worries me."

"You can't trust him! He's probably been screwing this Grace woman as well."

Jenny shrugged her shoulders.

"When he came back and discovered what she'd been saying, he was furious. He started shouting. She screamed at him. There was a terrible scene. He was threatening her. She ran outside. He chased after her and when he came back, he had blood on his knuckles."

"I told you he was violent."

"I hadn't seen it before. And I didn't like it. That's what made me want to talk to Neil – about us. I feel we've got to get things straight. And the sooner the better."

Ellie was realistic.

"Jenny," she said, "you've got to get Graeme off your back. One way or another."

"It's easier said than done."

"No. You've just got to stand firm. Tell Graeme: 'That's the end! It's over!' And then take the consequences. You've got to stand your ground. Don't run away! Even if Neil blows up sky-high, you hold firm. You tell him that Graeme has been blackmailing you since Christmas ... and that you haven't been able to get out of his clutches ..."

"I haven't."

"Well, there you are. You'd only be telling the truth! Tell Neil what Graeme got that woman to say about him. Tell him every single word. Tell him all the lies Graeme is spreading. Trying to undermine his authority as Scout-leader – which he is – and then let Neil deal with things in his own way. He'll have to get rid of Graeme! You can't live under this constant threat."

"It's a pity we can't murder him ourselves!"

"That would certainly put an end to all our problems!"

Ellie laughed.

"But then I'd lose my gardener," she added. "I couldn't afford to lose him. Arthur's no good with his hands ... not in the garden anyway!" She thought for a moment. "Tell you what! Graeme's coming round to my place tomorrow afternoon to cut down a tree. I could have a word with him. Tell him to lay off. Tell him not to say anything to Neil. Tell him to cool it ..."

"Would you?"

Jenny sounded desperate.

Ellie began to realize the degree of stress her friend was under. She tried to sound relaxed. Make a bit of a joke of it.

"I'll do a bit of blackmail on him in return. I'll tell him that if he doesn't lay off you, he'll lose all his customers. I'll phone round and do the dirty on him. He won't like that!"

"You don't think it'll make him even more angry?"

"All bullies are cowards underneath. Graeme's no different. Put a gun to his head and he'll back down. You'll see."

Jenny resumed her knitting.

"I just wish he was out of the way – completely."

"I'll do my best," said Ellie, "but you've got to come clean with Neil. You've got to talk. You don't have to tell him the full story. Just enough to make him see what Graeme's up to."

"Do you think I should speak to him tonight?"

"Why not? The sooner you get rid of Graeme, the better."

As she said these words, Ellie felt very deceitful. Very two-faced. She knew that she had no intention of giving up Graeme

– as a gardener – or as anything else. He was a most pleasing distraction. When Arthur was away, she quite looked forward to Graeme coming round. He was a good lover and quite good fun. She was a middle-aged woman and she was determined to enjoy everything that was going. It suited her book to get Jenny out of the way.

But if Graeme was coming round tomorrow – to be talked to about Jenny – and for one or two other things – then Arthur would have to be out of the way. Ellie didn't want an audience. She wanted Graeme on his own. So Arthur would have to go! Either he would have to go back to work – or out to the golf course. Either way, it should be no problem. Ellie could wrap Arthur round her little finger. Besides … Arthur had some explaining to do! What was he up to in Paris when he should have been in Turkey?"

Ellie smiled.

She would make Arthur sweat a little …

For both Neil and Arthur, it would be a rough night.

She looked at Jenny, knitting away, deep in thought.

"Would you like me to make us another cup of tea?"

25 *Ain't it grand … ?*

Monday was another beautiful summer's day. Not a cloud polluted the sky. From early morning, there was every promise that it would be 'a scorcher'. Grasshallows had indeed had a splendid summer – along with the rest of the country. Who would want to go to Spain when one could fry at home? What could Greece or Tenerife offer that one could not enjoy on one's own doorstep? It was the sort of weather which restored one's faith in Great Britain. It was the sort of morning when almost everyone woke up feeling glad to be alive.

Even Raynes, who had spent the previous evening with Debbie in an expensive French restaurant some fifty miles away from Grasshallows, awoke with a tremendous sense of well-being. The combination of snails cooked in garlic, veal and ratatouille, raspberry pavlova and Irish coffee had done nothing to undermine his constitution. In fact, he felt on top of the world. And he had proved it twice! As he emerged from the basement flat to face the glories of the new day, he felt only a deep sense of goodwill to all mankind – and particularly to that curvaceous and willing portion of womankind which had brought such a sparkle of sunshine and laughter into his otherwise dull, pedestrian life.

To hell with what Ellie had said! You had to pay for everything in this world. You had to pay one way or another – wholesale or retail! And which was the more honest? What was Arthur getting from his matrimonial investment? Henpecked by a dominating bitch! Deceived by an unscrupulous woman! As soon as he vanished round the corner, there was Graeme preparing to cut down her tree! What sort of bargain was that!

If Raynes could at that moment have been a fly on the wall of the Fosters' home, he would have seen his most cynical thoughts amply fulfilled. Arthur had indeed had a rough night. Ellie had given him the edge of her tongue. She had mercilessly flayed him for being in Paris. She had berated him for his drunkenness. She had cast scorn upon his sentimentality. She had cast doubts upon his manhood and suggested that he would be better out of the house. By breakfast-time, Arthur was inclined to agree. He would leave that morning – without a moment's hesitation. As she said, it was no use moping. Much better to drown oneself in work. And, anyway, he had a bit of unfinished business in Paris – but he wasn't telling Ellie that!

By 9.30 am, Arthur was on his way.

* * *

Other people were also travelling that morning. At 8.30 am, Mrs Fisher was down at the bus station, seeing Colin off on his journey to King's Lynn to stay with his uncle and aunt. He was to be there for a week – or for two weeks if they could bear him! By that time, Mr Fisher would be home on leave and they could do something together as a family.

Colin had set off with a knapsack full of Agatha Christie's novels, several empty notebooks and an 'Encyclopædia of Murder'. He felt very sorry to be leaving Grasshallows so soon after Allan's death, but he reckoned that Inspector Raynes would probably be able to manage the case on his own without

164

him. He had to confess his deep disappointment that Raynes had failed to arrest Mrs Foster before now. She had been his No. 1 suspect. '*Cherchez la femme*' was one of Colin's chosen maxims in detective fiction – and he had often been proved right.

However, over the weekend, he had begun to have second thoughts. The case was perhaps more subtle than he had realized. He was now of the opinion that it might be Jenny and Neil. It was not the sort of thing one said in public. He had simply expressed his views to Johnny Cotton. But the more he thought about it, the more convinced he became. When he got to King's Lynn, he would give the matter more thought and then he would write to the Inspector and give him his considered opinion.

* * *

At the bus station, they had met Mrs Armstrong and the twins, waiting to catch the 8.45 am coach to London. Pat and Doug were full of excitement and mischief. They had already vanished once, causing Mrs Armstrong to lose her place in the queue. They had now vanished again and were stalking each other through the bus station. Mrs Fisher said to Mrs Armstrong: "Don't you sometimes wish you had a couple of girls?"

Mrs Armstrong was philosophical: "At least you know where you are with boys! I'm glad to see them so high-spirited. I thought all this murder business might have got them down. But they seem to have taken it in their stride. It's amazing how resilient children are!"

* * *

At 8.30 am, Tom Hayward set out for work. He had still not recovered from the Inspector's traumatic visit but at least he had taken his advice. He had had a quiet weekend. There had been no drugs, no late-night videos. He had kept away from *The Red Dragon* and he had not seen Doug. He had also made a final decision to leave home and get his own flat. Then he would be his own boss. Now that he was earning good money, why should he have to pay half of it over in board money and then be treated like a kid? Tom reckoned that if he wasn't careful, his own mother might be the next victim. As he had said to Graeme, he couldn't stand her hectoring, patronizing manner. It went on day after day, always shaming him, always humiliating him.

But now it was a new week! He would be his own man. At the depot, he clocked in ten minutes early. He was told that his job would be to go round a certain part of Grasshallows with a pot of yellow paint, marking all the pavements and kerb stones in need of realignment. It was a pleasant job. Tom would be out in the sunshine and perhaps be able to have a short time sunbathing in Grasshallows Memorial Park. For a beautiful summer's day, it was just the job.

* * *

Jenny saw Tom as she headed down to the University in her car. She was a secretary in the Geology Department. It wasn't a very exciting place, but on a morning like this, she was glad she had a job to go to. Neil would look after the children and she could slip away.

They had talked last night – for the first time in months. Jenny had taken Ellie's advice; she had been very firm. She had not been apologetic or cringing; she had been very diplomatic. To listen to her, you would not have suspected her of anything disreputable. She was the victim! For months, she had been pestered and harassed by Graeme. His behaviour had been intolerable. Really! She couldn't stand it any more. Neil must do something – immediately!

She had liked that bit.

Neil had looked quite helpless – spineless, as Graeme so often described him. What could he do? Jenny told him exactly what he should do. He should go to the District Commissioner and have Graeme thrown out of the Troop. He was as much a disgrace as Tom. They should both go. Ellie had told her – that very afternoon – that he was constantly seducing women – even some middle-aged hag called Grace, who lived in a caravan up Picton Dale.

When Jenny mentioned Grace's name, Neil's face had gone a delicate shade of pink. It gave her the cue to attack: 'Had he had any dealings with that woman?' Graeme had said that he had been up there with some of the boys. What sort of leadership was that? What sort of husband was he? Could she not trust him – not even when he went to camp?

166

Neil had got very worked up in his own defence. He declared that there was no truth whatsoever in Graeme's allegations. They were completely false. He had never even seen the woman. He would never dream of going to see her. Jenny should know him better …

Jenny had pointed out that he had been very cold towards her ever since Christmas. She had been very sorry about that incident, but didn't he realize that his unkindness and coldness were driving her into Graeme's arms? Not that she was in any way remotely interested in him. But Graeme had made all sorts of dreadful suggestions – even that she should move in with him and his father – and leave Neil on his own. Was Neil going to put up with this? Was one little slip at Christmas going to destroy their home and their marriage?

It was amazing how virtuous she sounded!

That had finally aroused Neil! He had suddenly seen the terrible abyss opening before him. Jenny and the children leaving … going to stay with that old rogue and his double-crossing son. Graeme threatening his own wife and family! The snake in the grass!

Now he knew what other husbands must have felt. He admired Jenny for standing up to Graeme. She might so easily have given way. But she had put up with all that pestering – and said nothing – because he had been boorish and cold towards her. And all the time, that swine was undermining him – and even suggesting that he might have been having an affair with Grace!

Neil had been furious. Jenny had never seen him quite so angry. In fact, she had become frightened at the venom she had unleashed. Neil had crashed around the house vowing vengeance. He would certainly do something about Graeme! He would take action right away!

Jenny was glad she had taken Ellie's advice. It had certainly worked. She had lit the blue touch paper; and she was glad she would be out of the way when the inevitable explosion occurred.

* * *

Graeme reluctantly surfaced at about 8.00 am. He was still feeling low – but there was work to be done, money to be made and possibly a plump, wholesome body to be enjoyed. He had to keep the business up to scratch so that there would be nothing for his dad to complain about when he came home. Graeme had spent most of Sunday evening phoning up his regulars, arranging for work during the coming week. But this Monday – by his standards – was likely to be a fairly quiet day – just three calls.

He made himself a good breakfast and prepared some of his favourite sandwiches for his packed lunch. After looking at the clear blue skies, he included two bottles of orangeade. One for elevenses, one for lunch. He was thinking about Jenny – he had never stopped thinking about Jenny – but it was impossible to phone her at home. Neil would be there. He would phone her at work and perhaps they could meet later in the day on her way home?

At about 9.30 am, Graeme got into his red pick-up truck and drove over to the Armstrongs to tackle their lawn.

* * *

Johnny Cotton and Mark Todd went fishing. At least, they said they were going fishing. But they took neither rods nor bait! They took their packed lunches and disappeared. Shortly after lunchtime, they were seen in Grasshallows Memorial Park, talking to Tom. At about 2.30 pm, they were on their bicycles in Picton Dale. They called in on an old friend, but found she was out. They returned home sunburnt and smiling. They had caught nothing!

* * *

Grace had been uplifted by the brightness of the new day. She took it as a favourable omen. She pottered around during the early part of the morning and had a couple of gins. Then she caught the local bus into Grasshallows and arrived in good time. She had a secret date with a man. Where that meeting would be, and who would be the lucky man, was a secret that she kept close to her heart. But she arrived in town feeling that nothing could go wrong. At least, she hoped not!

* * *

Ian Mackay sat at home reading. He was a slow reader and he was bored stiff. He wished the holidays were over and he could go back to school. His parents were away working and he had promised to do the shopping, clean out the hamster's cage and – if time permitted – repaint the garden shed. But as the morning wore on, he felt a strong desire to go out and see someone.

He went round to the Armstrongs, but all he could see was Graeme mowing the lawn. He went down to Colin's house, but Mrs Fisher said Colin was away for at least a week. He then went round to see Neil – but Neil too was out. In despair, he retraced his footsteps to the supermarket where, fortunately, he bumped into Tony Mason, who also seemed to be at a loose end. Together, they went home, ate a whole packet of sticky doughnuts, watched a video and repainted the garden shed. When Mr Mackay came home, Tony was invited to stay for tea and both boys were rewarded with a couple of seats at the local cinema watching the latest horror movie. For Ian, the day ended better than it began.

* * *

Garry and Stephen were looking forward to a more exciting day. They were going to a model railway exhibition in Peterborough. The organizer of the Grasshallows section was going to pick them up in his minibus and take them there. Mr Hogg had left them extra money to buy food but, at 10.15 am, the organizer phoned up to say the minibus had broken down and they would not be able to leave till after 1.00 pm. After a rather aimless morning, they were eventually collected. In Peterborough, surrounded by all the joys of locomotion, they forgot about all their troubles. They spent all their money on extra track for their own layout and returned to Grasshallows at about 8.30 pm, tired and very hungry.

* * *

Simon and Geoff spent the morning at the police station. Inspector Raynes had decided to re-interview all the scouts he had seen in Picton Dale to see if there was any further evidence they could add. The more he looked at the case, the more it seemed to be leading to a dead end. Even with all the salacious information he had received from Graeme, he did not feel he was one inch further forward. So, with a good deal of patience and humility, he decided that there was no alternative to going back to the boys to see if there was any small point he had missed.

He had spent most of Sunday morning and afternoon reading through the transcripts taken at Mr Sheldon's farm, and he felt that he now knew the replies almost by heart. He had asked Detective-Constable Carlisle to contact the boys, but his efforts had been largely unsuccessful. People were away for the day … for the week … or else they were working. However, Inspector Raynes managed to see Harry Robb at 10.30 am and Simon and Geoff at 11.30 am. Predictably, they had nothing to add to their stories. Raynes looked forward to seeing Neil, who was booked for 2.15 pm – but Neil did not appear.

* * *

After a hard morning's work – with only a ten-minute break for elevenses – Graeme settled down for lunch. He got his sandwiches out of the front seat of his truck and sat down on the Armstrongs' lawn, with his back to the sundial. It was a large, ugly, concrete object but it was quite strongly built and he could lean up against it. He sat and ate his sandwiches and his meat pie and looked round – with some satisfaction – at the transformation he had achieved in a few short hours. The garden now looked beautiful. He had worked so hard that he felt quite sleepy. 'Out of condition,' he said to himself. 'Two weeks of holiday and your body's gone to flab.' However, the rest of the afternoon's work was peanuts. Half-an-hour on the pear tree, an hour and a half on Ellie, and a final forty-five minutes giving Mrs Fisher's hedge a short back and sides. No problem! He stretched out on the warm, soft grass and let his body completely relax.

* * *

Mrs Foster had been keeping an eye on Graeme. She had seen him arrive in his red pick-up. She had seen him unload all his tools. Judging by the condition of the Armstrongs' garden, she reckoned that it would be well after lunchtime before he could get round to her needs. So, whilst Graeme slaved away, she went into town and did some shopping – including a rather nice peach-coloured slip (a rather generous size 14, which appealed to her vanity!) – and then came home to try it on.

170

By now, Graeme was having his lunch so she went for a shower before slipping into something loose and casual. She put on some morale-boosting perfume and felt herself ready for anything. Looking out of her staircase window, she noticed that Graeme was now asleep, flat out on the Armstrongs' lawn.

'Lazy beast!' she said to herself.

*   *   *

Jenny had tried to ring Neil at lunch-time to ask him if he had contacted the District Commissioner yet about Graeme and Tom. But despite phoning six or seven times, she had got no reply.

*   *   *

At 2.00 pm, Harry Robb reported for duty at Tesco's.

*   *   *

At 3.30 pm, Arthur landed in Paris.

Considering how badly the day had begun, he was now feeling much happier. He had no illusions as to why Ellie had been so harsh and so rude. She was trying to cover up her own misdeeds by blaming him. It was bad enough having your son murdered – and having to go through that dreadful funeral. But to have your wife committing adultery as well! That was the last straw! He knew as well as she did that Graeme was not just coming round to cut down a pear tree. He was coming round to screw her! And whilst he was on his way across the Channel, they would be at it. The slimy little toad!

If Graeme could have realized the volume of hatred burning inside Arthur Foster, he might have thought twice before calling at Ellie's home. Arthur was determined to get even with his wife's lover – and he thought he knew how. Allan had told him a lot about Graeme's habits, and Arthur had decided just where he would put the boot in. It would be interesting to see how Ellie would react. Would she cry – or would she laugh?

At this moment, Arthur was laughing. Of course, she thought he was in Turkey selling pharmaceuticals. But he was getting his own back. One of his old customers had died in a car crash just a couple of months before. His widow was lonely ... she was French ... and at this moment she was looking for

171

comfort and reassurance. And both of these, Arthur was happy to provide.

* * *

Tom had spent a couple of hours sunbathing in Grasshallows Memorial Park. But by 3.00 pm, he had returned to his rather pointless task of finding dangerous kerbs and uneven pavements and marking them with bright yellow paint. He had done this many times before and had noticed how long it took for any repair to be made. Sometimes, he had marked the same pavements twice! He sauntered back and forth along the tree-lined avenues of Grasshallows' better-class streets till he suddenly came across Graeme's pick-up truck parked just off the London road.

Here was another wonderful excuse to have a break from work! A ten-minute chat with Graeme would fill up time nicely. Besides, he had wanted to ask him if he knew of any flats or rooms that might be rented. Graeme had been a good friend to him. He had not condemned him. He had not rejected him like everyone else. Last Thursday night, they had chatted till nearly 1.00 am.

He put down his pot and his brushes and went in through the nearest gate to see Graeme. But Graeme was nowhere to be seen.

He went into the gardens of several other houses – but drew a blank. Perhaps Graeme was seeing one of his lady friends just round the corner? The dirty dog! Tom picked up his paint pot and his brushes and moved on – outwardly amused but, inwardly, just a little bit jealous.

* * *

Neil was home when Jenny got back from work.

"Well?" she said. "Where have you been all day?"

Neil said that he'd taken the children out for a picnic. They had had a wonderful time down beside the river. It had been a beautiful afternoon; the water was really warm.

Having spent the whole day cooped up in a concrete block, typing lengthy notes about jurassic fossils, Jenny was in no mood to be conciliatory.

"Have you not phoned the District Commissioner yet?"

"No." Neil was sorry but he hadn't got round to it.

And had he kept his appointment at the police station at 2.15 pm?

Neil's face fell.

He had completely forgotten he was supposed to be seeing Inspector Raynes. His mind had been so occupied with the children that everything else had been eclipsed.

Jenny was furious.

If he had suffered last night, he would suffer again tonight. Why could he not be trusted to do the things he had promised? Why was he always letting her and everyone down?

The telephone rang.

It was Ellie.

Would Jenny like to come round for a drink later that evening? She was a bit worried about Arthur …?

Jenny was glad to have any excuse to get out of the house. If she stayed at home with Neil, it was bound to develop into another long row. Perhaps it would be much better if she got out of his way? He would have time to think things over. Perhaps he might even phone the District Commissioner?

Jenny scowled at Neil and waved him away.

Once the kids had been put to bed, she would be around.

'Having a drink' seemed a little on the conservative side. Quite frankly, Jenny felt like getting completely guttered!

* * *

Colin was hardly eating his tea. He couldn't stop talking. He felt a compelling need to tell his uncle and aunt the full story of the murder in Picton Dale. He had introduced each of the scouts in full detail and given a moderately accurate account of their doings – Grace excepted. He described his experiences in the middle of the night and his encounter with a real, live detective – Inspector Raynes. He gave a blow-by-blow reconstruction of the interviews at the farm and was now in the middle of Allan's funeral …

Colin's aunt looked at the mixed grill and chips getting steadily colder on his plate.

She sighed and looked at her husband.

It was bad enough hearing it the first time. She hoped he wouldn't go on about it for the whole week.

Mercifully, at that moment, the phone rang.

Mrs Fisher, phoning to ask if Colin had arrived safely.

Colin's aunt used the brief interval to reheat her nephew's meal. She didn't want him to go home complaining of cold food.

* * *

At 7.30 pm, Mrs Armstrong and the twins returned from London. Mr Armstrong went to collect them from the bus station.

"Has Graeme been?" asked Mrs Armstrong.

"The garden's beautiful. He's done a splendid job."

As they pulled up outside the house, the twins waved to Jenny who was getting out of her car and going in to see Ellie.

Ellie had already sunk two brandies and was looking rather the worse for wear.

Jenny was not looking forward to spending a whole evening discussing Arthur … she really couldn't see what Ellie saw in him … but anything was better than sitting at home looking at Neil! At least her tactics seemed to be working. For, as she slipped down the staircase and escaped through the front door, she had heard him deep in conversation on the phone. It seemed that at long last he had had the courage to speak to the District Commissioner. She was glad about that.

* * *

Grace returned to her caravan at about 8.00 pm. She had enjoyed a lovely day and, even now, as she walked across the fields, her thoughts were still of what she had been doing in Grasshallows. She walked past the former site of the scout camp without a second glance. The swallows swooped and dived around her but she didn't notice them. Even the sunset – especially beautiful that night – failed to attract her attention.

She climbed through the gap in the wall, headed past the ugly heap of sand and paving stones and took out her key. Normally, she left the caravan open but, having been away the whole day, it had seemed sensible to take precautions. But never once in all the years she had lived in the caravan had anything been stolen – except for the odd items removed by the scouts. Life in the country was so much more civilized

174

than life in the city. Here in Picton Dale, people were more honest and trustworthy. That was why she had moved out of Grasshallows. One summer in the caravan had convinced her of the virtues of living in the middle of nowhere.

Fortunately, she still had her creature comforts.

When she had got inside, she had a shower, changed into something more comfortable and put on the TV. She got out the bottle of gin and poured herself a generous measure, topped it up with a modest amount of tonic and downed it in a single mouthful.

She stretched out on the sofa and poured herself a smaller amount of gin and a larger amount of tonic. She shut her eyes and fell asleep.

She was awoken by the shrill buzz of the telephone. It had rung in the middle of the nine o'clock news. She turned off the TV and picked up the receiver.

It was probably her friend in Grasshallows phoning her to say thank you.

But it wasn't.

The voice on the phone was not one she had ever heard before. The voice seemed anxious and worried. Was that Grace Turner? She said it was. The voice said it had some urgent information to convey to her. It was about Allan Foster – the scout who had died at camp. The information would have to be given to the police, but it was essential that she should be told first. The voice said that it was difficult to reveal these things over the phone. Could she come down to *The Carpenter's* – the local pub – right away? The full details would be given to her there. The voice made her promise that she would be there by 10.00 pm. And that was it.

Grace was a simple, gullible person. She responded easily to suggestion. And the prospect of finding out more about Allan's death was too tempting to be resisted. She immediately put on a pair of slacks, a thick woollen jumper and a pair of trainers and set off back the way she had come just over an hour before.

One thing Grace was not frightened of was the dark. She was used to the deep mantle of darkness which now covered the countryside. Many a time, when she had been working at *The Carpenter's,* she had crossed the fields after midnight – in rain and snow. For her, there was no problem. It would take her half an hour at the most.

She reached *The Carpenter's* just before 10.00 pm and went into both the lounge and the saloon bar. Everyone knew her there and she greeted them accordingly. Various people offered her a drink, but she refused. She was supposed to be meeting someone there at 10.00 pm. Everyone thought that was rather amusing ... Grace Turner having a blind date! The teasing went on till Grace began to find it rather tiresome. She went to wait outside, but she could still hear the locals laughing and making personal cracks.

Eventually, it dawned on her that she was the victim of a cruel hoax. No one was going to come and meet her. She had travelled all that way for nothing. She felt hurt – and cried. One of the locals, coming out of the pub, tried to dance with her, singing: 'He'll be coming round the mountain when he comes ...' He tried to kiss her but she pushed him away.

There was nothing for it but to set off home. It was after 11.00 pm and, this time, she was conscious of every step. She wondered what sort of person could play such a dirty trick on her? She slammed the gates behind her and cursed loudly when her jumper got caught on a nail. At about 11.30 pm she once again climbed through the hole in the wall and stumped up the steps of the caravan. Home at last! And she wouldn't be answering any more anonymous phone calls!

The caravan was still nice and warm and the bottle of gin was sitting where she had left it. She poured herself another stiff measure, took off her sweater and walked through into her bedroom.

It was in darkness as she walked in. But immediately she was conscious of a human presence.

She screamed.

There was a man in her bed.

Even in the half-light, she knew who it was. He was sitting in the middle of her bed, wearing nothing but a pair of cotton briefs, leaning back against the headboard, with his legs slightly apart. His head was inclined to the left and, at first sight, he seemed to have a wicked smile on his face.

"Graeme!" she screamed. "What the hell d'you think you're doing here at this hour of the night? You gave me one hell of a shock!"

And, indeed, she was shaking like a leaf.

But Graeme said nothing.

He did not even move.

Grace turned on the light.

He looked a funny colour.

She went forward and touched his foot. It was cold, hard and lifeless. She looked at his eyes. They were half-closed, but she could see that they were staring. There was no point taking his pulse.

It was Graeme all right – but he was dead. In her bed.

She immediately perceived the purpose of the telephone call. Someone had wanted to get her out of the way. It was more than a cruel hoax. Someone was trying to involve her in a second murder. She was in deep trouble.

Grace rushed back into the sitting-room and grabbed the phone. She dialled 999.

The measured voice replied: "Fire, police or ambulance?"

"Police!" said Grace. "I must have the police. And I must speak to Inspector Raynes!"

26 ... *to be blooming well dead!*

Raynes was not surprised.

He had been expecting something of this sort – but not quite so soon. Ever since he had heard about the last-minute exchange of tents, he had been sure the murderer had made a mistake and killed the wrong person. Graeme was the obvious target ... the motives: hatred, fear or revenge. The death of Allan had simply confused the issue. One could not spend one's time investigating a murder which might have been intended; you could only deal with the one which had actually occurred. Now – barely a week later – the murderer had corrected his mistake. He – or she – had drawn strength from the fact that the first murder remained unsolved. So why wait? Strike whilst the iron was still hot! Whilst the police were running round like headless chickens! But perhaps the murderer had been too bold? This time, Raynes would be looking for the real murderer – not a shadow.

As he dialled Carlisle's home number, he drew consolation from one minor fact. The number of suspects was down to sixteen – and Graeme was not one of them.

Mrs Carlisle answered the phone.

"I'm sorry to disturb you. It's Richard Raynes. I'm afraid we've had another murder. Could you please wake up your husband? I'm sending a car round to collect him. It's all hands on deck."

Raynes mobilized all the necessary forces – dragging them out of their beds. He wrapped himself up warmly and went downstairs to the hotel car park. The night porter saw him walking down the passage.

"Is something wrong, Inspector?"

"No. Just a piece of unfinished business."

"Funny time of night to be doing it!"

"You can say that again!"

As he got into his Rover and started the engine, he felt a strange sense of satisfaction. This was the real thing. The murderer had committed himself – or herself – once again. Two sets of clues were easier to follow than one. But at least the killer had a sense of humour. Fancy dumping Graeme in Grace's bed! What a nerve!

* * *

Raynes drove up to Picton Dale as fast as he could go. By road, the caravan park was about two miles beyond *The Carpenter's,* involving a rather circuitous route through country lanes. He was determined to be there first this time.

He parked his car beside a red pick-up and walked down to Grace's caravan. She was standing alone outside the van, wrapped in a blanket but shivering violently.

"I can't go in again. I've been and looked at him twice. It's definitely Graeme."

Raynes climbed into the van and turned right into the small bedroom. He switched on the light. Graeme was lying on top of the bed, propped up against the pillows. His head was lolling slightly to the left. His eyes were almost closed but his mouth was open. The body was cold and waxy to the touch. He seemed to have been dead for quite some time. Rigor mortis had set in.

The corpse was wearing only a pair of blue cotton briefs. There was no sign of any other clothing. Raynes looked at his neck to see if there were any marks of strangulation. There were none. He pulled up his head and looked down his throat. No sand! But there was a smell of something. Raynes tried to identify it. A rotten sort of smell. Of course, if the body had been dead for some time ...? He looked the body up and down to see if there were any bloodstains or evidence of bruising. There were none. There were no visible signs of violence.

Raynes looked thoughtful.

This was not going to be easy.

He switched off the light and climbed out of the van.

"I wasn't dreaming?" said Grace.

"No, you weren't dreaming. It's him all right. What time did you find him?"

"About half past eleven."

"I see. Where had you been?"

"Down to *The Carpenter's*. I got a phone call about quarter past nine to say that someone was wanting to see me. They said it was urgent. Something to do with Allan. They said they had to see me at once. It couldn't be said over the phone. They told me to be in the lounge bar by 10.00 pm at the latest."

"So you went?"

"I flew down. But when I got there, there was nobody. I sat around. Had a couple of drinks. Asked if anybody had been asking for me. Which they hadn't. Made a bit of a fool of myself actually. People thinking I was cracked." She smiled sadly. "Of course, I'm used to that. But, anyway, no one came. I stayed till closing time. One of the locals tried to pick me up. I had to fend him off. And then I came home ..."

"Across the fields or by the road?"

"Across the fields. It's quicker. I must have got home some time after half-past eleven. It was very dark. No moon. I was bloody angry – and cold. I just walked into my bedroom and there he was. It was an awful shock. I just screamed. Thought I'd wake up half the caravan site. But no one stirred. It's pretty deserted here during the week … People only come up for the weekends …"

"Did you touch him?"

"Not at first. I just stared. Thinking he was having me on. I didn't even put the light on. 'Oh, Graeme, you bastard!' I said. 'What a fright you gave me!' Then I realized he wasn't moving. I put the light on and there he was. It was really scary!"

"So you went over and touched him?"

"Just his foot. I lifted it up and dropped it. He was completely dead. Then I phoned you. I'm sorry I was so hysterical. I couldn't believe it was happening to me!"

"And after you phoned me?"

"I went in and looked at him again. Just to make sure I hadn't been dreaming. And I hadn't. He was still there. It was horrible. I couldn't make up my mind if he'd died in my bed or whether someone put him there. It was an awful shock."

Raynes listened to her story carefully. He knew that she had every reason to hate Graeme. Indeed, she had vowed vengeance and murder as recently as Saturday morning. Was she telling him a lie to cover up her guilt? Had she enticed Graeme to her caravan – and then killed him? Had she invented the cock-and-bull story about a phone call? Gone down to *The Carpenter's* to create an alibi? Called him only when she was sure the murder scene was just as she wanted it to look? Grace was something of an actress – so all these histrionics could easily be put on. Even if she had murdered Graeme, it was inevitable that she would be very upset. The violence – and then the reaction. Grace's involvement could not be ruled out.

But what about the phone call?

"Was it a man or a woman who called you?"

"A woman."

"Not a boy? Not one of the scouts?"

"No. It was definitely a woman."

180

"Did you recognize the voice?"

"No."

"It wasn't Jenny?"

"I don't think I'd recognize her voice – not on a phone anyway."

Raynes stared up at the dark clouds which were rolling across the sky. Jenny or Ellie? It must be one or other of them! Anyone else – and the case would be blown wide open. Perish the thought! He could imagine the flood of complaints which would be launched against the police. Two murders in one week! And two funerals! He shuddered visibly.

"Are you cold as well?"

"No. Just a bit worried about who this woman could be."

"She seemed very hard."

"Did she?"

Raynes noted that Grace was still shaking. Cold and nerves were taking their toll.

"I think," he said, "that you'd better go and sit in my car till the others arrive."

"Others?"

Raynes nodded.

"Half Grasshallows police force is on its way out here. Most of them will probably get lost in the country lanes but, by daybreak, this place will be crawling with policemen ..."

"How exciting!" said Grace.

Raynes smiled. She would survive. He led her back to his car. Removed the keys so she couldn't drive away. Showed her how to work the stereo system. Then he left her and returned to the caravan.

* * *

What he was looking for, he did not know. But he wanted to have a little bit of peace before the place was crowded with experts. He climbed back into the van and went into the bedroom. He searched the cupboards, looked under the bed, sniffed at Grace's perfumes and pulled open all her drawers. He saw nothing remotely suspicious.

He did another careful study of Graeme's body, moving him as little as possible. He returned to the living-room and searched through the cupboards there. He was amazed at the numbers of bottles Grace had stashed away – mostly cut-price gin. Eventually, he decided that what he was looking for was Graeme's clothes.

If he had driven out from Grasshallows to see Grace, he would hardly have come out in a pair of underpants! He would have been wearing some shoes! And how would he have come out to Picton Dale? He would have come out in a car – or van. Not on a motor-cycle. Graeme was a businessman. He would have a Ford Transit or something similar. Even if he had arrived as a corpse, someone must have brought him. His mind went back to the red pick-up he had seen parked next to the Rover. Surely that was the vehicle he had seen at Graeme's home on Friday? What was the registration number? If he had driven up to Picton Dale, Grace must have been involved. And his clothes must be hidden somewhere.

He was looking round the toilet and shower cubicle when the main force began to arrive. Carlisle sounded a little breathless: "We got lost!" he said.

"I thought you would," said Raynes, "these lanes are like a bloody maze!"

"Well, who is it?"

"Have a guess."

"Graeme Wilson?"

"Right first time!"

"So they got him after all?" He paused. "You were right."

"I often am," said Raynes modestly.

"Well, where is he?"

"In Grace's bed. Go and have a look."

Carlisle stood at the foot of the bed.

"Artistic," he said. "An artistic touch."

"I hadn't thought about it."

"It has a woman's touch – just as you said last time."

"Why d'you say that?"

"Well, they've taken his shoes off – and his socks – so that he won't mess the bed. But they've left him with a little privacy – not exactly starkers. And look at the way he's propped up against the pillows. Someone's made him nice and comfortable."

Raynes lifted his eyebrows a shade.

"A nurse perhaps?"

"Ellie?"

"It's possible. Grace had a phone call from some woman, summoning her down to *The Carpenter's Arms* at about 9.15 pm. Someone wanting to spill the beans about Allan. She charged down to the pub, but no one appeared. She came home after closing time – and this is what she found ... at least, that's what she says she found."

"You don't believe her?"

"I'm not believing anything or anyone at this moment. The phone call could be pure moonshine."

Carlisle continued to look at the body critically.

"Is that how you found him?"

"Yes."

"Someone tried to shut his eyes?"

"Yes. I noticed."

"What did he die of? Not sand again?"

"No. There's no sand. But apart from that, I'm not sure. There's no sign of blood. No signs of strangling. No daggers in his back. I couldn't see any sign of someone hitting him with a blunt instrument. It's all very neat and tidy. I'm just wondering if he's been poisoned or taken an overdose. I can't think of anything else."

At that point, there was a sound of heavy footsteps and the jangle of expensive equipment. "Anyone at home?"

"It's all yours," said Raynes.

He climbed out of the van and made way for the police surgeon and the photographer.

Raynes and Carlisle stood aside from the crowd and looked out over the dark fields. It was a cold, miserable night.

"How did he get here?"

"I think that's his red pick-up in the car park. The one sitting next to my car. I think it's the one we saw on Friday morning."

"We can soon find out."

"Well, either he drove out here ... or he was brought out here. If that's his van, he obviously drove here. He's been dead for some time. Three or four hours, I should say. Perhaps more?

So – either he came out here to see Grace – and she did him in. Or he was lured here whilst she was away – and someone else did the dirty. Or – a third possibility – he died somewhere else and was brought here as a corpse. There's no reason why we should exclude Grace. I think we shall have to take her into custody. At least for the night."

"I can't see her doing it all on her own."

Raynes shrugged his shoulders.

"If it was poison, there's no saying she didn't give him a drink and lace it with something pretty potent. She's got gallons of liquor in there. I didn't see any bottles of arsenic – but she's had plenty of time to throw them away. To wash out any glasses. To wipe away any fingerprints. Graeme could have come out here to beat her up. I think it highly likely. He wanted to get his revenge on her for spilling the beans to Jenny. She could have stalled him. Said: 'Hold it! Give me a moment! I can explain …' Graeme sits down … waits … gets a drink. Dead. She strips him, drags him into the bedroom. Hides away his clothes – puts them in a dustbin perhaps? She has plenty of time. Most of these caravans are empty during the week. Yes. I think Grace is a fairly prominent suspect."

"But surely she didn't murder Allan?"

"Well, I don't think so. But we may have to modify our views."

Raynes went over and spoke to the police sergeant who seemed to be the most senior man on duty. He said: "I want to know who owns the red pick-up in the car park. Could you put a call back to headquarters? It's quite important. Next, I want a full search of the area for a set of man's clothes. They could be anywhere on the site – in a bin, burnt, stuffed underneath a caravan or at the back of a hedge. I want a real search. Thirdly, there's a woman sitting in my car – the red Rover – beside the pick-up. She is to be taken back to headquarters for questioning. Her name is Grace Lawrence … or Turner … She has quite a few names. I want her treated nicely. Find some sympathetic officer to take her back to Grasshallows. Right away! Is that understood?"

"No problem," said the sergeant, who immediately started giving the necessary orders.

"I'm sorry to be disturbing your marriage," said Raynes to Carlisle. "Your wife must hate me for dragging you out!"

"I don't think she minds when she knows it's in a good cause."

The police surgeon clambered out of the caravan.

He looked at Raynes.

"Quite simple. An aerosol. There may be more to find when we get him out on the slab, but it looks quite straightforward to me. Polish, I should think."

"I smelt his breath. I thought it was perfume."

"Furniture polish, more likely. His tubes got clogged up and he stopped breathing. I've seen it quite a few times before. These silly kids! They put polythene bags over their heads and breathe it in. They can't believe that something so simple can be so deadly. A couple of squirts and you've had it. They try to experiment – just to see if it's true. Next thing – they're dead too."

"Thank you," said Raynes. "That makes things easier. What time d'you think he died?"

"Can't say exactly." The police surgeon looked thoughtful. "Twelve hours?"

"Twelve hours!" exclaimed Raynes.

"At least," said the surgeon. "By the time I've done the autopsy, I shall be able to be more accurate. But I should say at least twelve hours."

Raynes scratched his head.

"That ruins all my theories," he said.

"No substitute for facts," said the surgeon. "That's what I say. Well, if you gentlemen have got no more surprises for me tonight, I'll be on my way. See you tomorrow!"

Raynes and Carlisle watched him go.

Raynes sighed.

"Twelve hours," he said. "That makes it sometime yesterday afternoon. Lunchtime or after. Now where was Graeme supposed to be at that time?"

"Could he have come here during his lunch break?" suggested Carlisle helpfully. "Stopped off at *The Carpenter's* for a plate of soup or a pint, and then come up here to see Grace?"

185

Raynes scowled. "Could be."

He walked up and down for a while, and then returned to the efficient police sergeant.

"We're looking for polish ..."

"Polish?"

"For aerosol cans of any sort. There may be some in the caravan or, once again, they might be in one of the bins. I'm sorry to be so vague."

"No problem!" said the sergeant, who was used to bizarre requests. "Look sharp, Evans! We're looking for polish!"

Raynes continued to walk up and down.

"We've got to solve this one quickly," he said. "As quickly as possible. Now that Graeme's dead, the motive's obvious. It's got to be revenge. It must be one of his victims. It can't be anyone else ..."

"It doesn't look like one of the scouts?"

"A nasty red herring, Carlisle!"

"Could it be Jenny? Jenny and Neil?"

"If he died up here," said Raynes, "my money's still on Grace. You know her feelings. You heard what she said. But if he died in Grasshallows, that still leaves only two or three people. I'm trying to remember what Graeme said at that dreadful reception ... you remember ... after the funeral. People were booking him up for work – in a most haphazard fashion. He was doing a lawn for Mrs Fisher; a tree for Ellie. A pear tree! And what about the Armstrongs? What did they want?" He paused. "No – that was it! It was a hedge for Mrs Fisher and a lawn for the Armstrongs! That was it."

"I beg your pardon?" Carlisle could hardly follow the Inspector's train of thought, having spent most of the reception listening to Mr Hogg and Mrs Todd complaining about the police.

"At lunchtime ...," said Raynes. "At lunchtime, Graeme would have been at Ellie's. I'm sure he wouldn't have got any further. She would have given him his lunch. I wonder if Arthur was there? I bet he wasn't! The Armstrongs were away; they were talking about going up to London. I wonder if they went ...? But Graeme was going to Ellie's! That's the main point! What did you say about a homely touch? A feminine hand arranging the pillows? It's a wonder she didn't tuck him in and round it off by giving him a couple of hospital corners!"

"That might have given the game away?"

"It wouldn't make much difference now," said Raynes. "We're almost there. Twenty-four hours at the most. We must interview each of them separately tomorrow morning. First, Ellie and Jenny – then Neil and Tom. We must make sure they have no way of communicating with each other. Their alibis are bound to have cracks. It'll be a real pleasure busting them wide open. We must make sure that we give the impression that Graeme died some time in the evening. Between six and 9.00 pm. We won't let on that we know the real time. If they know, they're bound to blurt it out."

"And if it's Grace?"

Raynes sighed. "Well, if it's Grace, we shall know tonight."

He was interrupted by the arrival of the police sergeant.

"Message from headquarters, sir. That red pick-up belongs to a Mr Ron Wilson. He's had it for a couple of years. He's in jail at the moment. That's probably why his son's got it …"

Raynes smiled appreciatively.

"That's splendid!"

"… And we've found three aerosols in the caravan. One a fresh air spray. Bouquet of flowers. An oven spray and a lavender polish. Would that be what you're looking for, sir?"

"That's very good," said Raynes. "Pop them into a plastic bag and send them back to forensic. I'm afraid you'll still have to look in all the bins. We're still not sure what he inhaled." He thought for a moment. "Is the fingerprint man still here?"

"Nearly finished, sir."

"Well, tell him to give the pick-up the once over for any tell-tale dabs. Once he's done that, it'll have to go back to town. Could you see about that?"

"No problem!" said the sergeant. "Will that be all?"

"I should think so," said Raynes.

Carlisle smiled.

As the sergeant walked away, Raynes said: "I wish our life was as easy as that!"

"Some are born to give orders, others to obey them."

"Very true." Raynes looked round the caravan site with a quiet satisfaction. "You know, Carlisle," he said, "there is a certain poetic justice – a deep and delicious symmetry – about this case. It began in the fields. Now it is ending here. Graeme was one for the ladies. All his life. What better finale than to end it in a lady's bed?"

Carlisle agreed.

"I should think there'll be quite a few ladies breathing a sigh of relief when they hear the news. Not to mention their husbands!"

"I'm sure you're right," said Raynes, "but the tragedy is that hardly a tear will be shed. It's very sad, but I'm sure Graeme won't be missed."

"Except by his dad."

27 *She sailed away*

"Why have you arrested me?"

Grace was sitting in one of the interview rooms in Grasshallows police station. It was after 3.00 in the morning.

"I haven't arrested you. I've taken you into protective custody. You can't stay in that caravan. And it's difficult to find you any other accommodation at this time of night."

"You put me in a cell!"

"Some of our cells are very comfortable. Did they give you toast and tea? Two extra blankets?"

Grace nodded.

"Well, there you are! VIP treatment."

Raynes switched on a cassette recorder. (Carlisle had gone home to bed). He looked at Grace: "One or two questions …"

"At this time of night?"

"You weren't sleeping?"

"No."

"Neither am I. My job is to bring this case to a speedy conclusion. If you could be helpful and truthful, we'll soon get it done." He suppressed a yawn. "Now what were your movements yesterday?"

"You mean: 'Where did I go'?" She looked thoughtful. "I had a late start. But then, I always do. I got up at about 9.00 am; made myself some coffee; cleaned out the van; had another cup of coffee; did myself up. I was going out, you see?"

"What time was that?"

"About twelve."

"Go on."

"I walked across the fields to *The Carpenter's*. Had a gin. Had a couple actually. This nice man – he's one of my exes – he treated me. Then I caught the bus ..." She caught Raynes' eye. "... The 2.00 pm bus into Grasshallows. They only go once every two hours. I caught that. Did some shopping ..."

"Where?"

"Mostly window-shopping. On the way up from the bus station. I went into Littlewoods. I always get my cheese there. I bought some chocolates – for a friend. I had tea in a little cafe in the High Street ..."

"Which one?"

"*The Steeple*. Gosh, you are being nosy!"

"I want every detail."

"Well, then I went to see my friend. The one I'd bought the chocolates for. He's retired. A widower. He used to be a greengrocer. He's really a nice old guy. He phones me up sometimes when he's lonely and I go round for a chat ..."

"Just a chat?"

"Well, you know men, Inspector, just as well as I do. They always like a cuddle ..."

"So you gave this old fellow a cuddle?"

"I always do. He gives me lovely grapefruit. Beautifully fresh. He still gets them from his shop."

"At what time did you arrive and what time did you go?"

"I got there at about twenty past four and I left about 7.00 pm. I caught the 7.20 pm bus home. We had a couple of gins before I left. The rest you know."

"Tell me again."

"I got home about 8.00 pm. Put on the TV. Had another gin. Fell asleep. Then that woman phoned ..."

"At about 9.15 pm?"

"Yes. Saying that I'd got to go down to *The Carpenter's* right away because she'd got something important to tell me about Allan."

"You didn't recognize the woman's voice?"

"No."

"I'll ask you again. Did it sound like Jenny Gray?"

"I couldn't tell you, Inspector. I've only met her once."

"And that was all? Just a request to come down to the pub?"

"She said it was very important. She made me promise I would be there by 10.00 pm. So I just went."

"You got there by 10.00 pm?"

"Just before. I know the route across the fields quite well, but …"

"… after two or three gins …?"

"Exactly!"

"Now when you got to *The Carpenter's*, there was no one there?"

"Well, there were quite a few of the regulars there. And some passing trade. They were all in the lounge bar. I asked Dan – he's the owner – if anyone had been asking for me. He teased me. They all did. 'Everyone's been asking for you, darling.' Some of the men gave me dirty looks. At least, their wives did! It wasn't very pleasant. So I sat there till closing time. Then I hung about outside. I had a bit of trouble with Neddy – he's a ploughman up the Dale. He's all right when he's sober, but last night he wasn't. He got very persistent …"

"I get the point."

"He didn't. Anyway, I left him and walked back across the fields. Quite slowly. I was bloody angry. When I got back to the van, it must have been half past eleven. Then I found Graeme."

She shuddered at the memory and burst into tears.

Raynes waited patiently.

"I don't think I could ever live in that van again. I'll have to get another. What a dirty trick to play on someone!" She sniffed. "It was obviously someone who knew Allan was my son. And someone who knew Graeme was blackmailing me. Don't you think so, Inspector?"

"It seems very likely …"

Raynes paused.

"… but I have to consider another possibility. That Graeme came to see *you*. That perhaps he was there waiting for you when you came back from Grasshallows at 8.00 pm. Perhaps he had come round to beat you up again? Perhaps even to kill you? You took him into your caravan and gave him a drink …"

"He'd never have got another drink from me!"

"… and you poisoned him!"

"Me?"

"You were certainly vowing vengeance on Saturday morning. You told me that if you got the slightest chance you'd kill him." Raynes looked grim. "Well, suppose, last night, you got your chance? He sat down for a drink and you laced it? With what, I don't know. Then you arranged him neatly on your bed. Took away all his clothes. Removed every item connected with the murder. Cleaned away all the fingerprints. And then went down to *The Carpenter's* to create an alibi. Which you did – rather well!"

Grace listened to him with growing amazement.

"I wouldn't have done that, Inspector."

Raynes shrugged his shoulders.

"It's quite possible."

"Well, I didn't. I didn't have the opportunity. When I saw Graeme, he was dead. I didn't put him on my bed. Someone else did. And it was that woman who did it!"

"I shall deal with her tomorrow," said Raynes – suddenly feeling very tired. He yawned. "In the meantime, you'd better give me a full list of your contacts. Who gave you the drink at *The Carpenter's* at lunchtime. The appearance of the bus-driver – both ways. The address of your greengrocer friend. And Dan and Neddy! We'll check that lot out first thing tomorrow morning. And when they've confirmed your story, you can go."

"You don't believe me, Inspector?"

"After what's happened, I don't believe anyone!" Raynes snarled. "And remember! You don't have a proper alibi from 8.00 pm till 9.30 pm. Graeme could have been with you then …"

191

"He wasn't!" She was crying again. "I may be an immoral woman, Inspector. I may be an alcoholic … but I'm not a liar. And I'm not a murderer!"

Raynes remained cold and unimpressed.

"That remains to be seen," he said.

28 *How now, brown cow?*

Upstairs, five hours later, still feeling very tired, Raynes faced Ellie. She looked angry, cold, contemptuous. She had been visited by the police shortly after 7.00 am – before she had had any breakfast. She had been given very little time to dress or make herself up. She therefore looked a mess – and she knew it. Worst of all, she had been kept waiting for almost two hours before Raynes was ready to see her. His breakfast had consisted of merely one croissant and a cup of strong black coffee. He had not even had the time to read the headlines in *The Daily Telegraph*. He was burning on a very short fuse.

"I suppose I have Mrs May to thank for all this?"

Ellie had decided that attack was the best method of defence. But Raynes was totally unsympathetic.

"Don't be bloody stupid! Mrs May's got nothing to do with this! You've been arrested in connection with the death of Graeme Wilson … and anything you say is being taken down by Detective-Constable Carlisle and will most certainly be used in evidence against you."

Ellie tried to register shock and surprise.

"Graeme? Graeme Wilson?"

"Yes. And don't pretend you don't know anything about it! You're in this up to your neck. You told Graeme that Allan was Grace's son. That information – and the way it was used – almost certainly led to Allan's death. Now I find you playing a leading role in Graeme's death. I think you have a lot of explaining to do, you middle-aged hag!"

Raynes' abuse had a marked effect on Ellie. It increased her contempt for the Inspector and her determination to be as awkward as possible.

192

"I haven't the slightest idea what you're talking about."

"Do you drive?"

"Yes."

"What?"

"An Escort."

"Would it surprise you to know that your car was seen up Picton Dale at about ten o'clock last night?"

"Was that when Graeme was killed?"

"I want to know whether you were in your car up Picton Dale at 10.00 pm last night?"

"I wasn't."

"Where were you?"

Ellie chose her words carefully.

"I was with Jenny Gray. She came round to my house to have a talk about things ..."

"And where was Neil?"

"He was looking after the children."

"So you two were sitting in your house just chattering away – till when?"

"Till about 11.00 pm. It was perfectly normal. Jenny often comes round for a chat."

"Were you talking about Graeme?"

"As a matter of fact, we were."

"You knew he was dead?"

"You've just told me."

"I'm talking about last night. Did you know he was dead?"

"I didn't know."

The fact that she paused to think before answering his question, convinced Raynes that she was lying.

"Think again, Mrs Foster!" he said.

"There's no need to. I've told you the truth."

Raynes shook his head.

"No, you haven't. But let's go on. What were you and Jenny saying about Graeme Wilson?"

"I can't remember."

Raynes shook his head.

"I thought you had a remarkable memory, Mrs Foster. You can remember people you saw in restaurants several weeks ago. You can remember how many husbands they had. And yet you tell me you can't remember what you and Jenny were talking about last night!"

"We had quite a lot to drink."

"Did you?"

"So obviously we weren't driving!"

"Obviously!" Raynes was sarcastic.

He continued: "I think that you and Jenny were talking about Graeme trying to persuade Jenny to leave Neil. The fact that he has even been trying to blackmail her into leaving. You know that, don't you?"

"Jenny'll never leave Neil."

"But she was thinking of it, wasn't she?"

"Not that I know of."

"How would you advise her?"

"I'd tell her to think of her husband and children."

"You wouldn't want to be two-timing your best friend?"

"It's hardly likely now – if he's dead."

"But he wasn't last night!"

"He ..." Ellie paused on the brink.

Raynes swooped.

"You knew he was dead?"

"I said nothing!"

"Mrs Foster," said Raynes, "you are in a very delicate position. You are suspected of being involved in the death of Graeme Wilson. If you persist in lying, you will simply increase my suspicions and you will not leave this building till you have signed a complete confession."

"You're getting nothing out of me," said Ellie.

"So I see," said Raynes.

"I told you, Inspector, last time I was here, that I had no dealings with Graeme Wilson. He is simply – quite simply my gardener."

The lie was delivered with the utmost sincerity. Raynes thought of Graeme's list. He smiled.

"And he was supposed to be doing your garden yesterday afternoon, wasn't he?"

"As a matter of fact, he was. You have a good memory, Inspector ..."

194

"A pear tree was to be cut down. And Arthur didn't want to lose it. Where is Arthur?"

"I haven't the vaguest idea."

"He's gone back to work?"

"He's gone somewhere."

"When did he leave?"

"On Monday morning."

"Before Graeme arrived?"

"Graeme didn't arrive."

"He didn't?" Raynes was interested. "So the pear tree is still standing?"

"It is."

"So Graeme didn't get as far as your house on Monday?"

"No."

"Did he get as far as the Armstrongs?"

"You ask them!"

"I'm asking you." Raynes was getting steadily more irritated by her stonewalling. "Mrs Foster," he said coldly, "as one of Graeme's many lovers, you were looking forward to his arrival. Even more so, with Arthur being away. You weren't thinking about any bloody tree; you were thinking about the pair on the bed! Perhaps you'd even got out your brown cord dungarees? Ironed them specially for the occasion …?"

Raynes noted that he had scored a direct hit. He could see Ellie biting her lip in anger. Who had told him that?

"You're not going to provoke me, Inspector."

"Graeme told me a lot about you after your last visit. Perhaps he told me too much? Perhaps you heard about it? Perhaps you also suspected him of killing Allan? Perhaps he boasted of his achievement privately to you? He knew you wouldn't go to the police. He thought he was safe with you. But you were upset with the way he was treating Jenny. You didn't like him trying to break up her marriage. A little affair was all right. But this was serious. Graeme had even stooped to blackmail. You're fond of Jenny. You didn't want to see her hurt. You poisoned him!"

"I did no such thing!"

"Last night – or perhaps yesterday afternoon – you phoned Graeme. You asked him why he hadn't come round to cut down your tree. He said he'd been too busy – or too lazy. You told him to come round immediately. You had something to say to him …"

Ellie shook her head.

"… You can't deny he's been avoiding you lately. He's obsessed about Jenny. He knows you don't approve – so he's been keeping out of your way. But you coaxed him round for a quiet chat – and you laced his drink. Jenny then came round and you hatched up this rather nice little plot to get rid of the body. Why not dump it in some comfortable corner in Picton Dale?"

Raynes looked at Ellie. He detected the faintest glimmer of a smile. He paused. She laughed.

"What a ridiculous story! You're making it all up!"

"So it wouldn't have been you driving Graeme's red pick-up through Picton Dale at 10.00 pm?"

Ellie shook her head.

"I've told you. I was sitting with Jenny – in my own house – from 8.00 till 11.00 last night. We didn't stir outside my front door. We had more important things to do."

"Such as what?"

"To talk."

"So Jenny would have been present when you made your phone call?"

"What phone call?"

It was proving a difficult interview – as Raynes had known it would be. There was not the slightest doubt she was lying and covering-up. She would go on lying. His only hope was to accumulate enough facts and then use them to trip up Jenny. If Jenny could produce contradictory evidence then that would be the way to break down Ellie.

"You deny making a phone call?"

"I deny everything!"

"Do you deny seeing Graeme yesterday?"

Ellie hesitated.

"You did see him?"

"I don't see why I should tell you!"

Raynes put on his most gentle voice.

"Mrs Foster, you'll have to tell me eventually. It's no use you trying to shield Jenny."

"I'm not shielding Jenny!"

The reply came back so quickly that Raynes was sure she was telling the truth.

"Well," he said lamely, "someone transported Graeme's body up to Picton Dale. They left his red pick-up in a car park up there – so there must have been a second car to drive the person back. What kind of car does Jenny drive?"

"A Polo."

"Did she come round to your house in it?"

"I couldn't say."

Raynes reckoned that there was nothing worse than a hostile witness. It was partly his fault. He knew that he hadn't treated her very nicely. But Ellie was a determined character. If she had decided to stonewall his questions, then it made little difference whether he treated her kindly or not.

"You know," he said gently, "this is not going to look very good in court. All these denials. All these lies. They're going to make the jury very hostile."

"Who said I was going to end up in court?"

"Well, it's obviously going to end up in court! We're dealing with two savage murders. You're going to be in the witness box – or the dock – and all that you've been saying this morning is going to come out. Detective-Constable Carlisle's got it all down in black and white. It won't make pretty reading. Even if we don't get you for murder, we'll get you for perjury or obstruction. You'll be sent down for a couple of months. I shouldn't like to see all your exploits written up in the local rag. 'City Nurse in Sex Drama with Dead Man!' You'll probably lose your job! Perhaps Arthur too?"

"If you haven't any evidence, you can't charge me!"

"Don't worry about that!" said Raynes cheerfully. "We've got plenty of proof. I'm just waiting for you to condemn yourself out of your own mouth – then you'll be charged. After that, it's simply a question of chipping away. We'll get the truth in the end. But it's much better to come clean. Makes things a lot easier for everyone."

Ellie looked less assured. Doubt had come into her eyes. Perhaps the Inspector did know more than she thought. She pursed her lips together.

"I know it's difficult," said Raynes.

"I didn't kill Graeme," said Ellie. "And I certainly didn't kill Allan." Her voice had the ring of truth.

"But you know who did?"

Ellie gathered her courage together.

"I'm innocent – and that's all I'm saying!"

29 *A little bit of sugar*

After Ellie had been taken out, peace descended on Raynes' office. Carlisle checked through the notes he had made and the Inspector ordered a large jug of coffee with three cups and saucers. He had decided that Jenny, being a softer and more gentle person, needed different treatment to Ellie. Whilst he was waiting, he opened that morning's correspondence. Most of it was rubbish. He threw it into the wastepaper basket. He looked at Carlisle who was still staring with some annoyance at his notes.

"Having problems?" he asked.

"You were both going a bit quick for me," Carlisle replied. "I've got all her answers down but I haven't got all your questions."

"Don't worry about that!" said Raynes. "We can put them in later. Better re-writing the questions than the usual police practice of re-writing the answers! Can you make sense of them?"

"I think so."

"The next one should be a little easier."

Like Ellie, Jenny had been collected from her home before 8.00 am and, on Raynes' orders, they had been kept in separate rooms in Grasshallows police station. It was now nearly 10.45 am and Jenny was feeling fairly desperate. She had been given two cups of tea and offered some toast. But no one had answered any of her questions about why she was there or how long they would keep her. A friendly policewoman had kept her company and chatted away about children and the Guides, but after two hours even this company had begun to pall, and when she was told that under no circumstances could she phone Neil, she had burst into tears.

However, soon after, word came down that Inspector Raynes was ready to see her and she was ushered into an upstairs room where there were two men in plain clothes and a rich aroma of newly-made coffee. Both men stood up when she came in. They explained who they were, apologized for the delay and offered her a splendid cup of creamy coffee which she could hardly refuse.

Jenny felt that it was better to be doing something rather than sitting around doing nothing; but she realized that her ordeal was about to begin. However, it seemed to be starting in a friendly fashion. Inspector Raynes was polite and smiled a lot. He even cracked the occasional joke with his colleague which made her feel more at ease. Eventually he got down to business.

"Mrs Gray ... may I call you Jenny? ... as you know, I am conducting investigations into the death of Allan Foster. I've already spoken to your husband, but I haven't had a chance to speak to you. At first, I didn't think you were in any way involved in this tragic business – but as time has gone by, it seemed to me that your relationship with Graeme has had some bearing on events. Could you perhaps tell me something about it? I know he was trying to entice you away from Neil."

Jenny found Raynes easy to speak to.

She explained the frustrations she sometimes felt at home and her irritation with Neil. The fact that so often she seemed to come a poor fourth in his life. There was the Scouting – that came first; then his teaching; and thirdly, their children. He adored the children. She supposed that really she ought to be grateful for such a hard-working husband. And, in a way, she was. But something was missing. The sparkle of adventure. That was something Graeme provided. They had known each other for years. But knowing what sort of person he was,

199

she had been wary. But last Christmas, she had let herself go and – despite Neil's bitter reaction – she had to admit that she had drawn quite a lot of comfort and excitement from her affair. Graeme had been very considerate and charming. She wasn't blind to his faults, but he had seemed genuinely fond of her.

What had started as something of a joke – her leaving Neil – had begun to be serious. Graeme had kept saying what fun it would be if they could live together in his house. His father wouldn't mind. Graeme had a good job and they could perhaps go up to London once a month for a night out. It sounded very exciting. Graeme had begun to speak disparagingly of Neil – his moodiness, his small-mindedness, his obsession with Scouting. He had also begun to hint that Neil was seeing another woman. Who she was, he did not say – but he had promised that he would introduce her to Jenny so that she could tell her face-to-face what Neil had been up to.

It had all seemed rather far-fetched – she didn't think Neil was like that – but on the Sunday night before Allan died, she had driven up to Picton Dale to meet Graeme. He had produced this 'dreadful female' – middle-aged, dyed hair, scraggy neck – who had described in lurid detail what Neil had been doing to her. That had been bad enough. But, the moment Graeme had got up to get them both a drink, this woman had apologized to Jenny and said it was all a tissue of lies! She had never even seen her husband! Graeme had been blackmailing her over Allan and there was not one word of truth in what she had said. Apparently, Allan was her son. Jenny could hardly believe it – Allan was such a nice lad. But she had heard from Ellie that Allan had been adopted ... so it was possible. And this 'female' had told her that Graeme had said that if she didn't tell Jenny all these lies about Neil, he would destroy Allan's reputation once and for all. For Allan's sake, she had agreed to go through with it – but on meeting Jenny, she had realized that she couldn't lie to her.

Graeme had realized what had happened whilst he was away at the bar. There had been a terrible scene – shouting and screaming. The woman had run out and Graeme had chased after her. He had come back with a cut on his knuckles where he had hit her. All in all, it had been a terrible evening and she had felt shattered. Graeme had sworn blind that what the woman had told him about Neil was true. But she didn't believe him. He denied having any plan to hurt Allan. But, two days later, Allan was dead ... and since then, everything had fallen to pieces.

Graeme had phoned her once or twice, but she had been non-committal. Neil had withdrawn into himself and she had not been able to discuss anything with him. Ellie had been a tower of strength throughout the ordeal. She had told Jenny again and again that it would be madness to leave Neil and, over the weekend, she had persuaded her not to accept Graeme's offer.

Raynes shook his head sadly.

"And now he's dead, it's all over anyway?"

"Yes."

Jenny was so taken up in her own tragedy that she did not notice what she had said. Raynes felt sure that both Ellie and Jenny had agreed on what they would say to the police – they would have only one story and a common alibi. That had probably been agreed on Monday night. But Raynes had allowed Jenny to speak at length. He had put in the odd question; muttered an occasional word of surprise or comfort; he had acted as a sympathetic listener – so much so that he had lulled her into a false sense of security so that she was not expecting any trick questions.

Before she had time to realize her mistake, Raynes rushed in with a second question: "Do you know the name of this 'dreadful female' as you call her?"

"I don't know her surname, but I believe she's called Grace. She was standing beside you at the cemetery on Saturday."

"That's right," said Raynes. "Grace Turner."

Raynes proceeded to ask her some more very boring questions about the scene in *The Carpenter's Arms* on the Sunday night. What Grace had said ... And then he sprang his second trick question:

"Didn't Ellie phone her on Monday night?"

"Yes, that's ... No!"

Jenny went red with embarrassment.

She realized that she had fallen into a trap.

"No, she didn't."

"Are you sure about that?"

Jenny's lips were tightly drawn.

What had she said?

But Raynes was very kind about it.

"You don't have to lie to me, Jenny," he said. "Ellie came in here determined to keep mum, but she realized that it was such a serious matter that she would have to tell me the truth. And I'm sure you feel precisely the same." He gave her a warm smile.

Jenny felt very upset inside. She had promised Ellie to say nothing. They had decided that there would be a pact of total silence about what happened on Monday night. They had agreed that this silence would be in everyone's best interests. But here was the Inspector saying that Ellie had changed her mind. Surely the Inspector would not lie?

He spoke gently.

"You've already admitted that you knew Graeme was dead ..."

"Did I?" She was surprised.

Raynes nodded to Carlisle who turned back a couple of pages in his notebook. He quoted: "'And now that Graeme's dead, it's all over anyway?' Mrs Gray replied: 'Yes.'"

Raynes continued: "Since Graeme's death has not yet been announced publicly, there is no way you could have known anything about it unless you were involved."

Jenny's eyes were filled with tears.

"Oh dear," she said. "What shall I do?"

"I think it's fairly obvious," said Raynes. "Do what Ellie very wisely decided to do. Spill the beans! Let us have a complete picture of what you did last night and you can walk out of here a free woman."

Jenny was suspicious.

"But if she told you, why d'you need me to tell you as well?"

Raynes looked surprised.

"Corroboration!" he said. (Always dazzle the punters with big words!) "We've got to have your evidence to put Ellie in the clear. She told us she was innocent but we can't just take her word for it. Someone else has to confirm that what she said is true. You are the only person who can do it. You were with her all Monday night. You know what happened and you must tell us."

Jenny hesitated. For all his gentleness and soft-spoken words, she was beginning to have her doubts about Raynes. Was he trying to entrap her? What had Ellie said? Or not said? Their pact, made the previous night after a couple of rum and cokes, had seemed totally cast iron. But now, in the cold light of day, it seemed rather fragile. She realized that the Inspector was beginning to sense her inner confusion.

"I must point out to you, Jenny, that it is a criminal offence to obstruct police inquiries and to withhold vital information. This is a double murder – two of your husband's closest colleagues have been killed. I think I'm entitled to your complete support. You're a person who hates lies. And so am I."

He had wielded the big stick. Now he waited – letting her slowly make up her mind. His eyes moved to the coffee jug. He smiled. "Perhaps if we had another cup of coffee it would help?"

Jenny shook her head.

"No, I don't want any more coffee. Thank you."

What she wanted to say was: 'Let me out of this place! Let me go home! Let the world go back to normal! Please let me go now! Let me go back to my children ...' But she knew she couldn't say anything so pathetic and childish. He was not going to let her go until she told him the truth. As he had said, she wasn't very good at lying ...

The silence became oppressive.

Raynes said nothing. He looked steadily at her – his brown eyes boring into her soul. She knew she couldn't bear it lasting much longer. Something had to give.

"I didn't want to get involved in all this," she said at last. "I just wanted to help Ellie."

Raynes nodded encouragingly.

"Ellie phoned me up and asked me to come round to her house about 8.00 pm. Arthur wasn't there. He'd gone back to work yesterday morning. Flown back to Turkey, I believe. Anyway, she phoned me just before tea and asked me to come round. I had no idea … no idea at all!"

She twisted her bangle round her wrist.

"She didn't tell me at first. We talked about Graeme and Neil – just as we did on Sunday afternoon. And then she said to me: 'You don't have to worry any more, love. Graeme's dead!' I couldn't believe it. It was a terrible shock. I asked her how it had happened. She said she had found him lying dead in Mr Armstrong's garden. She'd seen him sleeping there and had gone across to waken him. She was wanting him to cut down a tree or something. I think she said she kicked him – but there was no response. So there he was – dead. She said she'd spent the whole afternoon wondering what to do about it."

"She didn't want to phone the police. She said it'd only cause more trouble. She'd decided that the best thing was to get the body out of Grasshallows – well, out of town – so that there wouldn't be any connection with anyone round here. She said we'd all suffered enough. And that's true!"

"She told me she'd had a brainwave. That was why she'd invited me across. She'd decided to put the body in the caravan of that Grace woman who'd told all the lies about Neil. She said that she lived up Picton Dale and Graeme had told her roughly where her caravan was to be found. On the south side, near a pile of sand. So her plan was that we should load Graeme's body into the pick-up and take it up there right away. She couldn't do it on her own. She needed me to help her."

Raynes nodded. This was an incredible story. He was longing to ask lots of questions, but he didn't want to interrupt the flow of the narrative. No wonder Ellie had kept silent! She would be wild with fury when she heard that Jenny had blabbed.

"So you set off for Picton Dale?"

"No, we phoned up first. Ellie wanted to make sure that Grace was out of the way. She used to work behind the bar at

The Carpenter's and she was often down there having a drink – so Ellie thought she would lay a wild goose chase."

"Were you there when she phoned?"

Jenny nodded. "She didn't say much. She said she'd got some news about Allan which she might like to hear. She made out it was important. She said if Grace came down to the pub, they could have a quiet chat about it. The woman agreed. So Ellie arranged to meet her about ten."

"Well, after that, we had to deal with Graeme. That was the awful bit. I couldn't believe it was Graeme in there. Ellie'd wrapped him up in green polythene stuff and strung it all up with green string … you know, the sort of thing gardeners use. I half-knew it was him. You could see it was a body. But she wouldn't let me see him. She said it'd only depress me. Ellie's used to dealing with dead bodies. She sees them often enough at the Infirmary. It didn't worry her."

"She sent me off to get Graeme's pick-up. It's like a small lorry – red. It was parked down near the main road. She'd moved it there earlier in the day so that the Armstrongs wouldn't see it when they came home. I hadn't driven anything like that before – but it was quite easy. I had a bit of trouble reversing, but Ellie helped me get it backwards into her driveway."

"Graeme was in her garden shed – along with all his tools and his lawnmower. So we carried him round the corner and put him in the back of the pick-up. Then we put in all his stuff and Ellie drove the van out to Picton Dale."

"You drove there in your Polo?"

"Yes. To bring her back." Jenny was impatient to continue her story. Raynes had been brought up with the saying: 'Confession is good for the soul', and Jenny was the living proof of the truth of that saying. Once started, she could not stop.

"We got to the caravan site. It was difficult finding the place. It was so dark. No lights anywhere. No moon. No nothing. Ellie went off to find the caravan and I was left with Graeme. She also wanted to make sure Grace had gone. When she got back, we got Graeme out of the back of the pick-up and carried him down the path. It was a bit awkward getting him into the bedroom of the caravan. The door's quite narrow. But we managed."

"How did Ellie get into the caravan? She didn't tell me."

Raynes relished the *suggestio falsi*.

"I think she had a chisel or a screwdriver with her. But she didn't have to use it. The door was open."

"So no one can accuse you of breaking and entering?"

"No. It was open."

"Were you wearing gloves?"

Jenny nodded.

"So no fingerprints?"

"I wasn't in the caravan for more than a few moments. Ellie told me to get out whilst she did the gruesome bit – getting the body out of the plastic bags. She said there was no need for me to get upset. It was bad enough for her. So I waited outside – on guard, so to speak. Ellie did her thing and then we scooted away as quickly as possible."

She had clearly enjoyed the adventure.

It had lifted a burden from her young shoulders.

"What did you do with the polythene?" asked Raynes.

"We folded it up and left it in the back of Graeme's truck. We left it in the car park."

"Yes, we found it," said Raynes grimly. "Then you drove home in your car? What time did you get home?"

Jenny thought.

"About 10.20 pm, I think. It didn't seem to take long – but Ellie's always very well organized. Looking back, it seems like a dream. A nightmare, perhaps? I couldn't really believe it had happened when I woke up this morning. Then the policeman came and said I had to come down to the station. I didn't think we'd get away with it."

"No," said Raynes. "The police are brighter than you think." He returned to the events of the previous night. "So you returned to Ellie's and had a couple of well-deserved drinks?"

"We certainly needed them. It was an awful business, when you think about it. Graeme dead and being dumped out there in that woman's bed! I thought it was very funny at the time …"

"And now?"

"It's just catching up on me." She shivered a little at the memory. "No, it was a stupid thing to do. Spiteful, really.

It must have given her a terrible shock. But we had to get Graeme's body away from Ellie's house. We couldn't just leave it there ..."

Raynes was longing to ask 'Why?' – but that question might reveal that Ellie had not been so forthcoming as he had made out. He wanted to avoid that revelation at all costs. Jenny had been worth her weight in gold.

He smiled at her.

"I know it's been a sad and messy business – and I'm sure you're glad to be out of it. Graeme's caused you and many other people a lot of misery in his short life. If you'd taken his advice, you'd have bitterly regretted it. He was completely incapable of being faithful to anyone. Ellie was right. He'd have broken your heart. You're far better off with Neil. All marriages go through rough times. Half the joy is looking back and seeing how you managed to come through those rough times. Now that Graeme's out of the way, Neil'll be a happier man and that will help the two of you. Keep trying! It'll all come right in the end."

Jenny's eyes were full of tears.

Raynes felt very sorry for her – but it was not his job to be a marriage guidance counsellor. It was bad enough being a policeman!

"Now," he said in a kindly fashion, "you are free to go. I'm most grateful to you for your help and Ellie will be glad that you've confirmed her story ..." (Like hell! he thought.) "Detective-Constable Carlisle will arrange for a car to take you home. You'll be back in ten minutes." He looked at his watch. "Just in time for lunch! But before you go, can I just make two requests. Firstly, that you say nothing to anyone for at least forty-eight hours – not even to Neil? And secondly, that when my colleague has typed out your statement, you will be kind enough to come back and sign it?"

Jenny nodded.

She said: "I know you'll think me stupid. But can I ask you one question?"

"Certainly."

"How did Graeme die?"

"Don't you know?"

"No. Ellie didn't tell me."

Raynes put on a puzzled look.

"To be quite honest with you, she didn't tell me either. I don't think she was quite sure herself. It may have been murder. But he could equally have electrocuted himself on the cable of his lawnmower. These things often happen. It's something our medical people are looking into right now. We'll let you know as soon as we know."

"Thank you so much, Inspector."

"Thank you, Jenny. You've been a great help."

Carlisle went out to see about a car and to escort Jenny off the premises, whilst Raynes walked up and down his office, rubbing his hands with glee. When Carlisle returned, he said only three words:

"Bring back Ellie!"

30 *Ten green bottles*

However much Raynes desired to see Mrs Foster again, the confrontation was postponed until 2.30 pm. The simple fact was that, having had no proper breakfast, the Inspector suddenly realized that he was not only tired, but also extremely hungry. Although the police canteen was his idea of a gourmet's private hell, he knew he must have something to eat.

Carlisle was also anxious to get Jenny's interview typed out by one of the secretaries. He thought it might be helpful to have it down in black and white. The Inspector agreed.

There were also other matters to be considered. What to do about Grace who was in protective custody – and Tom, who had been brought in at the same time as Jenny and Ellie? Raynes decided to let both of them go. A public announcement would have to be made about Graeme's death and his father, Ron Wilson, told. All in all, it was an extremely busy lunch hour.

Ellie returned to Raynes' office much subdued. During the course of the day, she had gone through several changes of mood. First, she had been amused and petulant, anxious to

spike the Inspector's guns. Then she had been angry and contemptuous – especially when he had treated her so rudely and
in such a cavalier fashion. Towards the end of the interview
she had become rather frightened, when she thought of the
consequences of what she and Jenny had done. She had lied
and stonewalled with as much determination as she could. Then
she had been led away and kept waiting in a rather dreary
room under the watchful eye of a young policewoman. She
had been there for almost four hours. She had been escorted
to the toilet but not permitted to use the phone. She had had a
decidedly poor lunch of ham salad followed by a slice of stale
apple pie. Now the day was passing by and she was still being
kept waiting. No one seemed able or willing to answer any of
her questions. It was therefore something of a relief to be taken
back to the Inspector's office.

Raynes watched her sit down. He could tell that she was
dejected and fearful. He put together the sheets of paper on
which Jenny's interview had been neatly typed.

"Well?" he said. "Are you prepared to tell me anything
more?"

"I told you I was innocent. I didn't kill him. Isn't that
enough?"

"Unfortunately not," said Raynes. "You may be innocent
of murder, but you're not in the clear – not by any means. It
is a grave offence to move a body, to destroy evidence and to
obstruct police investigations. You have done all three. On
each count, you could very well face serious charges and a
severe sentence."

He looked at her. She remained sullen and unco-operative.

"Your friend, Jenny, has been much more helpful. She has
told me the whole story – or nearly the whole story ..."

Ellie shook her head.

"I don't believe you."

Raynes picked up one of the sheets and read out a paragraph
from the transcript of Carlisle's notes. "Are you saying that she
lied? That she made all this up?" Raynes read another short
paragraph.

"We agreed to say nothing."

"I know."

"I can't see how she would break our promise and speak to you. Not unless you tricked her in some way?"

Raynes lied happily.

"She told us the whole story of her own free will and volition. There was no compulsion at all. She was glad to get it off her chest. As you will be …"

Ellie's reserve lasted for a further minute. She had spent most of her four dreary hours wondering if it was really worthwhile holding out. The Inspector already had an inkling of what she had been up to. He could do all sorts of unpleasant things – like charging her with obstruction. She could end up in a cell or in a remand centre. People would gossip about her. That was not the sort of publicity Ellie wanted. Perhaps Raynes was right?

"What have you done to Jenny?" she asked cautiously.

"Done? We've done nothing," said Raynes. "She went home in time for lunch."

Ellie began to feel very much alone. What was to be gained by keeping silent? The questioning could go on all day. And at the end of it, she would probably have to give way. Better to confess now …"

She looked Raynes in the face.

"Well, it was like this …"

The story that she told was the same as Jenny's – with one or two more details, a little more spite and a touch of earthiness which Raynes appreciated. She told the story slowly and Carlisle had no problem getting it all down. By the time she and Jenny sat down to enjoy their rum and cokes, you could feel the release of tension. Ellie may have appeared hard and callous, but Raynes could feel that she was deeply relieved to pour it all out.

Raynes said: "There are still one or two questions unanswered. Why didn't you phone the police right away when you discovered that Graeme was dead? Why didn't you ring for an ambulance? Why go through all this farce of shifting the body and attaching the blame to someone else?"

He looked at Ellie. He could see that there was something still troubling her.

"Come on," he said, "tell me. There is more to this than meets the eye, isn't there? You know who murdered Graeme? But you are still hiding something? Something you didn't tell Jenny? What is it?"

Ellie looked down at the floor.

"I don't know what I saw, Inspector." She hesitated. "Everything looked very ordinary to me – but I know it wasn't. I was cleaning the house on Monday morning. Arthur had gone. We'd had a bit of a row over the weekend and I think he was glad to go. I had Graeme coming round to cut down that tree and – I won't deny it – I was looking forward to his visit. I was planning on a little something after he'd done the job."

"I saw him arrive at the Armstrongs at about half past nine. I waved to him. He waved to me. He got started on their lawn. It was quite a job because no one had touched it for almost a month and all the flower beds were full of weeds. It was a real jungle."

"Well, I went out and did some shopping. I got back at about a quarter to one. I came through the front door. I dumped all the stuff in the kitchen and went upstairs to change. To change into something nice for Graeme. Something nice and a little bit naughty … I looked out of the staircase window and saw that he was sitting by the sundial having his packed lunch. He seemed quite happy. He was certainly alive."

Raynes nodded thoughtfully.

"Five minutes later, I was just about to go into the shower and I had another peep at him. He seemed to have finished his lunch and was having a sleep. It was a really hot day and he'd done a power of work in those three hours. I'll say this for Graeme – he was a good worker! And then, whilst I was watching, this person ran across the lawn to Graeme. I only saw his back view. He ran across the lawn and bent over him. He wasn't there for more than half a minute. I couldn't think what he was doing. Then he ran away again."

"It didn't bother me too much. I went in and had a shower. Put on some lacy black underwear. A shot or two of Paloma Picasso and then I was ready. I looked out of the window to see how Graeme was getting on. He was still lying in the same

211

position, still asleep, and a bird was pecking into the last of his sandwiches. I thought to myself: 'That lazy bugger's never going to get round to my tree!' So I put on my dress – a nice, loose, summery one – and went downstairs."

"I gave him another quarter of an hour and then I went through to the Armstrongs. We have a connecting gate between the two gardens. I said to him: 'Hi! What about getting some work done?' But he didn't reply. I walked over to him and kicked his foot. His right foot. I said: 'There's a woman waiting for you!' He still didn't move. It was at that point I began to get alarmed. I could see his eyes were open and staring. I've seen enough dead bodies in my time to know a dead one when I see one. 'Oh, no!' I said. I went down and took his pulse. Nothing! Graeme was dead!"

She paused.

"I didn't tell Jenny all that."

Raynes gave Ellie a more kindly look.

"Of course not."

"I let her think he'd electrocuted himself on his machine."

"It does happen."

"Quite often. Might be a good way of murdering someone!"

Raynes raised his eyebrows. There'd been quite enough murders round Grasshallows for one summer! He looked at her. "But Graeme wasn't electrocuted …"

"No. I guessed that. What did he die of?"

"Inhalation of the contents of an aerosol."

"An aerosol? I didn't see one."

"Of course you didn't. The murderer took it away with him!"

Ellie hesitated.

"You think the person I saw was the murderer?"

"I do – and so do you. That's why you're covering up."

Ellie bit her lip.

"Was it someone you recognized?"

"Not precisely."

"Was it Tom?"

"Could have been …"

"Neil?"

"No." She sounded uncertain.

212

"Well, would you be kind enough to tell me whom you did see?"

"I'm not really sure, Inspector." She hesitated again. "My house faces south. The sun was in my eyes so I didn't see properly. I thought it was one of the Armstrong twins. But he wasn't in uniform." She paused ...

"But it was one of the scouts?"

Ellie took a deep breath.

"Yes."

31 *We're on the Scouting trail*

Although Raynes considered it quite possible that Ellie was lying about the scout-like figure who had been seen on the Armstrongs' lawn, he was quite prepared to give her the benefit of the doubt. Her story had confirmed that of Jenny's on almost every point, so he was fairly certain she had been telling him the truth.

It was natural that Graeme's death, taking place so near to her home, would make her a figure of suspicion. It was natural that if she suspected that a member of the 14th Grasshallows Troop had indeed done the murder, she would want to hide the evidence and protect the Troop from further scandal. Had Grace been a complete stranger – or if Ellie had dumped Graeme's body in some country lane, she might have succeeded in her cover-up. But the phone call had been too obvious for words! There were only three women on Raynes' short list. Ellie had not been clever enough.

He decided to let her go.

* * *

After she had left and Carlisle had gone away to dictate his notes, Raynes settled down to read the forensic report on Graeme. It did not make very cheerful reading.

Graeme had indeed eaten his sandwiches. Egg and ham. He had eaten a pie and part of an apple. He had also drunk copious draughts of orangeade. It was quite understandable – after all his labours. But the orangeade had a familiar ingredient. It contained tiny, tiny grains of the same pill which had been

213

found in Allan's stomach and in the empty orangeade bottle at camp. This time, they had been crushed more finely. Graeme had drunk deeply and absorbed the drug. Probably, because he was dehydrated, it had worked more quickly. He had gone to sleep and whilst asleep – or on the way there – the murderer had quite literally polished him off! Lemon-scented furniture polish from an aerosol, easily obtained from any supermarket, had been pumped down Graeme's throat. His bronchial tubes had become completely congested. He had died – perhaps within thirty seconds of the attack.

One or two things registered immediately in Raynes' mind. First of all, his instincts had been correct. Graeme was indeed the intended victim of the murder on the camp-site. Allan had been a tragic mistake. Which showed that the motive for the first murder was not to silence Allan's gossiping tongue but something totally different.

The second point was that the murderer was still showing a homely touch. A plastic funnel! Now furniture polish! The methods used were very simple and very deadly. Taken in conjunction with the pills, the killer could move in extremely fast, confident that his victim would put up little resistance and he could be up and away within a minute. His style and panache were to be admired!

Raynes noted that the murderer must be very determined to have renewed his attack so soon after his previous failure. Determined or desperate? He had shown remarkable ingenuity in remounting his attack – not only within the week, but also in broad daylight. Was he so sure he could get away with it?

As he said 'he', Raynes told himself not to be so sure the murderer was male. Even though he had been told that the assailant looked like a scout, Ellie could still be shielding Jenny. The transporting of Graeme's body to Grace's caravan was a monstrous hoax; could it not also be a convenient blind to conceal a more devilish deed?

Once again, he thought about the pills. They were the link. Because they were so easily available, he had not concentrated on that point as fully as he should. He had concentrated on relationships rather than on concrete facts. But someone, somewhere, had a supply of sleeping pills. That could be the murderer's weak point.

More miserably, Raynes conceded that he was still as far away as ever from discovering the motive for the killing. He could guess that it was Graeme's promiscuous behaviour. Some woman he had used and abused. But the motive could be something completely different. Who was the avenging angel? The St George who was determined to slay the dragon? Even though Ellie had implied that the villain might be one of the boys, could it not perhaps be Neil? A revenge killing? But that did not explain why he had killed Allan.

The only comforting thought that occupied Raynes' mind was that, having at last succeeded in killing Graeme, the murderer would presumably now be satisfied! Hopefully, there would be no third killing!

* * *

When Carlisle returned with his second pile of neatly typed papers, Raynes pushed the report over to him. "Read that!" he said. "Batman strikes again!"

Carlisle read the surgeon's report through and whistled with surprise.

"The same pills!"

"Yes," said Raynes, "it's his only slip. Someone has to know about these pills, common as they are. Once we get the pills, we've got him. It's a question of routine police work from now on. No more theories. No more little grey cells! We're going to have to work through every single suspect – again! We've got to find out what they were all doing yesterday lunchtime."

He looked out of the window, seeking inspiration.

"I think we've got to accept Ellie's timing. The surgeon says the estimated time of death was between 1.00 and 2.00 pm. Each suspect must be asked precisely where he or she was at that moment – and that statement must be confirmed *positively* by someone else. Preferably not by a fellow suspect!"

"Now, as you know, I've put out a statement saying that Graeme's body was found in Picton Dale last night. The implication is that he was murdered in the evening. When that statement appears in the Press, the murderer will be rather surprised.

215

He or she will wonder what happened to the body after they left. Unless, of course, it was Jenny or Ellie ... or Grace. They know."

"You still suspect them?"

"I still suspect everyone."

Raynes glared at his colleague.

"Those on our list who are innocent will be completely unaware of our interest in their movements at lunchtime. They'll all be busy making sure they've got a good alibi for the evening. Except for the murderer ... he or she will know. That alibi will be a good one. Or it ought to be ... We must make sure that the officers who are conducting these inquiries know exactly what they are looking for."

"We're not doing it ourselves?"

"No use barking when you've got a pack of dogs to do it for you! Besides, it'd take far too long. We've got to strike immediately. The general public's going to be up in arms with a second murder ... we can't afford to wait a second! The force will probably enjoy doing a little real detection. Sharpen up their wits. Remember! They've got to look for these pills as well."

Carlisle looked relieved.

"Well," he said, "that'll make life a lot easier. You mean we just sit here like spiders at the centre of the web, waiting to see what turns up?"

"Precisely," said Raynes. "I've seen all our sixteen suspects. Some of them twice. The murderer's fooled me once. He may fool me again. I'd like a second opinion."

Carlisle looked thoughtful.

"But we already know where some of the boys were," he said, "... if it was a boy? The Armstrongs were in London with their mother. Colin was with his aunt and uncle in King's Lynn; and Simon and Geoff were here in this office! Well, I suppose they'd just left. About 12.15 pm. I can't see that they had the time to do anything."

Raynes sounded irritated. "And Garry Hogg had just been down to his father's shop ... Harry Robb was on his way to Tesco's to do his afternoon shift; Ian Mackay was at a prayer meeting ... and Johnny Cotton? Well, who knows what Johnny Cotton was up to?" Raynes shook his head. "We must have detailed times and movements for every single suspect and all their parents and relatives. Every chemist in Grasshallows must be visited to find out who has been prescribed these pills. No one must escape the net!" He looked at Carlisle. "And I'm putting you in charge!"

"Me?" Carlisle was horrified.

"Yes. You!" Raynes was cutting. "You're the one who believes in all this paperwork. Let's see if – for once – it can bring results!"

* * *

Carlisle was vindicated.

The police went out two by two all Tuesday evening and Wednesday morning, asking questions and taking notes. The reports steadily flowed in. Times ... places ... who possessed what drugs ... where and when. Every report was meticulously recorded. Each alibi was double-checked. The information received was voluminous. However, by Wednesday lunch-time, Raynes had spotted a vital discrepancy. He had already received a note about the pills which pointed in the same direction. Together, these pointers were conclusive.

Raynes immediately stopped the search.

"We've found the murderer," he said quietly.

"Are you sure?" asked Carlisle doubtfully.

"Yes. It all tallies. Beautifully! Just look!"

He showed Carlisle the two reports.

"Don't you agree? Think what we were told!"

Carlisle shook his head.

"What fools we've been!"

"Pulling wool over our eyes all the way along! Through every interview! And we believed it!"

Raynes stretched out in his chair feeling immense relief and satisfaction. Another success!

"What are you going to do now?" asked Carlisle.

Raynes was full of confidence: "I shall order an immediate arrest. But we'll not let on." He smiled. "You know how I like these traditional endings. What d'you say to a little soirée in the Scout hut? Tin mugs? Sweet tea? Damp biscuits? A cosy little chat around the camp-fire? I think we should invite all the parents – and Grace! Don't forget her!"

"Are you planning this for tonight?"

"Why not?"

"But you don't want to invite the boys?"

Raynes considered.

"No," he said. "We'll leave them out. They'll hear soon enough. But I think we have a duty to the parents, don't you?"

32 *We're out for blood*

The Scout hut belonging to the 14th Grasshallows Troop was situated in a particularly dispiriting part of Henslea. It stood behind an empty garage, surrounded by a wilderness of pebbles and mud, and was protected by a high wire mesh fence. The windows were covered by metal grilles and the door was reinforced with steel plates and iron bolts. It was more like a fortress than a social club.

Inside, the passage walls sported a terrifying combination of purple and cream, but the room in which Raynes was to conduct his meeting was decorated in more homely hues. There were bright red plastic chairs and a large collection of photographs portraying members of the Troop over the past thirty years. Pride of place was given to an excessively romantic picture of the Queen, which was flanked by the Scout flag and the Union Jack, both neatly furled.

Raynes selected a chair and placed it underneath the royal picture so that he would not be distracted during his speech. Detective-Constable Carlisle was instructed to man the door and a patrol car was stationed at the gate.

Slowly, the unwilling guests filed in.

Neil and Tom bustled about, getting everyone a cup of tea or coffee. A tin of biscuits was passed round but since they were mostly fig rolls, there were no takers. Gradually, the company began to settle down and Raynes looked at the circle of anxious faces, checking to see if everyone was there. Neil and Jenny; Ellie and her husband, Arthur; Grace and Tom; Mr

218

Hogg and his solicitor; and most of the parents whose sons had been at the summer camp in Picton Dale.

The Inspector spoke softly as he began his exposition:

"You have all suffered a great deal in this case," he said, "and so have I. We have had to endure two murders – both, in my opinion, quite unnecessary. The first murder took place at 2.30 last Tuesday morning, in the second week of camp. It came completely out of the blue, because all the scouts – with the exception of Ian Mackay – said that they had had a very happy time. Neil and Graeme both told me that it was one of the most successful camps they had ever had. So what was the motive for the murder of Allan Foster?"

"I must confess that the answer was not at all clear. Allan was a popular and able Scout-leader, who had very high standards and was well-liked by the boys. He had helped a number of them get their proficiency badges in mountaineering and, as Harry Robb said, the experience of dangling fifty feet down a sheer rock face is likely to give you a lasting bond of trust and gratitude towards the person at the other end of the rope! So why kill Allan?"

Raynes paused.

"At an early stage in my investigations, I heard that Allan had reported Tom Hayward for various misdemeanours which had come to his attention. I will not go into detail. Suffice it to say that these things were a private, internal matter affecting the Troop. Ian's father, Mr Mackay, also put in a formal complaint against Tom, but since he has not been murdered, it seems unlikely that this was a cause of the killing – although a certain lady (I shall not mention her name) did her best to persuade me that Tom was in many ways the Devil Incarnate ..."

Tom looked at Ellie coldly. Although her name had not been mentioned, he knew to whom the Inspector was referring. He swallowed uneasily.

Raynes continued: "At about the same time, I heard about a fight between Harry Robb and Garry Hogg. The fight seemed to be about Harry's sister, who was in line to become yet another of Graeme's conquests. But I soon discovered that the real reason for the fight was about an allegation made by Allan –

that there were some irregularities in the business practices of the travel agency where he worked."

Raynes smiled genially at Mr Hogg.

"But, like you, I could not imagine that a firm with such a fine reputation here in Grasshallows could possibly be guilty of any shady dealing. Had there been any shady dealings – such as ghost payrolling, for instance – that might have pointed to a motive. But at an early stage, Mr Hogg and his advisers came to see me and handed over all the accounts for the past five years. They were most insistent that everything to do with the travel agency was honest and above board. So I was faced with another dead end."

"A third possibility occurred to me. Perhaps Graeme himself wished to eliminate Allan for reasons known only to himself. Like everyone else, he had the means. He was one of only three people who knew that Allan was sleeping alone that night ... the others being Allan and Neil. So I kept Graeme in mind, even though I could not see what he could possibly hope to gain by Allan's death."

"Detective-Constable Carlisle and I interviewed all the boys – a very long and trying process – and we put one or two of them under fairly strong pressure to see what their answers might be. After years of listening to guilty people telling me lies, I came away from those interviews with the very clear impression that the boys were telling me the truth. And, looking back at the transcripts of those interviews, I see that I was right. We were told no lies." (Raynes had decided to let Neil off for his mistake about the bottles. He did not think it was a deliberate lie.)

"After seeing the boys, I felt it necessary to cast my net more widely. Several of the boys had mentioned the existence of a Mrs Grace Turner who lived on a caravan site about half a mile upstream from the camp. Mrs Turner has been very kind to the boys in a number of ways ..." (Raynes passed delicately over the question of corrupting minors) "... and they were very fond of her. When Detective-Constable Carlisle and I went to see her, we noticed that she had received severe bruising to her left eye ..."

"My right eye!" said Grace.

"Depends on which way you look at it!" said Raynes. "O.K. Your right eye!"

Grace smiled happily.

"She received this injury when Graeme Wilson assaulted her outside *The Carpenter's Arms* on Sunday night – the night *before* the murder. He hit her because she had tried to warn a young married woman that Graeme was 'no good' and that he would use her – and discard her – just like the rest. The young married woman was well aware of what Graeme was like and was at that very moment trying to extricate herself from a very unpleasant predicament – namely blackmail."

Ellie looked covertly at her friend, but Jenny had her eyes firmly fixed on a photograph on the wall. Neil took a sip from his tin mug and licked his lips nervously.

"Having interviewed both Grace and this young woman, I became aware of the very strong passions Graeme could arouse with his promiscuous behaviour. At first, it all seemed light-hearted and casual, but once you got into his net, it was rather difficult to escape. Mrs Turner was herself being blackmailed by Graeme. He had threatened that if she did not do what he wanted, he would publish certain facts about Allan in Grass-hallows which would not only cost him his job but, almost certainly, drive him out of the city. These facts gradually emerged. Bearing in mind that Graeme's father has a reputation for violence and fraud – he is in fact in jail at this moment – I felt that it was a clear case of 'like father, like son'."

"These revelations, coming when they did, made me begin to think that the murder was perhaps committed by some unknown figure – someone on the outside of the Scout movement – but not far outside! It seemed to me that whoever killed Allan was probably aiming for Graeme, but killed Allan by mistake."

Raynes paused again – to let the picture sink in.

"Right from the beginning of my investigations, I had considered this possibility. Any outsider would naturally assume that Graeme would be sleeping in his own tent – the third from the left. So, if violence was planned, it would be on Graeme's tent that vengeance would fall. In the dark, one body looks very much like another. Having killed his victim, the murderer might legitimately suppose that the body he had left behind was Graeme's. But, of course, it wasn't; because that night Allan had wanted to stay up late and read. So Graeme shared a tent with Neil. Now, if the murderer had chosen any other night to attack, Graeme would indeed have been the victim – and there would have been no need for a second murder."

"I did wonder if Graeme had any prior knowledge of the attack? Was that why he deliberately switched tents? Did he know vengeance was coming? I noticed that Graeme was remarkably calm and collected after the murder. He did not seem to think he was in any sort of danger. He seemed to think Allan was the architect of his own downfall. I could not understand his ... sang froid ... because – the more my investigations into Allan's death led to a dead end – the more pressing appeared the motives for killing Graeme. I began to turn my attention to his lady-friends – and their husbands. I asked Graeme to supply me with a full list of his conquests – which he did."

Mrs Armstrong's face remained a frozen mask.

"Some of you will know what names appeared on that list. I shall say no more than that. But it became increasingly clear to me that Mrs Turner was right when she said that Graeme used his landscape gardening as a cover for philandery – even if that proved a difficult word for my colleague to spell!"

Raynes winked at Detective-Constable Carlisle.

Everyone laughed – and, for a moment, the atmosphere was more relaxed.

"As I say, Graeme supplied me with that list last Friday, and I went through it carefully, trying to decide which of the ladies mentioned might have most to gain by murdering Graeme. In retrospect, I was going up a blind alley, because the most important name did not appear on that list. So my eyes were turned in one direction – unfortunately, the wrong one."

"The next thing to happen was the funeral on Saturday morning. I think I am right in saying that we were all present at the service? The murderer was certainly present ..."

Raynes looked round the assembled company.

His eyes were cold with anger.

"But, at that point, we still did not know that Allan's death was a terrible mistake. I had thought it might have been a mistake, but I could not be sure."

"The murderer – I use that word to cover male as well as female – had by now recovered a little from the shock of killing the wrong person. The fact that nearly a whole week had passed – with no arrest – gave him or her renewed confidence. The police were obviously baffled. Perhaps a second attempt on Graeme's life might prove equally successful? If the police had failed once, why should they not fail again? Our murderer was very bold."

"At the reception given for the scouts and their families after the funeral, Mr Armstrong asked Graeme whether he would be getting back to normal that week? Would he be back in business doing his landscaping and gardening? Graeme said that he intended to start on Monday morning. Mr Armstrong therefore asked him if he would like to come to his house on Monday, because his lawn was getting rather overgrown, and his flowerbeds were full of weeds. Mrs Foster had a tree needing to be cut down, and Mrs Fisher had a small section of hedge which required trimming. Graeme agreed to tackle all these jobs on Monday."

"The murderer found this information most useful. 'Strike whilst the iron is hot' seemed a good idea. So, on Monday morning, we find Graeme hard at work in the Armstrongs' garden. At lunch-time, he took his packed lunch out on to the lawn and settled down in the sunshine to enjoy a well-deserved rest. Little did he know that his bottle of orangeade had again been doctored. Some more of the little white tablets which had appeared in the bottle of orangeade in Allan's tent, were again being used. They had once again been ground down and mixed with the juice."

"Graeme drank copiously of his orange drink. He was thirsty and tired. He stretched out on the lawn to have a short siesta – never dreaming for a moment that he was in any kind of danger. Slowly, the pills began to work and he started to snore – his mouth half-open …"

"Oh, no!" said Mrs Robb.

"Oh, yes!" said Raynes. "And the murderer was at hand with an aerosol spray. As you probably know, the newspapers have been full of the dangers of breathing in the contents of an aerosol spray in a confined space. It doesn't seem lethal – but it is. It clogs up the tubes and prevents normal breathing. It seems almost unbelievable but, within a minute, a person could be dead. In less than a minute, Graeme was dead. The murderer slowly approached the sleeping body, touched it, shook it – just to make sure Graeme was fully under the influence of the sleeping pills. Then the murderer darted back for the aerosol and squirted it – jet after jet – down Graeme's throat. The murderer took his victim's pulse. It was gone. Graeme was dead."

There was a deep silence in the room.

"Now as you all know, Allan lived next door to the Armstrongs. All that morning, Mrs Foster had been keeping an eye on Graeme, watching his progress and wondering how long it would be before he moved on and cut down her tree. She saw him lying in the sun. 'Lazy beast,' she said to herself. A few minutes later, she returned to the window and she claims … she claims that she saw a person bending over Graeme. She thought nothing about it, but, half an hour later, Graeme was still lying there. So she went through the connecting gate, into the Armstrongs' garden, to give him a well-deserved boot up the backside – and then discovered that he was dead."

Mr Armstrong had taken some time to grasp the full import of Raynes' words.

"D'you mean to tell me that Graeme Wilson was murdered in my garden?" He sounded very indignant.

"I'm afraid so. He was murdered beside your sundial."

"But why wasn't I told?" He turned to Ellie. "Why didn't you tell me? And, anyway, what happened to the body?"

Raynes held up his hand.

"I'm just coming to that. Just let me finish the story and I'll answer all your questions."

Mr Armstrong looked very angry, but said no more.

"At this point," continued Raynes, "Mrs Foster panicked. There is no other word for it …"

Ellie nodded.

It was as good an excuse as any.

"... She assumed that Graeme had been murdered but she felt it would be eminently desirable if the body was to be found somewhere else. Mrs Foster does not like the police ... She certainly does not like me! ... so she decided to create a diversion which would put the police completely off the scent. She dragged Graeme's body across the Armstrongs' lawn, through the connecting gate and hid the body in her garden shed. She wrapped it up in a couple of green polythene bags and tied the package together with green string. For some people, this might have been a gruesome task, but Mrs Foster is a trained nurse and is presumably used to dealing with dead bodies ..."

Most of the parents looked very shocked by what Raynes had just said. They looked at Ellie with disgust. Arthur folded his arms and looked at the ceiling. Ellie bit her lip and said nothing.

"She moved Graeme's truck to a side street near the main road and returned home. Later, she phoned up Jenny, after she had come back from work, and asked her to come round to her house later that evening ..."

Neil turned to his wife with amazement.

"You never told me!"

"Shut up!" she said. "He hasn't finished."

"Mrs Foster told Jenny what had happened and what she had done. She told her of her plan to take the body out of Grasshallows and get rid of it. The plan was to take the body up to the caravan site in Picton Dale and leave it in the caravan belonging to Mrs Turner. Jenny would drive her own car to bring Mrs Foster back."

Neil was furious.

He ran his hand through his hair.

"This is ridiculous! Bloody ridiculous!"

Raynes ignored him.

"Before they went up to Picton Dale, Mrs Foster phoned Mrs Turner to say that she was a friend of Allan's and that she had an important message to convey. Could she come down to *The Carpenter's Arms* right away and speak to her?

225

Grace had never met Ellie so she did not recognize her voice. She imagined that the message was genuine, so she set out on a dark night to walk the mile or so down to the pub. When she got there, she made a bit of a fool of herself, asking people if they were waiting for her. Eventually, she realized that she had been the victim of a cruel hoax and, with a sinking heart, she walked back home only to discover – at the end of her journey – Graeme's body lying dead in her bed!"

Raynes paused.

No one said anything.

The whole company was shocked.

"This wicked action was carried out by Jenny and Mrs Foster. It is, as you know, a serious offence to move a body or disturb evidence at the scene of a crime. In this case, the body was transported several miles and left in circumstances which suggested that Mrs Turner was herself involved in the murder."

"You bitch!" Grace snarled.

"Bitch yourself!" said Ellie, who looked quite unrepentant.

Raynes was frightened Grace might suddenly leap up and attack her. He held up his hand again, commanding peace and attention.

"Now there might have been any amount of body-shifting that night, but Mrs Turner had the sense to phone me right away and within half an hour, the police were at the caravan, examining the body."

"Quite clearly, Graeme had been dead for some time. Because the body had been found in her caravan, the finger of suspicion was directed at Grace. But when she told me about the mysterious phone call – and the woman's voice – my suspicions were turned in a different direction. I asked myself how Graeme's pick-up had managed to turn up in the car park at the caravan site? Had Graeme driven it there himself? The engine was still warm – but the surgeon told me Graeme had been dead for several hours! It looked as if Mrs Turner was telling me the truth. She had been sent on a wild goose chase whilst the body was delivered to her door!"

"I asked myself:'Where had the body come from? What was Graeme supposed to be doing Monday morning and Monday afternoon? Surely he was at the Armstrongs, then at Mrs Foster and later, at Mrs Fisher? Which of these ladies would have been most likely to phone Grace and send her on a wild goose chase?' "

Raynes smiled.

"It didn't take me very long to put two and two together. Mrs Foster is a strong character but, under questioning, she admitted that she and Jenny moved the body ... but denied that either of them had any part in his death. Jenny also claimed that she had no knowledge of how Graeme came to die. In fact, the murderer used the same method – the same pills to drug his victim – the same desire to choke life out of a living body ..."

Mrs Robb was in tears.

"Poor Graeme!" she said. "What a way to die!"

"I've never heard anything quite so dreadful," said Mr Mackay. "I hope you know who did it?"

Raynes nodded.

"It hasn't been easy – but the pills enabled us to pinpoint the most likely people. Unfortunately, the pills the murderer used were fairly common. We found a bottle in Graeme's house. They belonged to his father. Mrs Turner also had a bottle of them which was stolen by one of the scouts who was visiting her. Detective-Constable Carlisle has been in touch with all the chemists in Grasshallows to find out who has been pre-scribed these pills."

"My colleague has also been responsible for checking the movements of each suspect on Monday morning and after-noon. All of you have given statements to the police – and so have all the boys. These statements have been checked and double-checked most carefully. I told you that Mrs Foster saw a figure bending over Graeme's body. I did not tell you whether it was male or female ... and Mrs Foster herself was not sure because the sun was in her eyes. But she claimed that, even though he was not in uniform, she thought he was one of the 14th Grasshallows Troop ... and she was right."

Neil looked at his wife with despair. There were tears in his eyes. Jenny put a comforting arm round his shoulders.

"So we looked at the alibis of each boy most carefully. The Armstrong twins were in London with their mother for the whole day. Colin Fisher was dispatched on the early morning bus to stay with his uncle and aunt in King's Lynn. Garry Hogg was with his brother at a model railway exhibition in Peterborough but they did not leave Grasshallows till *after* lunch. Simon Wallace and Geoff Stewart have almost perfect alibis because they were in the police station seeing me till 12.15 pm. Harry Robb was on his way to Tesco's to do his afternoon shift. Ian Mackay told Mrs Fisher that he had been up at the Armstrongs' house looking for the twins. Johnny Cotton was fishing ... or at least, he said he was. Tom Hayward was sunbathing in a local park." Raynes turned to Neil: "And where were you?"

Neil looked confused.

"I can't remember."

"You were at home," said Jenny. "You were looking after the children. At least, that's what you said you were doing!"

Raynes let him squirm.

"Looking after the kids? But you don't remember?"

He shook his head.

As he did so, Raynes looked across the room to see how one other person was responding to all these revelations. She was listening with an interested look on her face – but seemed quite oblivious of the blow that was about to fall. He turned back to Neil.

"You were supposed to be seeing me down at the police station at 2.15 pm. But you spent your lunch-time having a picnic with your children down beside the river."

Neil nodded.

"That's right."

"So it wasn't you."

Raynes took a deep breath.

This was it.

He said: "We checked through everyone's stories again and again. Some of them were vague, like Neil's and Tom's. Others – like Johnny Cotton's – were highly suspicious. But only one proved completely flawed ..."

There was a deathly silence in the Scout hut.

It seemed as if everyone had stopped breathing.

Raynes said very quietly: "Colin Fisher arrived in King's Lynn later than expected!"

33 *Where have all the flowers gone?*

The silence lasted for perhaps a further ten seconds; then Mrs Fisher screamed: "You're wrong! You're wrong! It's not true! Not my Colin!" She repeated her protests hysterically and then collapsed in a flood of tears. Jenny and Ellie rushed to her side to comfort her. Neil dashed into the kitchen to get her a glass of water and a box of tissues. Grace leant forward and spoke to Tom.

To cover their embarrassment, the parents began to talk to each other in loud whispers – each expressing their amazement or their sheer disbelief at the Inspector's allegation. All of them knew Colin; they liked him; and, in his short life, he had never caused anyone any trouble. Poor Mrs Fisher! What a terrible blow! They kept looking at her to see how she was taking it. Her sobs and moans diminished. She drank the water and wiped her face with the tissues. Mr Derek Coates-Smythe shook his head sadly, spoke to Mr Hogg and glared at Raynes with undisguised hostility. When things had calmed down somewhat, he said:

"I hope you can justify your allegation!"

Raynes nodded.

"I know this is going to be painful – but I shall be as gentle as possible." He sighed. "The fact is that Colin loves his mother very much. In his father's absence, he felt very protective towards her. He was an only son and he had that special bond that such sons have for their mothers."

"During the time that Colin has been in the Scouts, he has learnt a great deal about Graeme Wilson. He heard his dirty stories and his boasts about how easy women were to get. 'Treat 'em rough and they'll come running!' That was Graeme's philosophy. The other scouts had told him about Graeme's exploits – doubtless exaggerated – and made it

229

clear to him that Graeme's conquests were not just stupid, young girls but older, mature, married women as well."

"It became implanted in Colin's mind that Graeme was a dangerous brute, a pervert, someone who was a very real threat to decent women. Which of course was true. And I suspect that he had also heard from Allan that Graeme had even seduced … the wife of a close friend …"

Jenny had blenched – frightened that Raynes might say too much. But he had halted just in time.

"Imagine then, Colin's feelings when he discovered that not only had his mother asked Graeme to look after their garden, but that she had also taken quite a fancy to that 'charming young man'!"

"It was all my fault!" wept Mrs Fisher.

Jenny hugged her more tightly.

"Not at all," said Raynes. "You may have liked him. You may even have fancied him. But your name did not appear in his list of conquests. That's what put me off the scent! It was precisely because you did *not* commit adultery with Graeme Wilson that I eliminated both you and Colin from my list of suspects. I never suspected that Colin had anything against Graeme. I must say that he hid his feelings extremely well."

"Colin's deep! Very deep!"

"I know."

Raynes tried to sound as caring as possible – even though it was difficult to show sympathy for someone who had now committed two murders. He continued in the same restrained tone of voice:

"Now, because of Graeme's easy triumphs elsewhere, Colin reasoned – wrongly, I'm sure – that it would not be long before his mother became just another notch on Graeme's cane, or a scalp in his collection. This upset him very much. He was sure that, with your husband often away in Saudi Arabia, or elsewhere in the Middle East, you would be a sitting duck. And he could not bear the thought that you might deceive – or had perhaps already deceived – his dad. So he decided to eliminate Graeme as a way of saving you …"

Mr Coates-Smythe was listening carefully.

"He planned the murder well in advance. He had decided to do it during the annual summer camp. Having been there the previous year, he knew the lay-out, the timing and where people slept. He was aware that Graeme had his own tent and slept alone."

"It was therefore easy to arrange the sequence of events. First of all, he would put some sleeping pills into Graeme's orangeade. Most of the scouts seem to have had a bottle in their tents for the odd nocturnal gulp. Colin reckoned that Graeme would probably take a swig or two and the sleeping pills would drug his senses and slow down his reactions." Raynes looked at Mrs Fisher. "You have these particular pills in your house, I believe?"

Mrs Fisher nodded. "His father uses them. Whenever he comes home jet-lagged and can't sleep ... It would have been quite easy for him to get hold of them."

"Next he collected the sand and the funnel. There was no problem with either. The sand was obtainable from the river at any point during the camp. It could be dried in the sun and then put in some plastic container. The funnel he collected from the kitchen. He probably kept both hidden in his sleeping bag. He didn't rush his plans. They were simple and methodical. He took his time. At 2.30 in the morning, he struck."

"Ian Mackay told me that Colin very often sat up late at night, reading his books – so he was quite used to being awake in the early hours. His brain obviously functioned well at that time of night. His tent-mate was, he knew, a heavy sleeper. So that was no problem."

"At about 2.25 on the Tuesday morning, he crept out of his tent, carrying the container of sand and the funnel. He moved to the next tent which was Graeme's. He undid the canvas ties. He could probably hear deep breathing from the body within. His victim was fast asleep. Holding his funnel in his left hand – (we had determined that the murderer was right handed) – he slipped into Graeme's tent with the container of sand in his right hand. He moved up the side of the body and thrust the funnel into the victim's open mouth and poured in the sand as fast as he could go ..."

Mrs Fisher said: "No …! No …! No …!"

She could not bear to hear the Inspector describing the murder scene. She continued to weep uncontrollably.

Raynes resumed:

"Allan never had a chance. He couldn't breathe. He didn't breathe. He died. Fortunately, he knew very little about it. In less than a minute, it was all over."

There was silence in the room.

Even Mrs Fisher had stopped moaning.

Ellie left her and moved back to her seat.

People were imagining the scene for themselves.

"Very soon, Colin was back in his own tent. No one had heard him go. No one had seen him return. Whilst he had been away, he had returned the funnel to the kitchen tent which was beside the river. He had also removed the bottle of orangeade with its incriminating contents. He probably poured the contents out on to the grass and washed the bottle in the river and put it away in a crate three layers down where no one would notice. He then peeled off the plastic gloves … I imagine he used gloves because his fingerprints were not found on the bottle."

"He thought he had covered his tracks well. Why should anyone look at the empty bottles? The fact that I saw a bottle-shaped stain in Graeme's tent – but no bottle made me look at the empties extremely carefully. And, sure enough, in that bottle, three layers down, we found a few grains of the sleeping pill which had stuck to the inside. In daylight, Colin would have seen these tell-tale traces but, in the darkness, he thought he had washed away all the evidence."

"So Colin was now back in his own tent. He listens. He waits till he gets his breath back. Till his pulse stops racing. He wonders if there is any small thing which will give him away? No, everything has gone strictly to plan. So now he moves to part two – his little rigmarole of waking Ian." Raynes looked at Mr Mackay. "Ian takes some waking up?"

"He does."

"And in the process, he wakes up Johnny Cotton and Mark Todd. That little ploy was very convincing. It put everyone off. Including me! One assumes that if a person hears a murder

232

being committed in the next tent, then they must be innocent. They cannot be in two places at once. Colin was very convincing in his description of what he heard. It put him completely above suspicion. He told me no lies. He told me that he had looked at his watch. It was 2.35 am. And so it was!"

"But there were one or two points I should have noticed. First of all, he told everyone that he had looked at his watch the wrong way up. He thought it was five past eight. Miss Dorothy Sayers – not one of Colin's favourite authors – once wrote a splendid book called *Murder must Advertize*. Colin was almost subconsciously telling us his story was 'upside down'. But I didn't see it. We accepted his story as fact. But we shouldn't have done ..."

Raynes looked at Neil.

"You told me right at the beginning that I should take Colin's story with a pinch of salt! Graeme told me not to believe anything Colin said. His tent-mate, Ian Mackay said: 'Colin is not being helpful.' And Johnny Cotton obviously regarded him as a compulsive story-teller ... over-imaginative, I think, is the word."

"So Colin had got his story all ready. No one was going to accuse him. He was the chief witness for the prosecution! So he went back to sleep and waited for the balloon to go up. This could be the dangerous moment! But soon after he crawled out of his tent next morning, he saw Graeme as large as life. He was amazed. Was it all a dream? Or had he killed the wrong person? By 8.00 am, he knew the worst. Graeme had switched tents and Allan was dead."

"Not surprisingly, Colin broke down completely. He was not alone. All the other scouts were similarly devastated. Colin's tears were genuine – because he liked and respected Allan. Neil said to me: 'He just couldn't take it ...' His reaction was quite understandable. He was horrified at what he had done. And if he was caught? If he was found out? Nothing is worse than being punished for a crime you didn't intend to commit! So he let his sorrow take its course. It was 100% genuine."

"Later that day, he had to face my questions. Perhaps I should have asked him straight out: 'Did you kill Allan?' If I

233

had done that, he might have broken down or betrayed himself in some way. But I didn't. As I say, he told me no lies. I liked him. I thought he was a very bright lad. He said that he liked Allan who was helping him to get his mountaineering badge. He seemed to like Graeme. In fact, the only scout he didn't like was you, Tom – and I think you know why."

"Without seeming to do so, he diverted suspicion away from himself. Because he had no obvious motive – and because he was the only witness to the murder – he probably got off lightly. Colin would have heard that I laid into Garry Hogg and Harry Robb, virtually accusing them of committing the murder. He saw police inquiries moving steadily away from the scouts. He was able to go home. He began to feel he had escaped the drag-net. Others might be suspected – but they were innocent. So no one would suffer. And neither would he, providing he kept his mouth shut!"

Mrs Fisher nodded her head.

"He never said a word. Never a word."

Raynes felt very sorry for her – but he felt he had a duty to explain the facts and he really didn't want to do it twice. Perhaps, having shared her sorrow, the other parents would later be able to understand – and help.

"By the time we got to Allan's funeral, Colin had begun to feel more confident. The police had completely failed to find the murderer. And his mother had had a bright idea. She had suggested that he might like to go and spend a couple of weeks with his uncle and aunt in King's Lynn. Colin was more than happy to go. He liked his uncle and aunt, and a break would be nice. He could escape the memories ... and the police."

"But then he heard that his mother had invited Graeme round on Monday afternoon to trim a hedge. He suspected – quite wrongly – that he was being pushed out of the way. With him in King's Lynn, his mother and Graeme would be on their own. So he hesitated ... Should he go?"

"All of a sudden, he saw a brilliant way out of his dilemma! He had heard that before he came round to his house, Graeme would be working at the Armstrongs and then for Mrs Foster. He knew that the twins were going to be away in London with their mother. The coast would be clear. And yet, he would have the perfect alibi. So Colin agreed most willingly to go to King's Lynn. He would leave early in the morning – and no one would suspect him."

"I have discovered that his mother saw him off on the 8.30 am bus from Grasshallows' bus station. All he had to do was get off two or three miles down the road, catch a bus back to Grasshallows and buy an aerosol spray. Easily done! He knew where his victim was to be found. He tracked him down. Once again, he doctored his orangeade. This must have been done between eleven and twelve o'clock because Graeme had already consumed the contents of one bottle. Colin knew where to find Graeme's things. The lunch-time bottle and the sandwiches were in the front seat of Graeme's pick-up."

"He hid himself away and watched Graeme come out for his lunch. He saw him take it back into the garden and settle down beside the sundial for a welcome break. After a little while, he noticed that Graeme had fallen asleep. He gave him time to fall into a really deep sleep. Then he came over without the aerosol – to say 'hello'. If he had made a mistake in his timing, he could always escape. But Graeme was snoring away. Colin bent over to make sure. (This was when Ellie saw him.) Then he rushed away for the aerosol – and the rest we know."

"The moment the murder was done, Colin rushed back to the bus station as fast as he could. He caught the next available bus, and still managed to be in King's Lynn in time for tea. He probably said he had been shopping or down on the wharf. Colin had read his detective stories carefully. He knew how important it was to have a good alibi which others could confirm. The only trouble was that his alibi was not cast-iron. Mrs Fisher told one of my officers that she had phoned through to his aunt to make sure he had arrived safely, and was surprised that he was not yet there. If other people had had weaker alibis, Colin might well have been overlooked. But, for once, it was Colin's movements which gave grounds for suspicion. The bus drivers were interviewed earlier this afternoon and they confirmed that a young lad had indeed left the 8.30 am bus soon after it left Grasshallows – and a similar lad had travelled to King's Lynn on the afternoon bus. When we found that the pills had been taken from the Fisher household, it was very simple to draw the obvious but painful conclusion."

What more could he add?

"Colin was brought back to Grasshallows this evening for further questioning. I am sure Mrs Fisher and Mr Coates-Smythe will want to come down to the station to see him." He looked around at the assembled company who were beginning to breathe again. "I leave it to the rest of you to explain it to the other lads as best you can."

Raynes sank back into his chair. His job was done. He had spoken as gently as he knew how, but Mrs Fisher seemed completely stunned. She remained staring at the Inspector long after he had finished speaking. Even Mr Derek Coates-Smythe found it difficult to gain her attention.

Raynes knew what she was feeling.

He too was suffering from an inescapable sense of guilt. The worst thing a detective could do was to ignore his own basic instincts. From the start, he had been sure that Allan had been killed by mistake and yet he had made no effort to protect Graeme. He should have been alive to the possibility that the murderer would strike again. But he had been distracted by Ellie and Grace. He had asked the wrong questions. He had looked for a simple, obvious motive – when there was none. He had placed the murderer low on his list of suspects because he had assumed that if you were a witness, you were hardly likely to be the culprit. And yet, how many times had he been warned of the murderer's capacity for invention?

The fact that the case had been solved in a mere eight days would no doubt be a cause of great public rejoicing in Grass-hallows. But, in his heart of hearts, Raynes knew that if he had been more astute, he could have brought the whole case to a successful conclusion much sooner – and prevented Graeme's death. A detective was only as good as his last case – and in this one, he had made a lot of mistakes. At this rate, he would never qualify for a proficiency badge in advanced detection!

236

He walked over to Detective-Constable Carlisle, who was still standing beside the door. "Come on!" he said. "There's nothing more we can do here. Let's go back to the station and have a decent cup of coffee before the fireworks really begin!"